Surviving Love
By: M.S. Brannon

Photo Credit: Shutterstock
Cover Design: Robin Ludwig Designs Inc
Editing and Formatting: C&D Editing

http://msbrannonblog.blogspot.com
https://twitter.com/@MSBrannonAuthor
https://www.facebook.com/pages/MS-Brannon/361712440596820?ref=hl

ISBN-13: 978-1497452862
ISBN-10: 1497452864

I don't wanna feel no more
It's easier to keep falling
Imitations are pale
Emptiness all tomorrow's
Haunted by your ghost

Lay down, black gives way to blue
Lay down, I'll remember you

Fading out by design
Consciously avoiding changes
Curtains drawn, now it's done
Silencing all tomorrows
Forcing a goodbye

Lay down, black gives way to blue
Lay down, I'll remember you

~Black Gives Way to Blue, Alice In Chains

Chapter 1
Drake

My legs are moving; I'm stepping with one foot in front of the other. The weight of my baby girl in my arms is keeping me in the present as I walk from the funeral home toward the Chevelle. My body is weak—my heart has been broken into so many pieces I'm finding it impossible to stand after the agonizing loss of Presley. There is nothing left inside to bust because every vital thing that keeps me alive has shattered.

The cool spring breeze connects with Mia's face as she sucks in a breath then smiles, her grin stretching across her cheeks. I look into her eyes—Presley's eyes—and get the small, rejuvenating bit of energy I need to keep going for just one more day.

The night Presley died, I saw Carter's gun lying on the concrete. It took an act of God not to pick up the pistol and end all of my suffering. If I didn't have Mia, I can honestly say I'd be dead. Nothing in that moment felt worth living for until Mia's precious face flashed into my mind; the thought of abandoning my daughter snapped me back from the darkest thoughts of my existence. I know I can't give up on life right now.

My mind is disconnected and my heart is an empty shell, yet this little angel needs her father. I won't be like my parents. I won't abandon my child because of my own selfishness. I have one more life to live for and she's the only piece of Presley I have left. For Mia, I will go on. The road will be the hardest I'll ever travel, but I've got to believe in the hope of my little Mia, and the hope my family will help carry me to a future.

I lean down and strap Mia in her car seat. I press my lips to her forehead and whisper, "I won't give up on you, my sweet girl. Just be patient with Daddy, okay?"

I kiss her again on the top of her head and her small, soft hand touches my cheek. The water fills my eyes as this simple gesture from my one-year-old daughter tells me she understands. She may be a baby, however this little girl knows her daddy is barely hanging onto life.

I walk to the other side of the car and then drive home, wiping the falling tears from my face. As I pull into the driveway, I'm reminded of the night Presley died—that night four days ago that has stripped my soul raw and left me a hollow, empty nothing.

Mia has quickly fallen asleep on the short drive home, something she commonly does when she rides in the car. As gently as possible, I take her from her car seat and trudge up the stairs. This is the second time I've climbed the back stairs since Presley has died.

Will I always do this—connect every moment I have back to the night she was killed? Will this be how I'm supposed to measure time? The thought disgusts me and slices me open all at once. Will I ever escape the pain?

I kiss Mia before laying her down in her crib and then walk back to my room. I've spent the last four days holed up in this prison.

I stare at our bed. The night before she died, we spent hours making love in this bed. I held her as we connected ourselves inside and out. Now, it's just an empty reminder of something I will never have again. I stand there, staring intently at a symbol of the happiness I once felt. It's now the agony I will never escape.

I'm nineteen-years-old, and I'm almost completely dead on the inside. The smallest sliver of my heart that's still alive is reserved for Mia. I will never love anyone as much as I loved Presley. And now, I have a lifetime of solitude to suffer through.

However, when I close my eyes, she's still here. Everywhere I turn, Presley is there. I can smell her soft, delicate skin and taste her sweet cherry lips. If I close my eyes hard enough I can see her lying underneath me in our bed. I can feel her warm, tiny body attached to mine as I express every ounce of love I have for her through my kiss. She is my heart and the other half of my life, and now, that life no longer exists.

Tears break free once again and I allow them to fall down through the stubble grown across my face. The room is suffocating me. I'm choking on my own pain and need to leave. Just for a moment, I want to be numb of everything I've been through the last few days.

I storm from my room and numb the only way my family knows how. Booze. I need to get drunk, just like I needed it four days ago. The house is quiet and my thoughts are raging, I need peace. Solace and peace.

"God, just for a moment, can I please have that?" I beg into the open air.

I yank open the door and pull the half empty bottle of

3

whiskey left in the cupboard. Unscrewing the cap, I tip the glass to my lips and allow a few more tears to fall down my face.

"Here's to the rest of a useless life," I toast to no one and chug down the whiskey. It instantly burns and calms my insides. The raging ocean of emotions I can't seem to shake is finally subduing, and it's welcome. Jack Daniels is always welcome to ease my agony. Always.

I rip my tucked-in shirt from the waistband of my pants and move down the back stairs. The last time I wore this fucking shirt was when I saw Presley in rehab. I will never wear this piece of shit again. Still grasping the bottle, I rip open my shirt, popping buttons as my chest is exposed to the cold, damp air.

I walk to the driveway and see the spot where I last held Presley alive. My boots scuff the pavement when I walk toward the dreaded spot. I hold the bottle to my lips again and chug. Then again and again. It's burning my gut and suffocating my throat, but I keep gulping it down. My legs give out, collapsing to the concrete. The pain stings when my knees connect with the ground. I relish in it. It's more welcome than the pain in my heart.

"This is the only way I can get you out of my mind," I whisper out loud to no one, or maybe to her, but I don't fucking know. "I need you out of my mind. I need peace for just a day. I love you, Presley, but I just need peace." I expel a deep breath and choke back another drink. "Don't hate me, baby, but please…give me some peace."

I lay down on the cold concrete just as the rain begins to pick up again. I don't care. I want to be in this spot. I want to be with her. And I want to be numb. I choke back a few more drinks until the bottle is empty then close my eyes, envisioning only her honey-brown irises and the world I will no longer possess.

***

My head is throbbing and my gut is churning. I roll my neck to the side and feel the ache all the way down my shoulders. Where the hell am I? I crack my eyes open, causing a searing pain just to touch them. It's too bright. Everything hurts.

When I finally open my eyes fully, I can see I'm in the garage, sitting up on the couch with Jeremy asleep next to me. The Challenger is missing, which I find strange since Jeremy is passed out on the couch. The last thing I remember is falling onto the driveway with a bottle of Jack in my hands. I was begging to be numb and it looks like I got my wish.

I sit forward and roll my shoulders around, loosening them slightly, then expel a deep breath. Drinking is one way to kill the pain inside my heart, but now I feel worse inside and out. Fuck! I can't get a break.

Standing from the couch, I see my shirt is torn and my pants feel stiff. Jeremy awakens on the couch and looks just as bad as I feel. I can tell he hasn't slept in days and it appears he may have lost a little weight. I immediately sympathize for him. If he feels half as bad as I do, I can't imagine how I look.

"Hey," Jeremy whispers as he stands beside me. He rolls his shoulder around, just as I did, and stretches his arms above his head.

"How did I get in here?"

"You were passed out in the middle of the driveway. I

almost hit you with the car. The three of us drug you in here and I stayed to keep an eye on you." Jeremy moves to the mini fridge and pulls out two cans of Mountain Dew. He motions with his eyes, asking if I want a drink, and I extend my arm out, taking it from him.

My mouth is dry and I welcome the moisture from the soda as I chug most of it in one huge swallow. "Sorry I took up the couch. I know how you like sleeping in here. Where's your car?"

Jeremy looks me in the eyes then quickly looks down at his feet. "Jake busted in needing the car. God only knows where he's going, but it's no problem...staying in here. Reggie wouldn't let you be left alone. You were in pretty bad shape. The drunkest I've ever seen."

"Yeah, well, a bottle of whiskey will do that to you," I snap back, not realizing how cruel I sound. "Look, Jeremy, I'm sorry. I just...just..." I can't form a sentence. I'm afraid that, if I talk about her, I will break down again. I don't want to break down any more, however as her face passes through my memory, the tears once again surface.

Before I can stop myself, I collapse onto the couch and begin to sob all over again. The hurt living inside my chest is too much and I can't hold it in. I fold forward, cupping my face in my hands. The moisture of my tears is soaking my palms as the hurt keeps falling from my eyes. I want to stop this pain more than I want to breathe, yet it just keeps festering inside of me, refusing to let go.

The couch concaves next to me and Jeremy's warm hand comes to my shoulder. He doesn't say a word. His hand merely squeezes and releases with every onslaught of emotion bleeding from my wounded insides.

6

This is exactly what I need. My family will stand behind me no matter what. They will take my pain as their own just to relieve me of it; if only for a brief time. Jeremy and I never really had conversations beyond cars and girls, but once Presley got back from rehab, he's made it a point to talk to me more, and now, his comforting hand is speaking to me. It tells me he will always be there for me. I know I will be able to overcome this eventually, and it's moments like this that will keep a small sliver of hope alive inside of me.

Several minutes go by before I can calm myself down enough to speak. I wipe the tears away with the back of my hand and look over to Jeremy, feeling slightly embarrassed at my actions. Jeremy just claps me on the back, giving me a comforting smile in return.

"Sorry, man," I whisper.

"Look, Drake, there's something we need to talk about. Something you need to know and I want to tell you, but I don't know how." As Jeremy leans back against the couch, I can tell he's torn up with his thoughts. Actually, I've never seen him so upset. Something's obviously bothering him, however to be honest, I can't hear anything right now. My emotions are on overload and stripped raw. If one more thing gets added to my shoulders, it will break me for good.

"Hey, we've got time. Just tell me later, okay? I don't think I can handle anything else right now." I stand from the couch and move to the garage door.

Jeremy looks down to his feet and back up to me, "Yeah, brother, we've got time."

I walk from the garage and from the look of torturous pain written all over his face. I don't want to think about that now. I just need to think about moving ahead and not falling behind. I have a daughter to raise; I can't afford more shit weighing on my conscience.

Chapter 2
Drake

Once I clamber inside, I notice the house is dark and quiet. It's after three in the morning and I'm wide awake. Too wake. I don't like being this alert. It makes life too much of a reality, and I don't want anything in my life to be real at this moment. I'm still seeking peace for a few more hours.

I move to the living room and sit down in the recliner. As I flip through the channels, I come across The Notebook on a movie channel and my peace is soon interrupted. Fate has a way of making you face your challenges head on, which is what it's done with this on the screen.

I close my eyes, allowing the glow from the TV to illuminate my eyes behind my lids, and like a movie playing in my head, I'm brought back to the last time I watched this movie with Presley.

She was tucked into my side with her fingers slowly dancing across my stomach. I had initially thought I wouldn't make it through the first thirty minutes because, with every emotionally filled scene, she'd grip my shirt and her fingers would graze the skin of my abdomen. Her touch was driving me crazy.

I looked over at Presley's face and knew life couldn't get any better. I remember thinking how amazed I was with my life, especially after the drugs and rehab, because here we were and life was good.

When she finally noticed I was looking at her, she started to blush and whispered, "What?"

"Nothing," was all I had to say. Presley climbed over onto my lap and straddled her legs on either side of me.

When her lips pressed to mine, I was helplessly falling once again for this woman's charms. I'd fallen time and time again when it came to her and every time felt like it was the best.

I wrapped one arm around her waist and the other crawled up her back until my palm was wrapped around her neck, pushing her closer to my body and deeper into our kiss. I then stood from the couch and moved into our room, holding onto the very precious life of the woman I loved.

We made love for hours that night. I tasted, licked and caressed very inch of her soft skin. I remember thinking when we were all done and Presley was fast asleep in my arms, how blessed I really was. I'd never been a godly man because growing up in Sulfur Heights often left you wondering if a God exists. The crimes, drugs and hate living on every corner made you question faith all together. But that night, when I reflected on all the obstacles we'd overcome, I had known there had to be a God because no one on earth was as lucky as I was in that very moment.

What do I think about God now? For starters, I think he's got a demented sense of humor—he's a twisted, sick fuck. I can safely say that I hate God right now.

I've spoken to him many times, at first begging him to take care of Presley when she was in rehab, and then again, pleading with him for her to come back to me after she died. Only a God who's spiteful would do this to us. I may hate him forever. There's no way someone should go through everything Presley and I were forced to go through only for this be our ending. At the age of nineteen, she's six feet under and I'm left to raise our one-year-old daughter and live the rest of my life with a piece of me missing.

My lids open and I allow my eyes to focus again. The memories are too vivid for me to handle right now. I get up from the chair and move to the kitchen. Tucked in the back of the cupboard, I find another bottle of booze and chug it down just as quickly as the bottle of whiskey. I move to my room and strip myself from my clothes.

Tomorrow I will focus on moving forward, but tonight, I want to stay right where I was before she died. I want to keep myself in the past just for a few more hours.

***

Reggie has informed me that I only have two weeks leave from work then I need to be back to reality. When he told me this, I thought to myself, *How the hell is someone supposed to go on with life as normal when nothing is normal at all.* However, after a week of walking around the house watching everyone else tiptoe around me, I will be ready for some normalcy.

The past ten days have flown by, probably because I can't live in my bubble anymore, but time has also stood still. Agony and torment do not take vacation, and now I'm forced to deal with it in my real life.

There is no more pretending. I have to deal with people outside my house, and they will surely ask how I'm doing. I'm not sure I'm ready for that, yet I need to work, and I need to move forward.

I called the plant manager last night, letting him know that I will be returning tomorrow. Reggie and Darcie have been a great help with Mia, knowing I'm slowly starting to come back to life but still struggling everyday with Presley's absence. I haven't talked to Jeremy since that night in the garage. I know something is off with him because he's absent more than he is around lately. Then there's Jake. His usual infectious personality has been gone since Presley died. I can't help but think something has happened between him and Delilah. Only Delilah can get him feeling this way. I wonder when he will actually realize she's crazy about him. Do I really want to see the two of them happy just the way Presley and I used to be, though? I'm not sure if I can manage that.

I head to the bathroom to take a shower, and for the first time, I get a glimpse of my appearance. I've avoided the mirror the last ten days, and now, when I see my reflection, I'm appalled. No wonder everyone is looking at me like I will break. I look horrible.

I pull off my shirt and jeans, standing in my boxers to study myself in the mirror. My skin is ashy and pale, my eyes are sunken in and large bags are pooling under them. My chest used to be defined and ripped, but now it looks like someone has let the air out of my body. My rib cage is the only definition I have in my chest, and my skin sags slightly, hanging from my bones. My arms look weaker as do my legs. I look like I've been starving myself for days, which is pretty much the truth. Food? It hasn't even been a thought for several days.

Tipping my head up, I try to remember the last time I ate a meal and cannot remember. I've been solely surviving on Mountain Dew and small bits of food here and there. My appetite has vanished along with everything else. I'm literally a husk of a human. There's nothing left inside and out. I'm nothing without her. I'm…nothing.

I quickly hop in the shower, washing and rinsing my body. When I get out, I can hear Mia crying from her crib. I get dressed and walk into her room, which is just off the bathroom. She's standing in her bed, arms up, begging me to pick her up. It's late, and the only way she'll fall back to sleep is to be rocked in my arms.

I reach in her bed and hold Mia against my chest. She rests her head on my shoulder, yawning through her tiredness. Sitting down in the rocking chair, I begin to sway my daughter back and forth. Then, for the first time in days, I get the courage to sing the lullaby only Presley has sung to her.

Swallowing the lump in my throat, I let the words to Billy Joel's "Lullaby" fall from my heart and into the air. Mia immediately is comforted as her body relaxes deeper into mine. I continue to rock her as I quietly sing words that have only been sung by her mother.

This was one of Presley's favorite joys of being a mother, rocking and singing Mia to bed. The time was only theirs, and until she died, I never interfered.

Now, it's up to me to keep the tradition going.

When I finish the song, I continue to hum the lyrics until I can feel the deep breaths coming from Mia's chest. I then lay her back in her crib and she rolls to her stomach, settling in. Before I leave the room, I take a moment to study my daughter. She is absolutely precious with her curly, brown hair wildly lying across her face. I run my fingers over her cheeks, brushing the strands away.

I'm overwhelmed with so many feelings when I look at my baby. Of course, love is present, but I feel disappointed in myself that I've allowed her mother to die the way she did. I hurt because Mia won't know her mother or how much she loved her. All I want is for her to be happy.

I lean down and whisper, "I love you, sweet girl," then kiss her on the temple.

Mia is the only person in this house who has been created out of love. Unlike me or my brothers who've come from irresponsible and idiotic parents, Mia was created from the love of two people. The love Presley and I had for each other was bonded together to make this little angel. It's a love that will withstand the test of time, and in my lifetime, will be irreplaceable.

I will love no one like I love Presley, and Mia is living, breathing proof of our love.

***

Six in the morning has come way too fucking early as my alarm sounds loudly in my ear. I shut it off and sit up, putting my feet on the floor. Today is going to be a hard day; I just hope no one asks how I'm doing. I'm not ready to talk about it, and the last thing I want to do is cry like a fucking pussy in front of a bunch of hard-ass steel workers.

I lean forward placing my head in my hands, which lately, has been my typical sitting position. I'm always hunched forward, looking down on a life that's done just that to me—let me down. Keeping myself looking down is the only way I can keep my body from collapsing onto the floor. It's so hard to look into the devastated eyes of my family and not feel pain. If I keep my head down, I find it easier to stand and move these days. I've got to do what I can to keep myself upright.

I pull work clothes from my dresser, get dressed and shuck on my boots. I can hear Mia over the monitor, bouncing in her crib and talking away. She has yet to say any real words and I'm excited for when she does. I wonder what her first word will be.

Jake started placing bets before she turned a year old and is confident Axl will be Mia's first word. He is a delusional idiot sometimes. Darcie and Delilah are so sure a curse word will come out before any other word. Man, I hope not. I try really hard to bite my tongue when she's around, but on the other hand, Darcie and Jake can't control their language. It's literally impossible for them. I said she would say mama first and Presley took the bet thinking Mia would say dada. It hurts a little, but I'm excited nonetheless.

I open the door to Mia's room and her angelic face is full of smiles. "Hey, sweet girl," I say when I pick her up and cuddle her into my body, holding her for a minute before we have to get moving back into reality.

I lay her down on the changing table to change her diaper and dress her in a purple outfit. I think Delilah bought this for her birthday, yet I can't remember. Delilah buys Mia crap all the time. Actually, everyone buys Mia stuff regularly. My child will definitely want for nothing.

I pick her back up and walk to the kitchen, placing her in her high chair. I give her a sippy cup of milk and sprinkle some dry cereal on the tray while I get my lunch packed for the day. Mia wastes no time drinking down her milk and eating her food.

How am I going to get through the day? I place my hands on the counter by the sink then lean forward. Expelling a deep breath, I realize I need to do what I did when Presley was gone for three months in rehab. It was hard then, but that's the only way I know I can approach the next several months of my life. I will just pretend she's gone to rehab.

I finish getting Mia's stuff ready and then we head out the back door and get into the car. I called Mrs. Fields last night and asked her if I could start bringing Mia there again. She was happy to be seeing us again, although I'm not really looking forward to seeing her.

Mrs. Fields has been a great help and a dear friend to both Presley and I, however it will be hard to look into her eyes. I haven't seen or even spoken to her since the funeral. She's a motherly figure to me now, and I hope I can make it out of her apartment without crying.

Then there's the other reason I will hate going there— Carter. Being back at the apartment complex where he lives infuriates me, yet inwardly I hope he's there. I'd like just one minute alone with him. I want nothing more than to make him suffer. However, I don't think Carter is stupid enough to be at his apartment, especially since the police are looking for him.

When I pull into the parking lot, so many horrible feelings begin to escalate. Nothing good surfaces inside my chest—only pain, rage and anger. I sit for a second to gather my emotions, not wanting my daughter to see me upset, then exit the Chevelle.

Mia giggles when I pull her from her car seat and it instantly calms my rage. I can't do anything stupid to

Carter. I can't sacrifice losing my baby. I have to be responsible. I believe full well Carter will get what's coming to him. And I hope it's as agonizing as Hell.

Before I get a chance to knock, Mrs. Fields opens the door and Mia leans toward her arms. She's missed her babysitter, and I can't help feeling glad I won't have to worry about Mia while I'm at work. As Mrs. Fields grabs a hold of Mia and gives her a hug. I smile. It's the first time in days something has made me smile, and I feel good for once.

Mrs. Fields sets Mia on the floor next to a basket of toys and then turns her attention to me. Dreading every word coming from her mouth, I close my eyes to get my emotions under control, yet again. I feel a warm hand clasp onto my forearm, and when my eyes open, Mrs. Fields is holding me. Her arms are tight around my waist and her body is frail. She's a lot smaller than I remember, but I embrace her right back.

For the first time in my life, I'm feeling what it would be like to be held by a mother. It's overwhelming and comforting all at once. I've needed someone like Mrs. Fields my entire life. I have needed the touch only a mother could give to a child who's surrounded by pain.

I hold her tightly and let the tears bubble and fall from my eyes. I release all the pain and sadness onto this woman's shoulder as she rubs my back and whispers words of comfort in my ears.

After several minutes, I calm myself enough to pull away. I've broken down so much over the last ten days that I'm honestly tired of doing it. My eyes hurt and my body aches, yet for the first time since Presley has died, I feel like I can finally breathe again. Not completely or without pain, but there's a small sentiment of hope that I will be fine someday.

"I'm always here if you need me, sweetheart," Mrs. Fields speaks through her tears and pulls me at arm's length, looking directing in my eyes.

"Thank you," I look down to my feet then back up to her eyes. "I'm… I'm okay."

"You're strong, honey. A lot stronger than you give yourself credit for, I'm sure. When I lost my husband, I was young. I had just celebrated my thirty-fifth birthday, and just like that, a heart attack takes him from me. Then I was left to raise our teenage daughter on my own. So I know how you feel." She picks up my hand and cups it between hers. "It does get better. You just need to give your heart some time to heal. But I promise, it does get better."

I nod in acceptance then move to Mia, who's completely distracted by a puzzle, and lean down to give her a kiss. When she stands, handing me a puzzle piece, I place it in the designated spot then pick her up in my arms.

"Goodbye, sweet girl. Daddy will be back soon." Mia places her hands on my cheeks and leans down to my face, so our foreheads are touching. I pucker up my lips and she does the same then I give her a swift kiss. "I love you."

I hand Mia to Mrs. Fields and leave the apartment. One emotional breakdown over; now it's time to go to work and hope no more tears surface today. I'm so tired of crying. I'm simply fucking tired of it all. I'm just so tired. So damn tired.

***

When I pull into the parking lot, I take a deep breath

and release it before quickly walking to the main building and punching in my timecard. The plant manager must have been waiting for me because, as soon as I run my timecard, he's pulling me into his office. Great, breakdown number two coming right up.

Rich is an average height man with a big belly and receding hair line. He is also the most impatient, hard-ass I've ever worked with. I really like him. I often wonder if this is how Reggie will be when he hits his fifties, but I doubt Reggie will ever let himself get a gut or lose his bad-ass physique. However, the hard-ass persona will undeniably be a Reggie trait.

"Drake, I wanted to let you know I spoke to your brother, Reggie, after everything happened. I want to assure you myself that human resources are the only people who know what your absence was from."

Confused at why he's telling me this, I nod in acknowledgment.

"The guys think you were out on vacation for the last couple of weeks. So when they ask, you'll know what they're talking about." Rich reaches his hand up to my arm, but he soon tucks it into the pocket of his jacket.

"Thanks, Rich. Am I still working in crane three?" I ask, just wanting to get this awkward conversation over with.

Rich's smile peaks for a second before he's back to business as usual. "Yes. Now get your ass to work."

I happily head out of the building and walk quickly to my crane. After climbing in the cab, I get myself situated in the seat and fire the equipment to life. And for the first time in ages, I begin to feel normal again.

Chapter 3
Drake

It's Friday, and this week at work has been better than I've originally expected. No one even cares why I've been gone or even mentions it to me. I sit in my crane and concentrate on moving metal from one area of the plant to the other. I don't let my thoughts run away with me, finally feeling somewhat normal.

After dropping Mia off at Mrs. Fields apartment the first day, I was sure it was going to be weird. To my surprise, it's like nothing has changed. She talks to me about Mia's day and doesn't give me looks of pity or grief, which I'm grateful for. I think it's because Mrs. Fields knows from personal experience how I feel. She knows how much harder it is to move on with life if you always have to see the looks of pity coming from everyone around you.

After lunch, I head to my car to put my lunchbox in the trunk and check my cell phone. Darcie's number has been blowing up my phone, making my heart freeze inside my chest. Darcie is watching Mia for the day while Mrs. Fields goes to an appointment. She knows I can't check my phone during the day, so why hasn't she called the plant directly? My gut instantly drops to my feet. I can see I've already missed six calls from her. Something horrible has happened. I can feel it.

I swipe my finger across the screen and listen to her phone ring on the other end. An eternity passes by before she picks up and I immediately hear Mia sobbing in the background. "Drake! Oh, my God. You need to get home!"

"Why? What's happened?" I scream into the phone and start to climb in the front seat of the Chevelle.

"The DEA is here. They're tearing the house apart, looking for drugs. Jake's probably going to get arrested. He started beating the shit out of them."

Anger slams into my heart as I fire the Chevelle to life and fly out of the parking lot. "I will be there as soon as I can."

I punch the accelerator to the floor, propelling myself forward. I have no idea why the hell DEA agents would be raiding our home, and right now, I really don't care. I just need to know if my baby is okay.

It takes no time to get to our street, and from three blocks away, I can see police cars everywhere. The street is flooded with cars and officers are surrounding the house. Reggie pulls up behind me and we both start running up the driveway when we're immediately stopped by DEA agents.

"What the fuck is going on?" Reggie's face is flushed red as he screams to the officers holding us back.

I'm trying to look for Mia. Breathing a sigh of relief when I see Darcie holding her on her hip. She doesn't appear hurt. My anxiety lowers slightly knowing Mia is okay.

Before I know what's happening, Reggie is placed in handcuffs and ushered to where Jake is sitting, also handcuffed and sitting on the ground with police surrounding him. Some of them are battered. Damn! What the hell is going on?

I stand frozen as I watch Reggie argue with officers while Jake smirks with pride. I then quickly shuffle to Darcie to take Mia out of her arms. I give her a once over, looking for any sign of injury, but she's fine.

Just when I'm about to ask Darcie why the DEA is here, Jeremy opens the garage door and walks to the Challenger. When he pulls the backpack from his trunk, I feel my world once again getting pulled out from underneath me.

"There's nothing in the house. Here's what you're looking for," Jeremy says and is soon handcuffed with the rest of my brothers.

This is not what I'm seeing. I am not standing in the middle of my driveway, hearing my brother confess to being a drug dealer. I am not seeing packages of heroin scattered on the concrete. This has to be a nightmare. Jeremy wouldn't do this to me or to any of us. It's when his eyes connect with mine that I know. With that one glance, Jeremy's admitting his guilt. I'm angry. I'm worse...I'm outraged.

I toss Mia into Darcie's arms and scream, "What is this? You're a fucking drug dealer?"

My body is boiling with rage. I can feel the hate traveling its way over every inch of my body, making my muscles rigid and taut. As I step to Jeremy, the color red is blinding my vision. I don't see anything but red. Nothing else exists except for the overpowering urge to annihilate Jeremy. I want to destroy him. I want to plow my fist into his face then wrap my palms around his throat and watch the life escape from his body. I want to KILL him!

Presley's dead body flashes into my mind—the crimson color of her blood is everywhere. There's so much red. On my hands, soaking through her shirt, painted across her skin…it was everywhere.

Then Carter's face invades my thoughts. Could Jeremy be working with him? The night Presley was killed, I really don't remember what Jeremy was doing, but I *do* remember coming out of the house seeing him and Carter in a heated discussion. Mother. Fucker!

Reggie instantly recognizes my furious state and tries to keep me from moving. He begins speaking, but all I see are his lips moving. Nothing else is registering other than the unrelenting fury toward my brother.

"Are you the other supplier? Were you the other dealer working with Carter?" I push my way toward Jeremy as the only thing I'm focused on is killing him. Police officers swarm me, but I push against their human wall. "You asshole! You fucking killed her!"

As swiftly as I can, I force my hands and arms though the army of officers. If I can just get one hand on him, just get one hand to grip around his neck, I will squeeze the life from his body. I push harder, yet the more I press against the wall of officers, the more resistance I meet. I just need to get close enough to touch Jeremy. I ram my arms forward with all my strength before they are being yanked behind my back. The cold steel of the cuffs cuts into my hot, angry skin.

Pain begins to register in my shoulders, but I let it fade as the hate takes over once again. I shout through my rage, still only seeing red. I need him to feel every ounce of loathing I currently possess. The hate he put inside my body. "You goddamn fucking piece of shit!"

My body has a mind of its own as the hate replaces all the hurt. For the last few weeks, my body has been aching from loss, but that is all gone. From the moment Jeremy came out of the garage, every ounce of loss has been replaced with hate. I loathe my brother. That I'm completely sure of. I despise Jeremy.

I. Hate. Him.

I need to get to him. I want to kill him, and I know I can. I push against the officers again, trying to take them off guard, however they stop me short. The next thing I know, I'm being drug backwards toward the chain link fence. The metal of the fence clanks loudly as I'm slammed in to it.

"You fucking killed her!" I shout. "You fucking killed her!" I scream then scream it again. "You fucking killed her!" I can't stop. He killed Presley and now he's killed this family. Jeremy has singlehandedly destroyed our family, and it will never be what it once was. I will never forgive him. I can assure that. I will only hate. Because the minute I saw the bundles of white powder fall from his backpack, every shred of love, trust and devotion dissolved only to be replaced by hate, doubt and apathy.

***

Several minutes go by, hell, maybe even hours go by. I don't really know. All I know is that, from the moment my brother admitted he has been working as a drug dealer with Carter, betrayal and hate have become the only emotions remaining inside of me.

After the officers confirm I'm was calmed down

enough, they take the handcuffs off my wrists as well as Reggie's. The three of us—Reggie, Darcie and me—stand in the middle of the driveway completely dumbfounded and shocked. There are no words to say because no words can even come close to explaining how unreal the last hour has been.

I take Mia from Darcie's arms and hold my sleeping baby against my chest. The anger reappears when I think of what Jeremy has done to my daughter. He knew what he was doing when he got involved with Carter, and now he's taken a mother from her child. I am so mad that I can feel my skin heat and tense as the rage begins to boil under the surface. Turning my body toward the backyard, I take deep breaths in and out, expelling the rage slowly.

I can hear Reggie in the background; he's on the phone with his lawyer, Tom Willington, explaining the situation. I try to get a grip on myself. I can't let my baby see me lose it anymore. This poor child has been through so much in her short life that part of me is concerned she will grow up with issues. I know she's small, but will she be mentally scarred from the trauma? The thought disgusts and worries me all at the same time. I don't want her to be fucked up like the rest of us. All I want is for my baby to be happy and loved.

"Mr. Evans? Drake Evans?" I turn around to see two police officers are surrounding a short, older woman with ratty hair and wearing clothes from the 1980s.

Clasping Mia tighter in my arms, I'm immediately concerned. "Yes?"

"My name is Charlotte Raines. I'm with Child Protection Services." She hands me her card. My gut clenches and my heart races. The boiling anger is surfacing again, but I do my best to keep it at bay. "I've been called by the local authorities to remove this child from her home. They alerted our department of the unsafe living conditions and possible neglect while she lives in your care."

"You're not taking my child." My voice is low but laced with power. Over my dead body will they take my kid from me.

When the officers move to my arms, reaching forward to grab Mia from me, I step back quickly, evading their advances. "Sir, you will be arrested if you do not comply. Please, just give us the baby and you can visit with the office in the morning."

"Like hell I will!" I shout, startling Mia awake. Reggie and Darcie move to my side, blocking the police's ability to grab my daughter.

"What grounds do you have to take her?" Reggie asks, his voice as furious as mine.

"Unsafe living conditions and possible neglect," the CPS worker answers again.

This is not happening. If I lose Mia, I will have nothing. She is the only link I have to Presley and I'm the only blood related family Mia has. We're all we have left. I will not lose her. I can't lose her.

"I'm not giving you my daughter. She's never been neglected by anyone and this house," I motion to the back of our house, "this is the safest place she will ever be. So I will tell you again," I look right into the CPS worker's eyes. "You're not taking my daughter."

The CPS worker is joined by several more police officers and suddenly the three of us are being swarmed.

They divide and conquer, separating Reggie and Darcie from me. Then a man of my equal size approaches. He's built and it looks like his arms are about to rip the sleeves of his shirt. "One last time, sir—please hand over the child."

"Fuck. You." I seethe in his direction.

The smallest smirk comes from his lips when an equally large forearm is being secured around my throat. I'm holding Mia tightly to my chest, but I'm losing my battle with breathing. Then, from nowhere, the burley police officer rips my daughter from my arms and quickly hands her over to the CPS worker.

"NOOOOOO!" I scream in their faces. I move to charge the officers, but I'm soon restrained once again as four men tackle me to the ground. Two of them are sitting on my back, each one holding my arms behind my back while the other has his knee digging between my shoulder blades. My face is scraping against the concrete and pain is shooting everywhere in my body, yet I refuse to acknowledge it.

"You can't take her from me! She's all I have left!" I plead into the air as I watch the CPS worker disappear from my sight, carrying my crying baby down the driveway.

She's gone. I stop struggling as I watch my baby vanish from my life. The small glimmer of hope I've developed over the last few days has vanished as the rest of my soul is being ripped from my arms. My body falls limp into the cold pavement. My vision fades from red to purple then to black as everything I've ever had evaporates.

Chapter Four
Drake

Reggie helps me off the ground as the officers finally leave after a day of hell. The side of my face is torn up from my head being pressed into the concrete. I'm slowing dying all over again, but this time it's much worse. My insides are gradually falling apart, and I can't get a handle on anything I'm feeling.

When I lost Presley, I thought nothing could compare to losing her, but I was wrong.

There are no words to explain the helplessness I feel at having my baby ripped from my arms and watching her disappear from my sight. She is innocent. Mia has done nothing wrong, and tonight she has been forced to suffer the consequences of Jeremy's stupidity.

After trudging up the stairs, I furiously stomp to my bedroom, slamming the door closed. Agony is evaporating as the anger sets in. I turn to my wall and start punching the shit out of it. I slam my fist into the drywall, sinking it deeper and deeper with every blow.

This whole time Jeremy knew how distraught I was after Presley's overdose, and yet, he said nothing. That was the time for him to say something—to confess his mistakes. Wait? Did he know she was involved with Carter before she overdosed? Was he hiding this from me because he

28

wanted to save face with his drug connections?

The very thought infuriates me even more, causing my fist to drive into wall again.

Several minutes pass, and my breathing is labored. I have holes covering the entire wall in my bedroom, and I don't give a fuck. I exit my room and go to the kitchen to get a drink. I haven't tasted alcohol since the day of Presley's funeral, but now it seems like the right time to get annihilated.

I open up the cupboard, seeing the bottles are dwindling down to nothing. I'm not the only one nursing the hurt with liquor. Jake probably has been drinking, too. He's been off since Presley's funeral, and I know he's been coming home wasted every night from the bar—more than normal.

I reach for the last clear bottle in the cupboard and down the vodka. It burns the back of my throat. I choke slightly as I soak my mouth in an attempt to become numb. I take another long chug when Reggie rounds the corner into the kitchen.

I haven't looked at him in weeks. I haven't really looked at anyone in weeks. As I finally focus on him, I see that he looks worn out. Stress undoubtedly has taken over his appearance, making him look older.

"You might want to take it easy with that." His voice is demanding, pissing me off. What does he know anyways? His life has never taken a turn so horrible, therefore he really doesn't have a say on how I deal with my emotions.

"And why's that?" I ask without really caring what his answer is.

"I've reached out to Cindy—the social worker who

helped me get custody of Presley—and she's assigning herself to Mia's case." Reggie moves in closer and stands in front of me, crossing his arms over his chest—his typical authoritative stance. "Apparently, she's managing things in the department now and has the authority to get things moving."

"Thank you," I whisper back to Reggie and then take another sip. The liquor is starting to take effect as my limbs start to go numb. The pain from today starts to slowly wash away in my now vodka soaked system.

Reggie motions for the bottle by stretching his hand out to me. "Hand it over, Drake. You have a meeting with Cindy in the morning, and if you go in smelling like booze, I highly doubt things will go well for you."

Reluctantly, I pass the bottle over to Reggie and watch him screw the cap on then put the bottle back into the cupboard. He shakes his head at the empty cupboard. "Looks like Jake's been self-medicating, too."

"I better call Rich at the plant and tell him what happened. I sort of left without saying a word. Hopefully I still have job there. I can't afford to be without a job right now."

I move from the kitchen and quickly call Rich's cell phone, leaving a message. I know my job is now in jeopardy, however my family will always come before a job. Mia is my priority, and getting her back into my arms is the only concern I have now.

Once my message is left, I head to the bathroom, stripping my body of its clothes and standing under the warm water of the shower. I face the stream falling from the faucet and bend my head forward. Using my left hand, I plant my palm on the wall of the shower to keep myself upright as the water streams down my back. My shoulders, back and arms throb from the police restraining me, yet nothing hurts more than reliving Mia being ripped from my arms. The physical pain of her being jerked from my body hurts more than anything I've ever experienced.

I can feel the emotions bubble to the surface again when I think of my baby in someone's house. I can hear her screaming as she's being escorted down the driveway. Her arms stretched out toward me, begging me to save her. The sight and sound is gutting. I've been sliced apart once again. It's too much to handle right now. The constant ache settled in my chest feels like it's been sliced wide open, bleeding profusely now that I've lost my daughter.

I vowed to Presley days ago not to worry about Mia—that she'd always be protected—and I failed once more. I couldn't protect her. I've failed. I'm a failure.

I was doing so well—I haven't cried in a week—but this…is too much. I clench my fist at my side and punch the shower wall with the other hand as I allow the hurt to seep from my body once again.

***

Darcie, Reggie and I spend the next two days cleaning up the house. It is a total wreck as we walk over broken and dismantled objects from our life. Picture frames in the living room are shattered. DVDs are scattered all over the place. Worse yet, Mia's room is destroyed; her toys and clothes cover the floor.

I bend down to pick up a framed picture of Presley and Mia, becoming infuriated. The glass is splintered and it distorts the image held in the frame. This is the final straw.

My life needs a change, and it will have one, starting with getting my baby girl back. Looking at the broken picture is the wakeup call I need to get my life back in order. I once had order, and after everything that's happened, I need it to be restored. I need the control back. It's the only way I knew how to live before, and over the last three years, the order has been slowly dismantling, but no longer.

My appointment with Cindy at the CPS office went well. She has expedited the paperwork to the courts and I have a hearing next week. She feels confident I will get Mia back. In the meantime, I will need to hang in there—Cindy's words, not mine. I'm barely hanging on. She has informed me that Mia is staying with a good foster family and is well cared for, but I don't give a shit. She's not with me. Therefore, she's not well cared for. Only I know how to take care of my baby.

I've talked to Rich after everything that has happened. He's told me he can't guarantee me a position. I have a week to get my shit together, or they will replace me on the crane. I can't afford to be without a job, and the crane operator position makes a pretty good salary. I know Rich is going out on a limb to keep me employed, but my baby comes first. And if it costs me my job, then so be it.

***

It's been five extremely long days. I just got off the phone with Cindy, who has a hearing scheduled on Monday. The house has been put back together with the exception of the basement. The energy in the house is hateful, though.

Reggie and Darcie are at each other's throats because

32

she's siding with Jeremy. Well, not siding with him, but she understands why he has done what he did. I, on the other hand, won't even fathom any other idea than Jeremy is a selfish prick who royally fucked up. Reggie is appalled at Jeremy selling drugs to make money. He and Darcie go rounds about how it's no different than Jeremy hustling at drag races for cash, but Reggie doesn't see it that way. And neither do I.

We were raised by a drug addicted woman who ultimately chose drugs over us kids. When Reggie taught Jake and Jeremy the hustle game, he was clear from the start to never get involved in the drug game; it will only fuck up your life.

And now, Jeremy will have to eat those very words as he spends the next several years rotting away in prison.

My thoughts are disrupted when Jake comes trudging through the door. Darcie picked him up an hour ago from jail and apparently he received another slap on the wrist. Tom Willington has been able to get Jake off on the assault charges because the one person the DEA truly has wanted is locked up.

I have heard through random conversations that Ronnie was arrested the day after Jeremy. I'm happy about that. Ronnie won't last a single day in prison, especially when he's turned into someone's bitch. He's weak and I hate him. Just as I hate my own brother and the murderer of Presley. I've never hated anyone as much as I hate the three of them.

"Hey," Jake says while popping a can of Mountain Dew.

"Hey," I say back, not really wanting to have a

conversation, but I have missed my brother. "How was jail?"

Jake looks over at me like I've lost my mind, and I can tell he wants to snap at me, but right as the anger surfaces, it dissolves just as quickly. "Oh...it was a fucking joy. When do you get Axl back?" Jake looks at me through pitiful eyes and I know he's hurting just as much as the rest of us.

"I have a hearing on Monday, and if all goes well, I will get her back on Tuesday. It's been almost a week and I'm going out of my mind." Jake nods in agreement and slaps his hand on my shoulder.

"Are you going to Jeremy's sentencing?" I'm really not sure why he asks, however Jake's been in jail for the last week and really has no idea what my thoughts are toward our brother.

The anger skyrockets through my body and my fists instantly ball up. "I want nothing to do with him, and frankly, I hope he gets the fully twenty years. The fucker deserves it." I glare at Jake, my eyes set to kill and my voice laced with fury.

He backs off the conversation instantly, sensing my anger."Well... I'm off to shower. I feel gross and probably smell like a homeless man's ball sack." I try to smile at Jake's joke, but it's too hard. Smiling used to be easy, but now I'm too angry to do anything. The only person deserving of my smile is Mia.

I head back to my room and flop myself down on the bed. My mind is completely consumed with Presley...and now Mia. I don't have room to think of anyone else, especially a traitor like Jeremy.

Chapter Five
Drake ~ 11 Months Later

It's Saturday night, my one free night to forget about the pain in my life and get obliterated. I drive to *The Slab* and park in the back next to Reggie's Camaro then make my way to my designated seat at the bar. The noise hits me like a brick, but the sight of booze calms me immediately. I sit at the far end of the bar, closest to the opening and the farthest place from other patrons, and begin to drink myself stupid.

I don't talk to anyone. I don't want to make friends or have pleasant conversations. I just want to get drunk then go home and pass out. I don't have to care for my daughter tonight. I can sit and drink everything away, allowing my tense shoulders to relax slightly as I chug beer after beer.

Tonight, like every Saturday night, Mia and Mrs. Fields are having their weekly slumber party. Since Mia turned two, Mrs. Fields has asked if she can spend the night so they can do fun girl things together. Mia loves Mrs. Fields and I wouldn't come between them. Then, on Sundays, I go over for lunch and spend the afternoon with the two of them.

It's been comforting to have Mrs. Fields in my life, and I think she's picked up on that. Mrs. Fields's daughter lives several hours away with her only grandchild, and having Mia and I around gives her purpose. So for the last couple of months, I spend Saturday nights drunk and Sundays with the only two women in my life.

As for the rest of my family, I really don't have too much interaction with them—only when it requires me to do so. For the most part, they leave me alone. Of course, we still have conversations, and I know the remaining members of my family care for me, but they don't know how to deal with me. In true Evans fashion, they just leave me be and are probably waiting for me to make the first move.

The mood in the house has changed dramatically since Delilah has moved in. For a while there I was so sure Reggie and Darcie were going to split, as angry as they would get toward each other. There were many nights when something would get broken, voices would elevate and tears would inevitably be shed, yet the moment Delilah moved in, her happy personality became infectious to everyone. Well, everyone but me.

I am incredibly happy for Jake and Delilah, but it is hard to watch them be so happy together. I was once Jake—so head over heels in love, with the only person who mattered in life being the girl standing before me. I find it sort of ironic how life can change like that in a split second.

Now, I want nothing to do with any woman. I don't want to be happy, or fall in love, or even make a friend. I just want to survive this life the only way I know how—complete detachment from everyone except my daughter, and now, Mrs. Fields.

Tomorrow will mark the one year anniversary of Presley's death. It's impossible to think it has been an entire year since I've held the love of my life. It remains incredibly raw to me. I can still feel the weight of her dying body in my arms. I can still feel the blood as it soaked through my jeans and saturated my hands. I try to forget that night—more than I try to breathe—but it's always there the minute I close my eyes. I can't even think about the good times I spent with Presley because all I can see is the blood and death. It takes over my mind, haunting me constantly.

When I found out Jeremy was dealing and when I thought I lost Mia forever, my life took a radical turn toward hatred. Over the last year, I've transformed into a living, breathing villain to others. I never smile anymore. Hell, I don't know what it feels like to regularly smile anymore. The only person who can make me crack a smile is Mia, and she is the only person I will shed my anger for.

The only other times I can truly dissolve some of my anger is when I'm drunk, or when I'm in the garage beating the shit out of the punching bag. Often times, when my nights are sleepless and the dreams of losing Presley are too daunting to bear, you'll find me in the garage, slamming my fists into the bag. Needless to say, I've been in the garage every night since I got Mia back. As my world lies crumbled at my feet, I feel for a small moment that I can put it all back together when I beat the shit out of something.

As Darcie passes me a shot of whiskey and a mug of Guinness, I quickly slam the shot back and then chase the burn with a big swig of my favorite beer. The taste is delicious as I move from being pained and sober to free and intoxicated, releasing my demons if only for a moment.

And this is me. I'm a man who never looks up anymore. I don't care to see the world around me. I don't want to see happiness because all it does is piss me off. Any kind of happiness, even an intoxicated happiness, makes me extremely angry.

I keep my head down whenever I'm around others. I don't talk to anyone at work unless I have to. I barely talk to my family who lives with me, and I sure as hell don't talk to anyone when I'm in the bar. I don't want to appear inviting to anyone because I'm anything but. I just want to keep to myself and survive long enough to get to Saturday when I get drunk, then I will go home and pass out. It's the only night a week I can sleep without the interrupted thoughts of my dying girlfriend running through my head.

***

The light in the morning is always painful on Sundays. I'm nursing a pretty bad hangover this morning, more painful than most, but last night, the buzz wasn't coming fast enough. I needed to be numb. Six shots of whiskey and five beers later, I was passing out on the bar and Reggie took it upon himself to drive me home. I remember him dragging me to the couch in his office, but after that, it's all blank. However, I did get several hours of uninterrupted sleep. It's something I look forward to every Saturday night.

I stand from my bed and stretch then make my way to the shower. A year ago, I was literally skin and bones; all my muscle mass was gone. Now, I've bulked myself up again, maybe more than I was. Working the heavy bag is a perfect way to let off some steam and beat out all the pent up anger, and for the last year, that's all I have had inside

38

me—anger. Every night, after Mia's tucked away in bed, I go out to the garage for hours and slam my fists, legs and knees into the hard, leather bag in an attempt to shed the pain and rage. It works momentarily, yet it soon comes back when I'm reminded of how shitty my life has been.

After my shower, I grab my keys and head toward Mrs. Fields's apartment with the thought of the anniversary of Presley's death haunting the back of my mind.

Since I walked out of the funeral home the day she was buried, I haven't acknowledged her death visually once. I have yet to visit her grave, and in all honesty, I don't think I ever will. There is no part of my brain willing to accept that she's dead. I just want to live in my semi-peaceful oblivion with my head down. I have a constant reminder whenever I close my eyes at night of what I've lost; why would I go to a grave and relive that pain when I'm awake? Nothing good will come from it, so why put myself through that? Existing for my daughter has worked for the past year and I don't want to upset the balance. I just want to exist for Mia and everything else can simply fade away into nothing. Staring at a headstone in the middle of a graveyard won't bring Presley back, so what's the point?

Pulling into the apartment complex, I reflect on how it doesn't bother me as much as it used to. Now that Carter is rotting in prison, I've come to terms with being here and don't find it difficult to control my anger every time I pull in to park.

Nothing has changed since I've lived here. The building is still rundown, the shrubs overgrown around the broken pool, and the security gate still doesn't lock. When Presley was pregnant, I was so sure this was the happiest place on the planet because we were finally making a home outside the walls of where I grew up. The three of us were going to be a family and create happy memories I never had when I was a child. Again, I find it ironic how utterly wrong that was—my stupid, optimistic disposition.

I can hear cartoons on the TV when I walk into the apartment. Mia is sitting on the floor playing with her dollhouse people.

"Dadda!" she squeals then comes running into my arms. It warms my soul hearing Mia's first word, and that word is my name. The smile I almost never don always surfaces when I look at my daughter and it's spread across my face now. All I have to do is wrap my arms around my little girl and my smile breaks free from its aching prison.

"Hi, my sweet girl. How's my baby?" I kiss her cheek and she snuggles for a moment, resting her head on my shoulder, something she always does when I hold her. It's a very brief gesture, but incredibly precious and only ours.

She's grown so much in the last year. The doctor says she's in the ninety-eighth percentile for her height and eighth percent for her weight, but he told me she's completely healthy. Her baby face is starting to slim since she's constantly running, jumping or dancing with happiness. I am amazed at how well she's adjusted to life since her first year in this world was so traumatic. The doctor has reassured me how resilient children are, and that, with the proper love and care, Mia will grow to be a well-adjusted child.

I've had to complete a year's worth of random drug testing and home visits from Cindy with the Child Protective Services office. She was responsible for getting

Mia back into my arms so quickly when she was taken, so I did anything she asked to keep myself in her good graces.

The first test was very insulting; I clearly remember how impossible it was to keep a lid on my anger. I couldn't get Jeremy out of my mind. It was still very new to everyone, and the house was fueled with a toxicity we could not cure. However, I managed to keep myself under control long enough to get through the first visit, and after that, they seemed more manageable.

As always, Mia looks absolutely adorable dressed in her purple and pink outfit with cats on the front of her shirt. Delilah has been a godsend when it comes to the care of a little girl. She helps me shop for clothes and has taught me how to braid her hair.

I want to do everything for Mia now that I'm her only parent, so I've insisted on learning how to brush and care for a little girl's hair. It wasn't easy at first—I would have to chase her around the house just to get a comb through it—but we've established a routine of Mickey Mouse and fruit snacks while I attempt to tame her wild head.

She still looks a lot like me—her caramel skin matches mine, as well as her high amounts of energy—but her eyes are all Presley. They are the same honey-brown color, wide and expressive just as her mother's were. I get lost sometimes looking into her eyes. They remind me of a happier time and make me miss my love every single day.

Mia leans back in my arms with a look on her face that is very serious, and I know she's deep in thought. She lifts her hand and points to her shirt. "Titties?"

I panic slightly, thinking Jake has taught her something inappropriate for his own humor. He is always trying to get

Mia to say something stupid, and I have this horrible feeling when she starts preschool next year she will be teaching her classmates some colorful new words. However, when I look again to where she's pointing, relief washes over me.

Suppressing a laugh, I try to correct her. "Kitties."

The cutest giggle comes from her mouth, and she smiles with delight. "Titties."

"No, kitties," I attempt to correct again, putting more emphasis on the *K* sound. She looks at me like I've lost my mind then squirms out of my arms, resuming her play with her dollhouse people. Apparently, this conversation is over.

"I've been trying all morning to correct her, but she's quite stubborn." Mrs. Fields comes from the back room and walks up to me, giving me a hug. "She's a little spunky thing sometimes, but I always manage to laugh."

I return her hug, feeling a small amount of peace as she shows me affection. I've never really had a mother's love, but when Presley died, we established a relationship that very much resembles what a mother would have with a son. Even though she's old enough to be my grandmother, I still think of her as a mother.

I go into the kitchen and start pulling dishes from the cupboard, setting them at the small table in the dining area. We work in comfortable silence together as we get everything settled for lunch.

When Mrs. Fields dishes up the food, I pull Mia from the floor and put her in her chair. I place a bib around her neck and blow on her food in an attempt to cool it off while Mia waits contently for her lunch. When I place it in front of her, she giggles and digs in. Mashed potatoes immediately cover her face as she shovels her food in her mouth. The sight makes me laugh and reminds me of her first birthday when she shoved cake in her mouth. She just can't get enough and must take after her daddy with her unquenchable appetite.

Mrs. Fields joins us at the table and dishes up our plates. My mouth waters when I smell the roast chicken, mashed potatoes and steamed vegetables in front of me. I love Sunday dinners with Mrs. Fields because she always goes all out and never runs out of food. She knows how much I eat and I think she enjoys taking care of someone again. Before Presley and I moved next door, I got the feeling Mrs. Fields was very lonely. Then, when she started watching Mia, she sprung back to life and has enjoyed looking after us since.

We sit in relaxed stillness for a while until Mrs. Fields speaks, breaking the silence. "I'm sure you know what today is." Her voice is quiet and sad. I can feel my mood plummet when she reminds me it's been a year since Presley's died.

I clear my throat as I set my fork down then take a large drink of milk. "Yeah…I know."

"Have you considered going to her grave yet?"

I feel like my heart has collided with a truck. Of course I've considered it. I've considered it every single day when I shut my eyes and get reminded of what's missing from my life. "I'm not ready for that yet." It's all I need to say and the conversation is over. Mrs. Fields recognizes my heartache and doesn't pry any further. She gets it and never pushes.

"Did I tell you my granddaughter is graduating next

weekend?" And just like that, the subject has been changed.

"No. Are you going to make a trip to Wisconsin?"

"Yes, I've told you about my daughter, she won't come visit me here because this place holds so many memories from her childhood. It makes no sense to me, but I leave her alone about it. However, I will see my baby sister and hopefully my niece. It's been a few years since I've seen her. She and my granddaughter used to be so close." Mrs. Fields looks at the wall behind me, obviously lost in a memory, then she continues, "I will be leaving on Friday and won't be back until Monday. The ceremony is on Sunday afternoon, but there will be a little party on Saturday night that I want to help my daughter get ready for. I won't be able to watch Mia for a couple of days."

"Sounds good. I will ask Darcie or Delilah to watch Mia while you're gone." It's then I that realize I don't know much about Mrs. Fields personally, and I'm curious. "What's your granddaughter's name?"

A forced smile comes across her face. "Sophia Jane. She's such a beautiful girl. She's graduating from college and went to school to be a teacher." The look on her face tells me there's tension between the two of them, but I avoid it and shovel in a mouthful of potatoes.

We finish the rest of our meal in silence, and then I move to the kitchen to start clearing up the mess. Mrs. Fields and I have a system on Sundays—she cooks and I clean. It's the least I can do when she's done so much for me in return.

When Mia starts throwing food, I know she's done with her dinner. I pull her from her chair after wiping mashed potatoes from her cheeks, hair and clothes as best as I can.

While Mrs. Fields sits and rests on the couch, I take Mia in the backroom to change her clothes and diaper then sit down in the rocking chair. As always, I rock her back and forth, singing the lullaby Presley used to sing her to sleep. Moments into the song, Mia falls fast asleep. I hold her for a couple more minutes, embracing my baby in my arms, then lay her down in the crib.

Passing down the small hallway, I take the opportunity to look at the pictures on the walls. She doesn't have much hanging up, just a couple of her wedding photos, an older picture of a woman who I assume is her daughter holding a young child, and mountain landscapes. None of the pictures are recent and it makes me wonder why.

I move back to the kitchen to finish cleaning up the mess, rinsing and scrubbing as I put the dishes in the dishwasher and leftovers in the fridge. Once the kitchen is tidy again, I sit with Mrs. Fields for a few peaceful minutes before my food coma settles in and I fall asleep.

Chapter 6
Zoe

The blood is dripping down my face in a constant, steady flow. It's falling from my hairline, tracing over my temple and dripping off my jaw. The pain isn't too bad, but this "incident" is a time too many and I can't handle this anymore. I've been with him for a year—the longest I've been anywhere in the last four years—but these last two months have been unbearable. I'm stronger than this.

The second he put his hands on me, my mind was made up. I will not let a fucking man hit me. Granted, my mouth got me into trouble, however that doesn't give him the right to punch me in the head. I have nothing to stick around for; he was my only real connection to this place.

I start yanking clothes from hangers in my closet and tossing them into a large, black suitcase. I decided to move in with Terrance only a few months ago, so my trunk still has most of my belongings in it. My motto always is: if it won't fit in my car, then I don't need it.

When I get to a new place, I look for the cheapest living situation, knowing I won't be staying for long. For the last four years, I've lived a budgeted lifestyle, sleeping on an air mattress and cooking my food in a tiny microwave. I haven't used any of this stuff since I moved in with Terrance, and am actually looking forward to going back to the life I understand—a life where I only depend on myself.

When you move around as much as I do, it doesn't make sense to keep stuff that doesn't fit into your car. That way, when I'm ready to up and leave, there's not much to pack up.

I give the large apartment another last look, grabbing a picture frame of me and my cousin, Sophia. I smile to myself, instantly brought back to simpler times. She was my best friend until the night everything changed. I miss her every day, but like my mother, she won't have anything to do with me. The pain of being disowned is still there, yet I won't give in—not a single inch. I was telling the truth and they chose to believe the lie.

All of that is in the past and my future lies with me and my decisions. I won't let another person dictate my life again. With that thought, I grab my suitcase and haul it to my car, which, other than my trunk full of possessions, is the only thing that truly belongs to me.

Just after I was disowned from my family, I took a bus to Colorado because I had always wanted to see the Rocky Mountains. I wanted to live on a mountain, away from civilianization. That way, I couldn't be disappointed by people again. When I made it there, I immediately got a job as a waitress at a truck stop where I had spied a fire engine red 1970 Chevy Chevelle for sale across the street. I dug the color, style and the black racing stripes painted up the center. I needed that car. That car represented my freedom and the ability to do whatever the hell I wanted.

Soon after that, I got a night job as a bartender, making a decent amount of cash. The car's seller was asking fifteen thousand for the car, and from my understanding, no one was willing to pay the asking price. It wasn't in the greatest condition—it had some rust spots around the bottom—but the interior was nearly perfect and the motor was decent.

Living on nothing for months, I saved ten thousand dollars and made the seller a deal. He accepted a blow job and seven thousand dollars for the car. Not my finest moment and not the first time I whored myself out for something that I wanted, but what's done is done. I have no regrets. I have a car and my freedom.

It's so hot this morning, and I'm ready for cooler temperatures. I pull out the map and red marker from the glove box then place a big X over the state of Louisiana. I won't be coming back here anytime soon, if ever. I lay the map across the hood of the car and study all the red X's across the United States—I've lived in several different states since I left my family in Wisconsin.

I pull a dime from my jean's pocket and toss it onto the paper. The shiny metal spins around until it lands flat on the state of Michigan. I debate the choice since Michigan is awfully close to Wisconsin, and I don't want to run into family. However, this *is* how I decide what my next destination will be and I will continue this method until I find a reason to stay somewhere.

I fold up the map and toss it back into the car when Terrance comes tearing into the parking lot of his apartment. "Where the hell do you think you're going?"

"I'm leaving your ass, Terrance." I point to the gash on my head. "I'm not putting up with this shit." I move to get into the car and Terrance intercedes, snatching my arm in his hand, squeezing hard. "Get your fucking hands off me!"

My throat burns from my shouting as my body goes on alert.

"You're not going anywhere. You belong to me!" Terrance's dark skin glistens with sweat from the humid Louisiana air and his large muscles are noticeably tight with his bare chest on display. He's a handsome man with deep brown eyes; a large, muscular frame; and he's as tall as my five foot eleven inch frame.

Our eyes met a year ago when I was bartending at a night club. I thought he'd be the reason I'd stick around. It was a stupid mistake on my part; I fell for his smile and southern charm.

Terrance is a very charismatic person, and until a couple of months ago, he has been the perfect gentlemen. I can safely say I cared for him—well, until he put his hands on me this morning.

A few months ago, his personality flipped a switch and he was angry all the time. He saw me talking to his brother and accused us of doing more. Since that day, he's made my life hell, becoming super possessive, and then today, physically abusive.

"The only person I belong to is myself, and I'm done with your shit! Now let me GO!"

He raises his arm and slaps me across the cheek with the back of his hand, instantly stinging my face. Blood is oozing down from my lip and I can feel it swelling as it throbs with pain.

Terrance begins yanking my arm, pulling me away from the open door of my car. I need to break free from him immediately, so I turn myself toward him and drive my knee into his groin. It causes Terrance to bend forward in pain, releasing my arm as he grabs his balls. For good measure, I kick him in the gut just as hard and then fall into the driver's seat.

Firing the engine and tearing out of the parking lot, I say goodbye to Louisiana and head north toward Michigan.

***

It's dark when I cross the border into Michigan. I'm ready to rest for a couple of days, so I find a small motel along the interstate to crash for the night. After I check in, I pull my suitcase and air mattress from the trunk. I like to stay in cheap motels, but God knows what's living on the mattresses. I refuse to lie in someone else's stains.

I inflate my bed, and after a quick shower, I turn on the TV and mindlessly flip through channels. I land on an old movie and stare at it until my lids are heavy and I fall fast asleep. Tomorrow, when I wake, I will decide where in Michigan I will land.

I must have been tired because twelve hours later, I crack my eyes open and stretch my exhausted limbs. I then roll off my air mattress and use the bathroom. When I look in the mirror, my bottom lip is pretty swollen and there's a small cut on my upper lip. I lift up my hair and study the other wound on my head. The gash looks pretty good; I probably should have gotten stitches. This will definitely leave a scar. The bruise around it is a purplish-blue color, but it's easily hidden by my bangs. My skin is pale, yet it always is, and my long, chestnut-brown hair is disheveled. I look like I'm strung out on drugs. The sight of myself makes me laugh.

I pull out my cell phone and Google the cheapest places to live in Michigan. I study the list and one city in particular comes into mind, Sulfur Heights. Where do I know this city from? I rack my brain, sorting through memories, but I know I've never been there, that I can remember. Still, there is just something about that name…

The curiosity gets the better of me and I decide that's where I should land for the next few months, or until it's time to leave. I gather up my clothes, deflate my air mattress and haul myself to the car. I sift through my playlists on my iPod and find the perfect song to start my newest adventure, "Son's Gonna Rise" by Citizen Cope.

Drake

I accepted a new position at the steel factory where I work. I like the solitude of working in the crane, but the hours were not conducive to my family life. When things started picking up, I found I was away from Mia more and more, and that wasn't going to fly. I talked to Rich and he said there was an opening as a line supervisor. I would be responsible for managing the part time and seasonal guys working the line—the place I started when I first came to the plant. I would only work fifty hours at the most a week and no weekends. I was sold the minute he said no weekends.

The job is actually not too bad. Initially, I was worried about being around people again—I hate talking to anybody, especially those who know about Presley, but to my surprise, everyone that reports to me is fairly new. Most of them are young—well, younger than me anyway—and it's their first job anywhere. I've had to put a couple of young punks in their place, but all in all, most of the guys are just looking to earn an honest living and are pretty open to my feedback.

I get Mia's bag packed and then head over to Mrs. Fields's for their Saturday night sleepover. It's been a few weeks since they've had a slumber party because of my long hours at the plant and the little time I've had to see my baby. The nightmares of Presley's murder have been overwhelming me lately, making me need to drink more than I need air right now. I just want to sleep for a night without seeing her dying in my arms.

I pull into the parking lot and head for Mrs. Fields's apartment. The summer is in full bloom and the fourth of July is next weekend. I can't wait to take Mia to see the fireworks; she's going to love them. She loves anything pretty and sparkly.

I step into the apartment and Mia immediately squirms to get out of my arms. Setting her down, I meet Mrs. Fields in the living room where she is pulling a basket off the coffee table filled with nail polish of all colors. Mia knows exactly what that is and is really excited to get her nails painted. She's clapping her hands and is as bouncy as a giddy little girl can get.

"Hi, sweet girl," Mrs. Fields coos as she bends down, kissing the top of Mia's head. "Say bye to Daddy."

Mia comes running into my arms and lays her head down on my shoulder, something she always does when we hug, then she sits up and looks right into my eyes. They still stun me every single time. Presley is all I see when I look into Mia's honey-brown irises, and it always throws me off balance for a second. God, how I miss her, and at times, I wonder if the missing her part will ever fade.

"Bye-bye, Dada." Mia leans up for a kiss.

I bow my head down and give her a quick peck on the

lips then whisper, "Bye, sweet girl. Be good, okay?"

"Tay, Dada." She puts her hands on my face and says, "Wuv you, Dada."It melts my heart every time she tells me she loves me.

"Love you, too, baby." I kiss her forehead then set her down. She forgets about me as she runs to the coffee table, getting ready to get her nails painted. I smile as she sifts through the colors and requests all of them on her nails. Mrs. Fields just smiles and waves me off.

Two hours later, I'm drunk off Jack and Guinness, sitting at the end of the bar, wallowing in my self-loathing. Darcie and Gavin are having a hard time keeping up with customer demand, which causes Reggie to emerge out of his office and help out. He's like Darcie; never questions what I'm doing or bothers to try to make small talk. Reggie knows this is the only night I get to forget about the pain I have endured in my life and self-medicate with booze.

I erase everything from my mind; the trials of raising a daughter by myself, Presley's absence and my brother's betrayal. I rid it all from my mind, one sip at a time. I don't consider myself a drunk because I would never drink to excess if I knew I had Mia to care for when I got home. I do it so I can forget for one night a week and actually get some sleep. Maybe I should go to a therapist, perhaps Dr. Redman—the therapist Presley was seeing for her drug addiction. I consider it for a minute, however my thoughts are soon interrupted when Jake mentions Jeremy's name. I immediately get pissed. Reggie recognizes my anger and fills my shot glass with Jack, knowing how much I hate my brother and anything affiliated with him.

I slam my glass down, and for the first time in over a

year, I look up. I'm instantly captivated and shocked where I sit as I take notice of a beautiful woman standing next to me.

Chapter 7
Zoe

I've been in Sulfur Heights for a few days. I managed to find a rundown apartment on the Southside of town. Now, I'm on the hunt for a job. I've got about three thousand bucks in my pocket, but it won't last long.

When I rolled through town earlier, a bar on the outskirts grabbed my attention immediately and I've decided to see if they're hiring. When I pull in front of the bar, the name appears in dripping red letters, *The Slab*. What a weird name for a bar. The outside of the steel building looks rough, however there are ten or so classic cars and tons of motorcycles parked in front of the building. Yep, this is my kind of place! I seem to fit in with the rougher crowd and can usually handle what bikers and gear heads typically dish out.

I pull my car in the back next to another Chevelle and envy how nice it looks. Mine still has rust on the bottom and the motor could use some work. I have yet to find a good body shop to fix it because, for one, I need money; and two, I need to stay at a place more than a few months. Louisiana has been the exception, and it became too distracting. I was soon sucked into Terrance's world of drug dealing and the nice things his money could buy. I didn't even consider getting my car fixed. Maybe now that

I'm so close to Detroit—motor city itself—I will make time for it.

I flash my ID to the big man at the door and get my first look at the people of Sulfur Heights. The noise level is overwhelming at first; rock music is blasting from the sound system. Several men are gathered around the pool tables and to the left is a long line of customers waiting for drinks. Perfect. Hopefully I can convince the owner to hire me, at least for the weekends. Then I can find a day job during the week.

I make my way through the crowd, turning myself sideways to squeeze through the bodies. After several minutes, I'm able to make my way to the bar and look for an opening. Located at the end and off to the side of the bar, I find an open space to inch up to.

I immediately take notice of a man, probably around my age, sitting all by himself. There is no one around him, not even the waiting crowd is anywhere close by him. He's definitely in good shape because his arms are very toned, and even through his shirt, his back has slight bumps indicating muscles.

Before I approach, I take the time to study him further. He has short, black hair, slight stubble formed across his jaw, and his skin is the color of rich caramel. I can't really see his face because he hasn't raised his head from the mug of dark beer, but I can still tell he's handsome, his features chiseled and inviting. How could he not be with a body like that? My insides are reacting to the sight of him, melting and aching for more. I immediately get a hold of myself. Getting involved with a man isn't what I need right now, but fuck, he's so damn hot.

I move up to the bar and stand next to him. I don't bother looking over at him as I get a handle on my raging libido while I wait for a bartender to notice me. The three bartenders are scrambling to make drinks and handle cash. This time, I notice the hot guys working behind the bar. One guy is short—well, shorter than me—with a lean body and baby face. The girl working with them yells "Gavin" to get his attention.

I look to the other man working behind the bar and swoon slightly. He's damn hot, too; tall—at least five inches taller than me—and his arms are covered in tattoos. He has short, sandy blonde hair and the most intense look on his face. I am captivated by his movements and study the way he works behind the bar. It's clear he's been doing this for awhile. Then I notice the ring on this left finger—married. I don't mess around with married men, not since New York and the crazy bitch who tried to cut me with a knife. She should have turned that knife on her husband. He was the one deceiving us both.

My trance is interrupted again when another hot guy comes walking up to the bar and stands on the other side of me. He, too, has tattoos, but in a 1950s style. What I can see of one his tattoos are the feet belonging to a pin up girl on his upper arm. As I raise my eyes to his face, I notice that he is also drop dead gorgeous. My body reacts again.

What the fuck? Have I been sucked into a portal of my own personal Hell where all the men look like gods? This is a punishment. I'm sure of it. This is what I get for swearing off men when I came into Michigan. I have to suffer through being surrounded by hot men everywhere I turn.

The guy to my right has short brown hair, stands a couple inches taller than me and is shouting at the other male bartender. "Reggie! Reggie!"

Reggie, the married bartender, turns and fills a mug of dark beer, passing it to the quiet guy on my right. Neither of these men has yet to notice me standing in front of them and I'm secretly glad. I know it will be impossible for my body to refuse any of these guys if they offered to screw me in the back of my car.

I stand a few inches back from the bar, eavesdropping on the conversation between the two hot men.

"When are you going to start working here, Jake? Can't you see I need the help?" Reggie asks the man to my right.

"I already fucking told you, man. I've got my hands full with the shop. Until Jeremy gets out, I can't afford to leave anyone else in charge," the man known as Jake replies and then swiftly takes a drink from his beer.

The man to my right finally makes a noise and mumbles something incoherent under his breath. The anger in his tone doesn't escape my notice. He pushes at an empty shot glass and without saying a single word Reggie pours him another shot of Jack Daniels. The quiet man on my right slams the shot back as I stare at him, watching his large Adam's apple move as he swallows the liquor. That's when he finally looks to me and I'm nearly knocked off my feet.

His eyes suck me in immediately; they are black in color. All the madness and noise surrounding me dissipates. We look at one another, never breaking our gaze. I feel like I've fallen into a place where only he and I exist.

The sound of tapping on the bar brings me out of my trance and the man to my right quickly leaves, heading for the back exit. I turn my eyes to the bartender, Reggie, and snap myself back into reality. Shit, I need a drink, but first I need to get a job.

"What can I get ya?"

Fumbling with my speech, I eventually find my words to speak. "Jack and coke, please. Oh…and a job."

The bartender looks at the man to my left—Jake—and then back to me. "You got experience?"

"I've been bartending off and on the last four years. I've got pretty good experience," I say, noticing I have yet to see the man smile, but the weird encounter I've had with the mysterious man has thrown me completely off balance.

"Well, you'll need to speak to my wife, and if she likes you, then you're in." He reaches his hand forward, offering me a handshake. "I'm Reggie and my wife," he points to the auburn haired woman at the other end of the bar, "is Darcie. Come back tomorrow afternoon around one and you can meet with her."

I put on a smile. "Thanks. See you then."

I quickly gulp down my Jack and Coke, overhearing them whispering about a guy named Drake. I wonder if that's the name of the gorgeous, mysterious man who's left abruptly.

Drake

I'm not near as drunk as I'd like to be when I dash out the back door and walk to my car. I notice a Chevelle parked next to mine and wonder who it belongs to, but when the sexy woman's blue eyes flash into my mind, I forget the thought.

I'm not really sure what's just happened back there. I haven't thought, felt or even glanced at another woman in eighteen months, however there was an aching voice inside my head that told me to look up. That's when my eyes collided with hers, causing my body to react for the first time since Presley died.

I studied her translucent blue eyes then a jolting ache traveled straight to my dick. This woman oozes sex and my body has awakened to become in tune with every vibe she's giving out. It's too much to take; the thought of another woman turning me on. I feel sick to my stomach.

I pull into the driveway and immediately go into the garage where I slide my hands into my fingerless boxing gloves and start slamming my fists into the hard leather. My shoulders ache when I punch as hard as my arms will allow, using up all the energy in my body. Before I know it, my body is covered in sweat as it burns off the liquor in my system. I grab the back of my shirt and pull it over my head, tossing it to the floor.

Standing in my jeans and boots, I listen to "Crawling" by Linkin Park blasting from the speakers—one of Reggie and my favorite sparring songs. The guitar riffs and intensity of the lyrics gets us amped up to fight. Right now, I'm in a different fight, and that's trying to get this woman out of my head.

I hit the bag over and over because I can't stop thinking about what has just happened. I knew I would be confronted by this one day—by my body betraying me, dissolving my will to abstain from sex. I just haven't been expecting it to happen so soon. I'm not ready to give up my solitude, or my hate toward the world. In fact, I've got a lot of hate that remains inside of me. Sometimes, I think that's what is pumping through my veins instead of blood—pure fucking hate. I'm not ready to give up Presley. I can't give her up and nothing or no one will ever replace her.

I stay in the garage for another hour until my body is dripping with sweat and exhaustion takes over any other thought in my brain.

After a shower, I head to my bed, hoping tonight I will get a peaceful night's sleep before I have to confront the newest challenge in my life—my attraction toward a long legged vixen looking to set my world ablaze.

Chapter 8
Zoe

I lock up my apartment and move to the apartment's garage to get into my car. I have a one o'clock meeting with the owner of *The Slab*. I hope she will like me enough to give me a job.

I pull out from the garage and drive toward the bar. Although my apartment is rundown and trashy, I pay the extra money to put my car in a garage. In neighborhoods like this, I can't afford my car being stolen or stripped. I do have a decent alarm system installed, but you'd be amazed how brave people are nowadays.

When I pull into the parking lot of *The Slab*, I take notice how the building looks a lot different in the light. It looks like the rest of the neighborhood, rundown, but I soon realize it's comforting because it's how I've lived the last four years.

When I left Wisconsin, I left the life I knew behind and only depended on myself to make it through. I didn't choose to leave Wisconsin, my mother made that choice for me. Nevertheless, when I finally made it to Colorado, I was awoken to a world I never knew existed. I immediately fell into the rougher scene where it was okay to be promiscuous, to drink and to embrace life one misdemeanor at a time. Like there, I'm comfortable here, too—too comfortable. And the thought is scary. I don't want to get attached to anyone or anything, yet I can't fight the overwhelming sense of calm I feel here.

Now that the bar is empty, it looks a lot bigger than I've expected as I walk through the front door. The first thing this tells me is that there's money to be made—a lot of money. When I was in the bar last night, the entire room was packed and all I could see were tips. Big, fat, pocket filling tips will be in my future. That is, if I can get the job.

When I approach the bar, the shorter bartender from last night greets me with a smile. "How can I help you?"

I clear my throat and dazzle him with my most charming smile. "The other gentlemen working last night mentioned I needed to talk to his wife, Darcie, about getting a job bartending here." I tuck the long strands of my brown hair behind my ear and slightly bite my bottom lip, a move I've done many times to get the men to fall to their knees. Gavin is a perfect example of this as he becomes mesmerized by my actions. "Is she available?"

"I'll check. I'm Gavin, by the way." He again smiles big then extends his hand.

"Zoe," I tell him before he turns to leave the bar area, stumbling over a box on the ground. I suppress a laugh, and soon after he leaves, Darcie appears from the back.

She is a beautiful woman with long, auburn hair, a skinny frame, and when she gets closer, her green eyes captivate me. The icy cold look on her face, though, dwindles any hope of getting a job here.

"Are you the girl my husband talked to last night?"

I extend my hand out and put on the charm, something that always works with the men and I'm hoping will work with her, too. Here goes nothing. "Yes, I'm Zoe Ledoux and I overheard your husband and another gentlemen talking last night about getting another bartender. I just moved here and am looking for work." I hate putting on the fake, charming act for anyone, but I know the cold, bitch-face look I have doesn't go over too well when you're looking for employment.

"Please, spare me the shit. If you're going to work in a place like this, you need to be a little bit tougher than that."

My charming disposition evaporates as my real self takes over. I'm thrown slightly because she's quite blunt with me. Then again, when I take a second to think about it, she's a person I can actually relate to.

"Look, I've been bartending off and on for the last four years. I know what I'm doing," I snap back, revealing my true self and the limited patience I have for people.

"We'll see about that." Darcie returns with a snarky look before she continues, "You don't look like a bullshitter and I appreciate that. I have no doubt you have experience, but you have no experience in a place like this, do ya?"

I nod my head in agreement. Most of my bartending jobs were at dance clubs or restaurants with bars inside. I've never been to a place quite like Sulfur Heights. Yes, I have lived in some rough areas, but something tells me Sulfur Heights is different. How it's different, I'm not quite sure as of yet, however I'm not willing to give up because I need a job.

"Look, I will give you an audition, so to speak." Darcie looks over her shoulder when her husband, Reggie, emerges from the back. "We've got some pretty demanding customers. I will invite them here tomorrow when we're closed, and if you can put up with their shit, then you've got the job. Deal?"

I look between Darcie and Reggie then smile with the faintest look of delight. "Deal."

***

Twenty-four hours later, I'm walking through the front doors of *The Slab* again. I'm a little more nervous than the last time I came here. Darcie is willing to give me an audition, and if all goes well, I will be the newest bartender on the weekends. My skin is damp from the humid summer and it makes me extremely happy that I've pulled my long hair into a giant bun on top of my head. After my eyes adjust to the dark setting of the bar, I see Darcie coming from the back, lugging a case of liquor with her.

I walk to her and she greets me with a half-smile then motions me to come behind the bar. After a very brief explanation of where things are located, I hear the commotion of regulars coming through the back door. When I turn around to face them, six customers are lined up along the bar waiting for me to serve them. I'm slightly confused at first because four of them are employees, but I say nothing and wait for my instructions.

"All right, Zoe, are you ready to show us what you've got?" Darcie says while motioning to the rest of the group. "We will be the most challenging people you'll ever have to deal with." A quiet snicker comes from the blonde girl on her left as my eyes meet hers. I'm instantly irritated because I'm trying to focus on getting this job and this blonde girl has snickered. I hate inside jokes. "Now, let me introduce you to the group."

65

Darcie stands and walks up behind the man on the end. "This is Big Mike. He's our doorman, bouncer and driver of intoxicated employees. He will be your easiest customer today." She moves down another stool, "I think you already met him, but Gavin will be your partner in crime behind the bar." I nod my head to Gavin and give him a slight smile.

Darcie moves down the line and wraps her arms around the blonde girl. She is very pretty, goddess looking even, and I immediately become self-conscious of how I look. She has her hair braided down her back and her blue eyes are sparkling with delight. Actually, when I look at all of these people, they are all very good looking. Even the older bouncer guy; he's got a slight edge of danger about him, but all in all, he is quite handsome. "This is my best friend, Delilah, and probably the sweetest person you'll ever meet."

"Yeah, fucking right," snaps the hot tattooed man sitting at the end of the row. He rolls his eyes and looks directly at Delilah. Yikes, I'm sensing some tension from the two of them.

"Some people have no manners. Just ignore his childish outbursts. I do." Delilah glares slightly at his rant then turns her attention back toward me, smile intact. "It's nice to meet you." She extends her hand and I shake it, returning it with a smile.

"Childish! I will sho—"

"Now's not the time, Jake!" Delilah shouts back as she leans over the bar, making eye contact with him. I start messing with the bar towel in my hand, wishing I could hold it up to just disappear. It's starting to get a little awkward now, and they both look like they're going to kill each other.

"Oh, really!" Jake replies just as heatedly. He turns to me, eyes ablaze and I can feel the anger boiling off his skin. "I'll take that shot of Jack now, Zoe." I quickly pull the bottle from the holder behind the bar and fill a shot glass then pass the liquor down to him. Jake doesn't hesitate to swallow its contents, smiling with relief once it's gone. "Delilah, why do you always act th—"

"Enough! I swear that's all you two do is fight." Reggie's deep voice breaks up the argument, and I'm secretly thanking him in my head.

Darcie moves to stand behind Reggie, her arms draped around his neck as she kisses him on the cheek. Reggie relaxes and it's like she's melted the tension in his body with one peck of her lips. You can tell immediately they are a couple who're completely head over heels for each other.

It's utterly baffling to me how two people can be completely devoted to one another. I've been in many relationships in my young life, but none of them were ever truly love—well, not love like that. There always has to be something in it for me before I'll commit myself to a guy. Terrance has been the only man I've really committed to.

At first, it was the fascination of his lifestyle which quickly changed over to greed when I relished in the nice things he bought me with the money he made from selling drugs. It took several months, but I soon realized the life he lived was not the life I was willing to live also. Nor will it ever be. Getting punched in the side of the head was the final straw.

"And this is my brother, Jake. He will be…uh…well, never mind. I'll let you be surprised," Darcie snickers to herself and I become a little worried.

My eyes connect with his and Jake gives me the sexiest smile in God's creation. His deep brown eyes twinkle with enjoyment. I can feel my panties melt away from the heat his eyes gives off, instantly igniting me to my core, but Jake's not fooling anyone here. I've seen smiles like that my entire life and have learned my lesson the hard way. Yes, he is a gorgeous man and it would probably be a good time fucking him, but with a smile like that...he's a player, which is the worst kind of guy to get hooked on.

Sex is a powerful connection, and I have no doubt it would be mind blowing with him. The last thing I need is to get hung up on a guy, something I tend to do when the sex is amazing. I will be practicing abstinence for as long as I can hold out.

Darcie moves to her seat between Reggie and Delilah then motions for me to begin.

"Okay, what'll you have?" I ask, just as they all start firing away their demands. Oh, shit, this should be interesting.

Drake

I'm walking behind the line workers, overseeing their work as they sort the various metals into the correct places. I've got a few new guys who've just started this week and they need constant supervision. I can't keep my mind from wandering back to Saturday night, though. My reaction to the girl who strolled into the bar and upset my oblivious state of mind has me baffled. Although she wasn't there long, the very sight of her has been burned into my memory.

She's tall, a lot taller than normal girls. I'm guessing

68

she's just under or right at six feet. Trim legs that go on for miles; beautiful, full lips; flawless, pale skin; full breasts; and long, chestnut brown hair that curls in large waves down her back. With all that, it's the look her gray-blue eyes gave me that has me flying downward in a tailspin. I can't get that feeling out of my head. The more I think about it, the guiltier I feel for allowing myself to think of another woman only eighteen months after Presley's death. I've never thought another woman could ever pull me from my dark head, but this girl has. She's moved her way into my mind—completely throwing my world off balance.

Then there's Mia I need to consider as well. My daughter is young, and if I even consider moving past Presley, I have to find someone who will be good to my baby. Someone who's willing to love her the way a mother loves a child. I refuse to allow anyone around my baby until I know for sure this is something worth believing in.

What am I doing?

How am I even considering being with anyone right now?

I get angry with myself instantly as the guilt of thinking of another woman floods my body for the millionth time since I've seen the mystifying girl. I'm getting the urge to punch something, yet I have to control it. I can't afford to lose my job over stupid emotions brought on by someone I've never even met. I shake my head and turn my focus back to work.

When the day is over, I drive to Mrs. Fields's to pick Mia up from her house. The rest of the day was better once I was able to keep my focus on work instead of that damn girl.

When I walk into the apartment, Mrs. Fields is sitting on the couch watching Mia play with her dolls, but something is off. I look over to her to notice she looks horrible, sickly.

I fall to my knees and startle her out of a trance. "Are you okay?"

"Oh, Drake." Mrs. Fields jumps slightly and takes a tissue to her nose. Her skin is very pale and clammy. "I think I caught a little flu bug or something. I'll be fine. It's nothing my old bones can't handle." She smiles back to me, but it's not the usual smile she gives.

"Do you want me to get you anything?" I ask.

Before she can answer, Mia has finally noticed I'm here and comes running into my arms. "Dada!" She wraps her arms around my neck and I return her embrace. This is one of the best feelings in the world. "Nanny sick, Dada." Her look has turned to concern as she points to Mrs. Fields sitting on the couch.

"I know, baby," I reply, looking over at Mrs. Fields on the couch.

Mia wiggles out of my arms and walks over to her lap, tapping her on the knee before she leans forward, laying her head on her legs. She looks over to me then back up to Mrs. Fields, "You sick, Nanny?"

"Oh, sweet girl, yes, Nanny is sick, but I'll be all right." She runs her fingers through Mia's hair, brushing it away from her face then kisses the pad of her finger and places it on the tip of her nose. Mia giggles and comes back to my arms.

"Well, we'll get out of your hair. I'll see if I can get someone else to watch Mia tomorrow so you can get some rest. I know how impossible it is to recuperate with a two-year-old to care for." I am really worried about her, knowing she doesn't have anyone to care for her. She's alone here and has been for awhile. It's probably no big deal to Mrs. Fields because she's been taking care of herself for a long time, but I want her to know she can count on me for anything. She's done a lot for me and my family. It's the least I can do for her. "Please call me if you need anything. It's not a bother, okay?"

She gives me a weak smile and stands up from the couch. I stand as well, towering over her tiny frame, and then she wraps her arms around my waist. I hug her back gently as she whispers, "You're an amazing young man. You know that?" I nod, not in agreement, but to acknowledge her statement. "Drake," she moves her hand up to my cheek, eyes filled with water, making my insides ache with hurt, "you are such a wonderful person. No one can go through what you've gone through in life and still be walking on their own two feet. I know you're mad at everything and everyone, but you have so much life left to live. This is your chance, live it." Mrs. Fields breaks our connection and bends down, kissing Mia on her cheek.

"Bye, Nanny!" Mia shouts and runs to the door.

I pick her up in my arms and look back to Mrs. Fields, burning her face into my memory. She gives me the slightest smile then waves us off.

When we exit the apartment, I get the sickening feeling in my gut that's telling me my time with Mrs. Fields will be cut short. Like so many people I've connected with, my time is always cut short.

Chapter 9
Zoe

Today is my second night at *The Slab*. I started last night, and it went pretty well, however Darcie has informed me the crowd is always a little bigger and rowdier on Saturdays. This will be my final test, I guess. It was definitely busy last night and I was seriously excited about making two hundred bucks in tips alone. I may not need a second job if this keeps up.

My audition went pretty well. Two hours into it, it was clear to me why Darcie said they'd be the hardest customers to wait on. Every single one of them were obnoxious, even Reggie. Jake was hitting on me right and left, making the need to take a cold shower more and more immediate. Delilah, who started out happy and giddy when she started drinking, became a lunatic, and the next thing I know, she's snapping at me and shooting death glares in my direction. I finally discovered Jake and Delilah are a couple as they started screaming at one another again then, in a flash, were both kissing savagely, reciting their love for one another. Darcie just rolled her eyes and said they are always like that. I suppressed a laugh.

Earlier today, Reggie called, telling me I need to be at work around five and to be prepared for a large crowd. Apparently, there is some big race, and lately, the crowd has been coming to the bar once it's over. All I see are dollar signs as I think of the massive amount of money I will make in tips if it's going to be busier than last night.

I discovered Darcie is a lot like me, meaning she doesn't bullshit and calls it like she sees it. The three of us divided the bar into three different stations. Gavin handled the right side, I was in the middle, and Darcie was on the left. We didn't step on each other's toes and all seemed to work well together. I actually really enjoyed working last night, which is another disturbing first for me.

***

Five hours into my shift, the bar is jam packed with customers. I'm moving quickly, making drinks, filling mugs of beer, and handling demanding customers. They seem to have taken a liking to me—the guys especially— but the tips are pouring in, so I keep up the charming act just to put more money in the tip jar. One man in particular looks a little familiar, then again, he doesn't. There's nothing recognizable about him that makes him stand out; he's just an average, everyday guy, however that doesn't prevent me from thinking he's someone of interest.

"What can I get ya?" I ask the man as I wipe down the bar top.

"What do you suggest?" He licks his lips and I'm instantly disgusted. Now I know this guy because I've run across him at every single bar I've ever worked at. He's the quintessential bar tool, a douche bag. Jackasses like him think their shit doesn't stink and that they're God's gift to women, yet in all actuality, they're disgusting and probably horrible in bed. I've never been desperate enough to sleep with one, though, I've just come to that conclusion.

73

"Gin and tonic. They're my favorite." It's a lie. I hate gin, but it's my go-to suggestion to anyone with a major creep factor.

"Sounds good." He moves to touch my hand that's resting on the bar top, but I quickly move into action making his drink. I pour in the gin and tonic water and then top it off with a slice of lime. I toss the straw in the glass and slide it across the bar.

Four dollars and seventy-five cents."

He hands me a five dollar bill and tells me to keep the change. Cheep fucking bastard, only tipping me a quarter. I let it slide. He's a weird freaking dude and I don't want him coming around again.

Out of the corner of my eye, I see the mysterious man sitting at the edge of the bar. Darcie fills a mug of Guinness and passes it to him then she fills a shot glass with Jack Daniels and sits it next to the beer. He has yet to look up from the bar top, and I can't help but wonder what his story is. His body is very ridged and tense. Every once in a while he will clench his fists hard then relax. My curiosity is peaking as I watch him for several seconds, ignoring my customers. I'm completely captivated.

Drake

Delilah was dying to have some Mia time tonight and offered to watch her overnight at their place. I was happy to oblige, knowing I needed to get drunk. The girl from the bar was still invading my thoughts after causing me to stress out all week. I need to let off some steam that beating the shit out of a punching bag hasn't been curing.

Delilah and Jake have made their own home above a garage they purchased six months ago. Turns out, Delilah's father has a passion for muscle cars, and soon after she moved to Sulfur Heights, Mr. St. James and Jake hit it off by talking about their love of cars. He's made a few trips here without his wife, of course, and six months ago, he helped Jake purchase the shop he now owns and runs.

They converted the second floor of the building to an apartment and have been living there for the last couple of months. Delilah does have a way of warming up a room when she's around, and in no time, the apartment was transformed into a pretty nice place to live.

She helps Jake with the financials for running the business, similar to how Darcie and Reggie work, and she also volunteers down at the children's shelter. However, unlike Darcie—who will help down at the bar—Delilah refuses to get dirt under her nails and will never go into the shop. It's funny how completely different Jake and Delilah are, yet they are perfect for one another.

Who would have known that Jake could possess the skills all along to fix up cars? I was a little shocked when he said he was going to buy a shop and had little faith in my brother's new adventure. Back in the day, he just refused to do any of the dirty work, knowing Jeremy was there to handle it. But to my surprise, Jake is doing quite well running his garage. He actually does the work, and between him and the other mechanic, they get a lot done. Jake talks about the shop all the time and I can see the pride on his face.

Mrs. Fields was pretty sick most of the week, so I took a few days off to be with Mia. She was feeling much better by Thursday to watch her, but was so worn out by Saturday night that she didn't offer to watch Mia.

I never have to ask Mrs. Fields if Mia can stay with her on Saturdays; she's always volunteered to take her. So when Delilah wanted to watch Mia, I jumped on it immediately.

Around nine o'clock I walk into the back of the bar and step into Reggie's office. Empty. Damn, it's probably busy as hell again. I make my way into the bar to find the noise is deafening. When it's really busy, Reggie will work crowd control alongside Mike.

Before I begin to wonder who's helping behind the bar, I turn to see the girl who's been the cause of monopolizing all my thoughts, and she's mixing drinks! Fuck! I don't need this right now.

Darcie sees me immediately and sets a shot and beer down in front of the end stool where I normally sit. I flop down and choke the poison down instantly.

I can't believe she's working here and I didn't even see it coming. This is a prime example of life fucking with me. She's all I could think about for the past week, and now, there she is, standing before me.

I take a brief second to look at her. Her brown hair is twisted up and piled on top of her head. That's when I notice how long and delicate her neck is. I scan my eyes down the length of her entire body, noticing how lean and tight she is. She's very sexy and my dick reacts at the mere sight of her.

I fix my gaze on Darcie to get another shot when she returns my stare, obviously noticing me looking at her new bartender. My face heats with irritation when Darcie just smiles and passes me my drink. I roll my eyes, more at myself than to her, then chug down the booze. Another glass is set down in front of me and then another. Before I know it, I'm wasted and feeling numb. However, the relief that typically follows my inebriated state never settles over me, only unwanted feelings for a girl who could never be mine along with the guilt over a woman I can never have again.

***

The bar is even more packed as the time hits midnight. I can safely say I'm very drunk but still functional, which is exactly how I need to be. As I'm getting ready to leave, some douche bag strolls up beside me, trying to get Darcie's attention.

"Hey! Bartender!" the man shouts over the noise of the crowd. "Can I get a fucking drink?" He loudly taps his hand on the bar, getting Darcie's attention. I can't help but feel amused knowing Darcie doesn't take to bossy customers very well.

Darcie walks over to him with a shit eating grin spread across her face. "Hey, fuckstick, I'd be glad to make you a drink just as soon as you get in the line like everyone else." She moves back to the other customers, quickly filling their drink orders.

"Fucking bitch," the man mumbles under his breath.

All the anger boiling just under the surface of my skin erupts from inside of me, and I lose it. I snap my murderous glare to the douche bag. "What did you just say?"

He turns his body toward me, looking me straight in the eye. The very sight of his face pisses me off. He's a young prick with no respect or remorse for insulting my sister when he replies to my question. "I called her a fucking bitch, asshole. What are you going to do about it?"

Before I can stop myself, I'm already on my feet, towering over the guy, who I'm certain, hasn't been expecting me to be so tall. I wrap my hands around his neck then suddenly my mind flashes back to what I was feeling that night. That very night I wanted to put my hands on my brother. The night Jeremy confessed to being a drug dealer, making the hate I never fathomed surface and become a permanent part of my soul. I picture the satisfaction of killing my brother and this sends me into a blind fury. This man is *now* Jeremy and I want to choke him.

I pick him up by his neck and swing him back, slamming his body into the wall, then press my body against his. He's scared and I know he won't fight back, but all I see is Jeremy in his eyes and I want to kill him. My heart is beating wildly in my ears, drowning out any other noise in the bar. The muscles in my forearm bulge as I squeeze. With just a little more pressure, he'll be dead. The rage is too much for me to stop and it feels good to take it out on an actual person and not a punching bag.

I draw my fist back, readying myself to crush it into his jaw when Reggie comes to my side, heaving me off the man. I let go of his neck and he falls to the floor, coughing and gagging, crumpling at my feet. The air in my lungs is rapidly filtering through my body when I take deep adrenaline-filled breaths. Reggie grabs a hold of my arm, pushing me toward the back then into the back room.

"Goddammit, Drake, what the hell was that for?" His glare is intense as he stares me down.

It takes me a second to answer his question. The rage is suffocating my throat, preventing me from speaking. "He called Darcie a bitch when she refused to serve him," I say, thinking this will completely satisfy Reggie, but it does the opposite.

He begins to pace the room, runs his hands over his head, then moves back to stand in front of me—on the verge of exploding. "Did you see that guy's face? You almost killed him, Drake!" Reggie lets out a deep breath to prepare to lecture me again. "That was no excuse to choke a man out. You really need to get a hold of your rage before you really hurt someone."

I stand there, anger boiling once again. This is Reggie's way of telling me to get over the past and move on. His way of saying it's been a damn year and he's ready for me to get over it. The very thought enrages me further. He has no idea what I've been through since Presley died and I found out my brother betrayed me. I can't stand his condescending tone and I'm ready to kill him now!

"Fuck you!" I shout. I belly up to him, looking to finish what I started with that man.

"I know that look, Drake. Don't even think about it," Reggie threatens as he steps in front of me, meeting me eye-to-eye. Granted, he's a great fighter, but I've got betrayal and loss on my side—fueling my fist to hit harder. "Get a handle on yourself, or I won't allow you to drink down here anymore. Got it?"

Before I can take him down, Reggie leaves the back room. I begin to obliterate the wall, tearing up my hand and my sanity with every punch I give—trying to win the war against my blinding rage and broken heart.

Zoe

When we finally slow down enough to take a breather,

Gavin gives me pointers on how to use the credit card machine. It tends to be a pain in the ass, according to him, but I think it's his inability to use technology.

A loud noise grabs our attention when a fight erupts at the other end of the bar. The mysterious man has another guy in a choke hold, squeezing the life from his body. I am stunned where I stand, wanting to do something to help, yet I'm completely unable to move. The man's face is turning purple, and he is clearly losing his battle with getting air in when Reggie intercedes, pushing the mystery man out of sight. Darcie runs to the man on the floor, helping him up, before Mike ushers him out the front door.

I turn to Gavin, who looks sick to his stomach. "What's up with that dude anyway? It's kind a creepy the way he sits and drinks by himself. Serial killer tendencies if you ask me."

Gavin turns to me and shakes his head no. Curiosity peaks even more, and now I *need* to know his story more than I need food to nourish my body. Why would he just freak like that? Is he really a wannabe serial killer? Or is he a recently released psych ward patient?

"Seriously, Gavin, did you see him snap? I'm pretty sure I need to know what's going on with him so *I* don't piss him off." I think about him pressing me against the wall with his hands wrapped around my neck, but it's for an entirely different reason. What the fuck is wrong with me? I lust after psychotic mental patients now?

"Look, Zoe, that's Darcie's youngest brother and he's…" Gavin trails off, searching to find the right words. He scratches his head, running his hand over his short, reddish-blonde hair. He's in a deep debate with himself on

80

how to approach the subject. "He's had a hard life, okay? So just leave him alone. Just ignore him. Don't try to talk to him or anything. Darcie and Reggie are the only ones allowed to wait on him since the whole *incident*...he's just not right in the head these days." He lifts his hands, using air quotes when he says the word *incident*.

Damn, my curiosity is slicing my mind apart. What could that incident be? What would lead a man to be free yet walk a very close line to killing a stranger? He's got to be a serial killer or something. People only ever use the word *incident* when someone is killed. Fuck, who'd he kill?

Without another word, Gavin steps to the bar to help a customer, leaving me with my thoughts. That little tidbit of information hasn't helped me; it makes my mind run wild with scenarios of why he's so crazy. I want—actually, I *need* to know more. I've never been one to pry because I hate when people are in my business, however the details of this man's past are killing me. I've gotta know! What the hell would cause someone to flip on a stranger for no reason? I mean, he almost killed that man. The very thought really bothers and intrigues me all in one.

Darcie instructs me to take a five minute break and to come back with two fresh bottles of vodka from the backroom. Damn, I could really use a cigarette. I haven't smoked in a year, but I could really use one right now. Pulling a stick of gum from my pocket, I shake off the desire to pollute my lungs and head to the restroom.

When I come out of the bathroom, I round the corner and walk toward the backroom. The door opens abruptly, hitting the wall behind it as it flies open, and he's standing right there—the mysterious, mentally unstable guy. He walks out of the back room so fast that he practically collides with me. I freeze mid-step, grabbing the wall to regain my balance. I become frozen where I stand, unsure of what to do or say.

My eyes are connected to his, just like the night we first met. I expel a deep breath in an attempt to get a handle on my feelings. On one hand, I'm scared out of my mind because I just watched him almost choke a man to death, and let's not forget the infamous *incident* clouding his past. On the other hand, I've never been so turned on. He's very different and more dangerous from any man I've been around, and the combination is intoxicating. There's an edge about him, and the longer I look at him, the more I feel myself inching closer to that edge.

He stands in front of me for what feels like an eternity, just staring at me. His eyes are black as coal and studying me with a puzzling glance. I notice his skin is slick with sweat, filling the air with his manly scent. That, too, is very intoxicating. I look down over his broad shoulders, trace my eyes down his large biceps, and stop my perusal when I see blood dripping from his knuckles. He has to feel the pain from his torn up knuckles, but it doesn't seem to faze him. His chest is rapidly caving in and out with his deep breaths, though.

We are close, so close that, if I take a small step forward, we'd be touching. I feel lightheaded—drunk even—yet I haven't had a single drop of alcohol. Then he speaks, and again I become high off him.

"Who are you?" His voice is a deep baritone, his words quiet yet laced with anger.

"I'm Zoe," I respond just as quietly, starting to wonder

if I will ever be able to break my gaze with his.

He lifts his hand, inching it closer to my face. Now I'm scared and my body starts to tremble. I know what those hands are capable of. He just almost killed a man, but I yearn for him to touch me. Oh, man, do I want him to touch me. My insides heat with desire, a pure lust for this enigmatic man.

He's pulling me into his black abyss the longer I look into his eyes, and I can't think of a single reason for stopping him. I'm hypnotized. My heart is pounding and there are butterflies rapidly fluttering inside my chest. I can feel a lump slowly finding its way to the top of my throat.

Then, just as his bloody hand gets dangerously close to my cheek, I close my eyes and suck in a deep breath, preparing to feel either his pleasure or my pain. However, he pulls his hand away quickly then steps back, retreating out the back door and into the night. The mystery man leaves me feeling scared, aching to know more about him.

Chapter 10
Drake

What just happened? Who is this girl? And why do I want to know more about her? Then there's this fuck at the bar. I've never wanted to destroy someone so much in my life. Never mind the fact I almost killed the dude because I thought of my brother. I couldn't shut off my anger; it's constantly there just under the surface. This isn't the only time since Presley's death that I've come close to killing someone. The rage is always there—a living, breathing beast ready to escape at a moment's notice.

Six months after her death, I was coping fairly well, but I still couldn't talk to anyone. Much like tonight's situation, a man approached me, trying to make small talk. I ignored him at first, then he started talking about getting into the drag racing scene, and that was all I needed to hear. My sanity snapped and I tackled the man to the ground, punching him as hard as I could. It felt good to hit him. I wanted to hit him more, but before too much damage could be done, Reggie broke up the fight. I was annoyed because he thought he could just talk to me, however the mere mention of drag racing brought me back to why I have so much hatred inside of me—my brother. I lost it and tried to kill the unsuspecting man.

I'm lucky he didn't press charges, and until today, I've

kept a pretty good handle on my rage. Anything reminding me of Jeremy, and then this girl—well, it's all I can do to control myself. All of it is about to kill me. She's causing feelings in me to surface, but the infuriation that's always living inside me is the only emotion I want to let out.

I park my Chevelle in the driveway and walk to the garage. I'm not ready to go to bed—my head is too fucked up right now. I pull the shirt off my back and slip my hands into my boxing gloves. Slowly, I start hitting the bag. Controlled punches come from my hands as I land them against the hard leather of the punching bag. I need to come down from the raging high I felt when I was hurting that man, so I continue to hit the bag. Over and over and over— each time my hands strike a little faster and a lot harder. I'm burning through my adrenaline the best way I know how.

Just as the exhaustion starts to take over, I look over to the Challenger parked in the garage. It hasn't been here in months, but Jake needed room in his garage and has stored it here. I hate this car. I hate everything it represents in my life.

I move forward, standing over the hood. The black paint is shining and flawless, in pristine condition for when Jeremy gets home.

I snap.

Fury once again surfaces when I think of my brother and the pain he's caused me. I start pounding my fist into the hood of the car gorilla style, wildly swinging my fist into the metal, putting dents in it with every strike. Jeremy loves this car, and because he loves it so much, I will destroy it with my fists, just as he's destroyed me.

As I obliterate the hood of the Challenger, I think about what Jeremy has done to me. For years, he worked with Carter, selling heroin to make a living. He was too big of a pussy to get a real job and look what it's done for him. Now he's locked up for several years, rotting away in a cell and will never have a decent life again.

When I think about the night before he was arrested, it causes me to get even angrier. We sat in this garage and he allowed me to cry my eyes out to him, knowing how much I was hurting from her death, and said nothing. He acted like he cared what happened to her, but the truth is, he only cared that he got caught.

He doesn't feel the consequence of what he's done to me or my daughter or my dead girlfriend. He only feels the consequence of his arrested. He singlehandedly destroyed our family and my ability to trust someone again. He is the reason I'm so angry and set to kill whenever someone crosses me. He is the trigger for my rage, and until he's in front of me to take out all the fury first hand, I will continue to destroy everything that means something to him. How could I not?

When I step back from the Challenger, the hood is completely dented in and a small twinge of pride surfaces. I'm glad it looks like shit because it's the one and only thing he loved besides himself. If he really loved his family, Jeremy never would have started selling drugs—plain and simple.

Zoe

The sun is brightly shining through the window, waking me up. It's far too early for this night owl. I raise my arms above my head and feel tension in my shoulders and biceps. My legs ache along with my feet. We were so busy at the bar the last two nights that my body is screaming at me. It's been awhile since I've worked that hard—well, since Terrance asked me to move in with him and swore he'd take care of me. Unbeknownst to me, his idea of taking care of me is having a 1950s housewife, one who will wait on him hand and foot, then when she gets out of line, bash her head in. Screw that! I'm number one, and I won't live like that.

Then I think about the only thing that's been on my mind since I strolled through the front doors of *The Slab*—the dangerous stranger. I've been intrigued from the moment our eyes connected on the first night I saw him, but last night was completely different. I watched him almost take a life, saw the anger first hand, yet it did nothing to pull me away from him. In fact, it pushed me closer to him. All I want to do is know more about him.

As I roll off the bed and freshen up in the bathroom, my stomach is grumbling and my body is weary. I grab my keys and purse from the counter and head out to my car. I decide to visit a department store to get the darkest curtains possible then go to a drive-thru to silence my ravenous stomach.

I pull into the parking lot of a discount department store and exit my car. As I get closer to the building, a small, older woman is pushing a cart from the door and walking to her car. Is that...? No, that couldn't be her. Could it?

I toss my keys in my purse then pull the strap over my head, securing my purse across my body. I quickly walk toward the woman. Her hair looks the same, but she's a lot thinner from when I saw her last. Granted, it's been over four years since I've seen anyone in my family, but I know it's my aunt.

I cut her off as she crosses the aisle and our eyes connect. It's her. "Aunt Connie?"

She gasps when her recollection of me surfaces to the front of her mind. "Zoe? Is that you, honey?"

I move around to the side of her cart as I nod my head. She doesn't say a word, she just wraps me in a tight embrace. It's then that I remember the familiarity of Sulfur Heights. When Aunt Connie would come to visit, she'd always talk about this place. I remember that, as a child, I never wanted to visit her here; it sounded scary and dangerous. It's funny that all I'm thinking about right now is the scary and dangerous. Thinking about how much I want to be around it, to kiss it and feel it pressed against my body.

We release each other and Aunt Connie holds me at arm's length. Her blue eyes are glistening with tears as we stand in the parking lot, staring at each other.

I look down at her cart and notice it is full of sacks. I lean down in the cart and start pulling bags out. "Where's your car? I can help you with these."

Aunt Connie points to a small four door sedan and pushes the button on her key ring, popping the trunk. I place the sacks in the trunk carefully. Before I close the trunk lid, I notice a sack is filled with child's toys. It makes me wonder who she's purchased the toys for, but I'm soon reminded of the life I left behind four years ago. I'm twenty-two and it's very possible Sophia has had a kid. We are the same age and there was a time when she was my best friend, but when she chose to believe the lie, I knew our time as friends—as family—was over.

My stomach roars loudly and I'm instantly reminded of how hungry I am. I grab it and smile politely over to Aunt Connie. "Sorry, I guess I need to get going so I can eat. It's good seeing you, Aunt Connie."

I pull away from her, but before I am able to get too far, she grabs my hand, not allowing me to move away from her. "Please…I haven't seen you in four years. What are you doing in Sulfur Heights? Did you move here?"

My heart breaks when I look in her eyes. She's always been a good person, and growing up, I looked up to her.

She took in my mother when her parents died. She was selfless as she raised her. Aunt Connie did the best she could to raise her in a town like Sulfur Heights. She had her own family to care for, but Aunt Connie and my Uncle Ray did what they could to raise my mother and their child, Sophia's mother, Rebecca. As soon as Rebecca and my mom were old enough, they both deserted my Aunt Connie, leaving her and the town they hated behind. I don't remember either of them ever coming back to visit, and I can safely say I've never been here until a few days ago.

I don't know what to say. A part of me wants to tell her where I've been, allow her to hold me and take care of each other, but it's not possible. When I left Wisconsin years ago, I refused to lay roots down anywhere. I will only be in Sulfur Heights long enough to make some money then I will head off to the next state.

"I…I don't want to keep you."

"Zoe, really, it's no bother." She's still holding my hand as she inches her way into my plans. "Are you going to be in town long?"

"I've only lived here a couple of weeks," I answer honestly, wishing I could just leave right now.

"Then come over to my house today so we can catch up. I usually cook a decent meal on Sundays and today I was thinking of making Spaghetti." Her blue eyes are pleading, breaking me down the longer I stare into them.

"Okay," I whisper back and then capture Connie in a hug.

She wipes the tears from her eyes and hands me a piece of paper with her address on it. I tuck it into the back pocket of my purse and watch her enter her car. As she waves goodbye to me, I get the unsuspecting feeling it's going to be a big mistake to go to her house. I'm starting to wish I never even left my bed this morning.

I turn back to my car and climb inside, avoiding the store altogether. My ravenous appetite vanishes as I head back to my apartment, allowing the bright sun to pierce my eyes.

Drake

Last night was a nightmare, but after my shower, I decide to shake it off and move forward with today. I walk to the kitchen and pull out a can of Mountain Dew when Delilah, Jake and Mia come strolling through the back door. Mia runs to me, and I swiftly pick her up in my arms, kissing her on the cheek. She looks beautiful in her green summer dress and pigtails. She smells like baby lotion and her honey-brown eyes are glimmering with happiness.

I let Mia down and she runs to her room as Jake and Delilah make their way deeper into the kitchen. My smile, as always, leaves my face when my daughter is not seeking my attention. I finish chugging down my soda and break the silence.

"So how was she?" I ask, speaking to Delilah while refusing to lift my head up to connect with her eyes. Her eyes, out of everyone's, are always filled with the most pity.

"Oh, she was just a doll," Delilah says and giggles when Jake wraps his arms around her waist and pulls her into his body. He's planting kisses on her neck and she can't help but melt into his arms. The sight of their happiness infuriates me. Little gestures they do here and there always remind me of what I used to have, and how I will never have that again. The wound is still too fresh, gaping even, and until it's partially healed, their relationship will bother me. I crush the aluminum can in my hand and choke back the rage.

I don't acknowledge Delilah's comment. The best thing for me right now is to separate myself from them. I toss the can in the sink and move to exit the kitchen when Jake's irritating voice stops me in my tracks. "So...ah, Reggie told me you about snapped a guy's neck last night. Care to tell me about that?" His voice is snarky and condescending.

Jake is a good brother, yet he doesn't know when to leave well enough alone, and often times, I leave the room feeling worse than when our conversation started.

"There's nothing to talk about. Why do you care anyway?"

"Hmmm...let's think about that one, Drake. Because you almost killed someone. Because you have a two-year-old daughter to care for. Oh...and a family who cares what happens to you regardless if you don't." Jake moves in front of Delilah, pulling her behind his frame—his standard move lately when we have a conversation. Jake knows eventually our relationship will come to blows. His arms are tight and body poised for battle.

My actions mirror his as the fury pumps through my veins. "Leave. It. Alone," I growl back, raising my head for the first time in ages to look my brother in the eye. We are connected in a mental showdown, and soon, both of us will explode. I can feel the tension clinging in the air and it won't be long now. Jake senses it, too. His body becomes more rigid.

Delilah's tiny hand comes around Jake's midsection and she grabs onto his waist. Her head peers around his body and her eyes meet mine. I break slightly when I look into her eyes, knowing she is missing her friend as much as I'm missing my girlfriend. "Jake, come on. Let's not do this."

"You're right, D. I don't want to fight him. I've already lost one brother. I can't afford to lose another." Jake is still intently glaring at me as I wonder what his comment is supposed to mean. I disregard the comment about Jeremy, although it still pisses me off. But what does he mean? Does he think he can take me? Is he really that delusional to assume he'll kill me if he gets his hands on me?

"What the hell is that supposed to mean?" I step to him, closing the gap between our tense bodies. The tension is getting thicker, cloaking even, and it's about to go down.

Jake pulls Delilah's hands away from his waist and steps closer to me. We are within inches of each other, and the already tiny kitchen gets smaller as our egos begin to take life. "It means, brother, that if I fight you, I won't be the one lying on the ground when it's all said and done."

I step even closer, looking down on him, standing a couple inches taller than him, and try to kill him with my intense glare. The slamming of a door attempts to get my attention, but Jake's face brings all my rage back to our conversation. "You're a delusional fuck. And you're weak. You won't know what pain is until I unleash it on you."

A smirk flashes across his face and I immediately want to smack it off. "You're a real big man, aren't ya, Drake? Pussies sucker punch. Pussies choke men when they're not expecting it." Jake exhales a deep breath into my face. "That's how I know I'll kill you because you're nothing but a pussy," he spits out at me.

I grab a hold of Jake's throat and swing him back, slamming his body against the fridge. Contents inside rattle and unused paper towel rolls tumble from the top. Before I have time to react, Jake returns my fury with that of his own. His fist swings around then connects with my cheek. Pain erupts in my face, but I push past it, refusing to let go of his neck. I pull Jake back toward me and slam him into the fridge again, banging his head into it. Jake lands a blow to my stomach causing me to flinch in pain, but I still refuse to let go of his neck.

I begin to channel the rage living in every square inch of my body and let it explode from my arms. The harder I squeeze, the more Jake struggles to get out of my grasp. His eyes are losing their life as I keep myself from looking away. He looks just like Jeremy. He has now become Jeremy. This is exactly what I want to do with Jeremy. I want to stand over him and choke the life he has taken from me. I want retribution for Presley. I'm seeking vengeance right now, and because Jake looks so much like the brother I hate, I will take that vengeance out on him. Nothing else matters right now. Only his death. I can't see anything else, just the red of her blood and the dying look of his face.

Jake's blows to my stomach start to weaken as his body starts to slump and his eyes roll slightly to the back of his head.

"Dada?" The sound of her voice brings me back to the present like a brick to the head. I immediately let go of Jake and he falls to the floor, coughing and gagging. When I turn, Mia is standing in the doorway of the kitchen—horror and bewilderment encasing her eyes.

What have I done?

I look to the ground where Jake is crumpled at my feet, desperately trying to get the air back into his lungs. I turn to hold Mia, but she steps back slightly, afraid of me. The guilt of my actions takes over every other feeling I've ever had.

Just then, the back door opens and Reggie, Delilah and Darcie come storming in the kitchen. Delilah falls to the floor, pulling Jake up in her arms. "What did you DO?" she screams at me, her eyes liquid blue pools, her body raging in anger.

"He about fucking killed me!" Jake screams back, finally finding the air to let in and out his body. He pops to his feet, immediately sizing me up again.

"Jake!" Reggie screams. "Outside, NOW!" Reggie pulls Jake's arm back, tugging him toward the back door. Delilah soon follows him out the door, wiping her tears as she goes. "Darcie, will you take Mia. I need to have a word with Drake alone." Darcie says nothing as she scoops Mia up in her arms and retreats down the hall.

I connect my eyes with Reggie as the anger ignites once again. He leans back against the counter and crosses his arms over his chest as he finds the words to speak. "What happened, Drake?"

"He called me a pussy and I proved I wasn't." I turn my body to face his, waiting to pick up where Jake left off.

"So you about killed your brother?" Reggie pushes off the counter and meets me in the middle of the kitchen.

"Back off, Reggie," I seethe in his direction, readying myself to punch him.

"No! You need to get a hold of yourself. Last night was one thing, but now, you tried to kill your own brother, worse yet, in front of your daughter!"

I stand, lifting my eyes to meet his, wanting to hurt him as much as I want to hurt everyone around me. They have no idea what's going on in my life. No one knows what it's like to lose everything you love, all at the hands of your brother. Hate and anger is all that I have left.

"You don't know what this is like, so don't pretend to know how I feel. I am coping the only way I know how, so spare me the lecture."

"Look, Drake, I've never said I understand anything you're going through and I don't pretend to, either, but I will do what's necessary to protect my family. And if you can't get a handle on your anger, then I'll do what I need to in order to keep you away from my family. That includes Mia."

"Like hell you will." I'll be damned if anyone will

raise my daughter but me. I step to Reggie and brush my chest with his. Anger is all that's living inside of me.

"Back off, Drake," Reggie warns

I ignore his threat and swing my fist. He's not going to take my baby from me. I will kill him before I let that happen. Reggie deflects my punch and expertly moves his body, knocking me to the floor. I fall with a loud thud as Reggie falls immediately to the floor, locking me into a rear naked choke hold. It's his infamous MMA move that has caused many men to submit almost instantly. His right forearm is tightly wound around my neck as he holds it tighter with his other hand. I try to buck my feet up and turn over to my knees, but Reggie again is one step ahead of me. He wraps his legs around my waist, squeezing the life from my midsection and pinning my legs to the floor.

His head is right by my ear and I can feel his hot breath on my neck. He's breathing deeply as I'm trying to capture my breath. "Look at what you've become, Drake. You almost killed your own brother in front of your daughter. You need help."

"You...don't...know what...I need," I speak in a slurred tone.

"Drake," Reggie releases another deep breath and tightens his hold around my neck as I attempt to escape his arms, "you're hurting, I get that, but you can't go around beating the shit out of people because you're pissed. You need help, and instead of fighting us, let us help you. We're your family; that's what we're supposed to do."

I start to weaken when I think of what I've lost. The pain of losing Presley has been dormant as I allowed the anger for Jeremy to control my every move. It's been a long time since I've allowed myself to feel that hurt.

Falling limp in Reggie's hold, my emotional floodgate crumbles. My chest is aching and all the heaviness I thought was gone comes bearing down, suffocating me, and then I see her eyes. Presley's honey-brown eyes, and I fall apart.

Reggie releases his tight grip around my neck as I fall completely to the tile floor, rolling to my stomach and weeping into my hands. My body trembles as I grieve once again for the love that's no longer here. She's gone and I will never get her back. My beautiful love is gone and I can never hold her, kiss her, or tell her I love her. She's gone forever and all that's left is the pain of her absence.

"I…miss…her so much." I sputter my words through the wounds of my broken soul. "I just miss her."

Chapter 11
Drake

When I finally peel myself up from the floor, I take note that my entire family is sitting around me. In my devastated condition, I've had no idea Delilah, Jake and Darcie have come into the room. Reggie is still by my side with his firm protective grasp on my shoulder.

The feeling of love starts to sink back in. I do love my family and I want to try to be the family we were before all this happened. I love them, and in this moment, I know I need them to help me heal. I've been in isolation with my pain for the last year and a half, and I can't do it anymore. I'm tired of walking through this life cloaked in my agony. I need to let it go, and letting my family in is the best way to release some of the burden.

I make it to my feet and the rest of them follow suit. I immediately turn to Jake, my eyes are swollen and broken from my outburst, but an apology is necessary. "I'm sorry, Jake. I saw you and then I didn't. I saw him."

Jake doesn't say a word, only stares are me with an unreadable face. I can tell he is still furious with me, and the marks around his neck are a reminder of what I've just done. Delilah tucks her hand inside his and he looks down to their joined hands then back up to her eyes. The tension in his body relaxes, and when he turns to me, I feel him pull me in for a hug. "I forgive you, brother," he whispers to me.

Reggie hands me a business card with Dr. Redman's information on it. "Just call her. If it all gets to be too much, just call her or me…or any of us. Just don't let it fester, Drake. Because the next time, you *will* do something stupid, and I won't be there to stop you."

I take the card and nod in agreement. I take the time to hug and apologize to my family and walk back to Mia's room. She's sound asleep in her crib, completely at peace. This is the reason I need help—Mia. I can't go on holding in the anger over the past because then, I will never have peace. And I want peace. It's been eighteen months and I'm ready for some peace.

Zoe

After my brief run in with my aunt, I'm regretting even waking up this morning. I'm a stupid idiot for not remembering she lived in Sulfur Heights, but my mind was so focused on getting away from Terrance that I didn't recall it. Now I'm forced to face a member of my family when all I ever wanted to do was forget them. Aunt Connie was always nice, and I know she's not like my mother or her daughter, but she's still family and I vowed the day I was banished to never trust family again.

The August morning was sweltering and now the early afternoon is no better. I pull into the apartment complex and find my way to Connie's apartment. The ache in my gut is either telling me to run or to eat; I can't tell which as I lift my hand to knock on the door. The door swiftly opens and Aunt Connie is there with a big smile on her face.

She's freshened up and looks better than a couple

hours ago. Now I know what the pain in my gut is, I'm starving. The aroma of garlic bread and Aunt Connie's homemade red sauce has me drooling to taste her spaghetti. I haven't eaten a meal like this in ages.

I step through the doorway and get a quick look around. It's a pretty small space with a living area to the right and dining area on the left, which leads to a small galley style kitchen. I look around at the walls, but nothing really covers them. No pictures of grandkids or family portraits—nothing except old photos from the nineties.

Aunt Connie is stirring the sauce in the kitchen when I walk through, inhaling deeply. I can't wait to eat, my stomach is dying. "Can…can I help with anything?" I ask.

"Sure, honey, you can set the table. Will you go into the linen closet in the hall by the bathroom and grab the green table cloth from the top shelf, please?" I look at her with confusion, knowing we don't need to fancy things up for me, yet I don't say anything.

I turn down the hall, walking to the back of the apartment and stand just outside the bedroom. I take a minute to peek through the door and notice it's filled with children's toys, a crib and other little kid things. I remember earlier this morning she had toys in her sacks and now I'm really confused. She has no recent pictures anywhere in the apartment of children. In fact, the only kid hanging on the walls is Sophia, but she was in middle school when that picture was taken.

When I pull the tablecloth from the top shelf I notice it's vinyl and chuckle to myself. Does she really think I will make that big of a mess eating spaghetti? Although, when my stomach roars angrily again, I start to think the tablecloth is needed.

I stroll back up the hall just as the front door opens. Walking through the front door is the mysterious psycho and in his arms is the cutest little girl. My jaw slams to the floor and my throat feels like it's being choked. I'm feeling strangled as I stand frozen yet again. Our eyes connect, and I can see his transform from confused to angry in a matter of seconds.

Oh. My. God. This can't be happening. Is this really happening?

"Nanny!" The little girl squeals as the man releases her from his arms and she goes running to my aunt. I break my gaze from him and look over to the little girl. She's babbling to Aunt Connie, who is intently listening as she holds the little tyke in her arms.

Nanny? How's that possible unless this man is the father of Sophia's baby. But when I look at the little girl, I see that she looks nothing like Sophia. She looks a lot like him, but not even a faint trace of Sophia is reflected in that little girl.

I turn my gaze back to him as he continues to stand there glaring at me, almost murdering me with his eyes. Oh. Shit. The word Gavin has said to me last night comes crashing back at me. *Incident.* He's had an incident in the past, which I'm sure is something terrible.

I right my posture in an attempt to look taller than I already am, trying to give him the impression I won't take his shit. To show him I'm tough and I won't be another *incident* for his past.

"Zoe, come here, child. I want to introduce you to my friends." Aunt Connie breaks up our gaze, and I look over to her. I will my feet to start moving down the hallway while the man doesn't take his sight off me. I can feel his glare digging into my back, and it's sending heated vibes throughout my body.

When I approach Aunt Connie, the little girl in her arms is smiling big and her eyes are pulling me in, like the way his do. "Zoe, this is Mia, the little girl I babysit. Mia, can you say hi to Zoe?"

"Hi," she says with excitement and waves her hand wildly at me. I can't help grinning at the little girl and get sucked into her charms. Normally, kids freak me out, but she's doesn't seem so bad. "Zzzzzzoooooooeeee!" Mia wiggles out of Aunt Connie's arms and runs down the hall. She vanishes out of sight, but you can hear the clanking of toys getting shuffled around in her toy box.

"Drake, this is my niece, Zoe. She's in town for a couple of months and I ran into her at the store today. I thought we could sit around and have lunch together." Aunt Connie is smiling big, turning her head to look between the two of us. "Oh, Drake, what happened to your cheek?" I didn't even notice that the side of his face is slightly bruised and swollen.

"Jake," he answers. Aunt Connie nods her head in acceptance of his answer as I remain confused. Since I know Drake is Darcie's brother, and when I had my audition at the bar Jake was there, I can assume this is the same Jake they are referring to.

Suddenly, a large crash comes from the back room. "Mia?" Aunt Connie says then turns to us. "I will go check on her. Drake, can you put that table cloth under her chair. Lord knows I don't need spaghetti all over my carpet."

With that she scurries down the hall to check on Mia.

Drake snatches the tablecloth out of my hands and shakes it out. He then picks up the chair and sets if off to the side before laying the tablecloth on the floor and setting the chair back down on top of the cover. I still have yet to move, however I'm starting to unthaw as I look over at him. I wonder if my aunt knows he has an incident in his past. I wonder if she knows he's a psychopath.

Drake moves from the dining area and starts pulling dishes out of the cupboard. He's very comfortable here, almost like he lives here or something. He stacks the glasses and silverware on top of the plates then moves to the table, situating each place setting. Each time he sets a dish down, it sounds even louder than it did before.

Finding my courage, I decide to speak to him. "What the hell is your problem?" Okay, it's probably not the best thing to say to a brooding mental patient, but he's really starting to piss me off.

Drake snaps his head up, his eyes ablaze and angry. "You could have told me." His voice is low and menacing.

"Told you what?" I whisper back, trying to understand what he's talking about.

When Mia comes barreling down the hallway, breaking up the conversation, Drake's expression quickly changes to happy as he gets a look at his daughter. I turn to watch her as she runs full-on to me, carrying an orange stuffed animal that looks familiar. She lifts her arms, asking me to hold her.

I look to my aunt who's smiling ear to ear. "She wants to show you something."

I bend at the knees and pick the little girl up into my

arms. She's lighter than I've expected and smells like baby powder, but her eyes are what suck me in. They are so beautiful and nothing like her father's. Drake's are so dark they look black, but Mia's... well, they are a golden brown and shiny.

"Zoe!" Mia says excitedly. "Her like Elmo?" I nod my head up and down, realizing this weird looking doll must be on Sesame Street. "Her pretty," Mia states then squirms out of my lap.

Drake picks Mia up in his arms, places her in the chair and then puts a bib around neck. I help Aunt Connie bring the food to the table and then we all dish up our plates. I choose to sit on the other side of Aunt Connie so I don't have to be so close to Drake, however every once in a while, our eyes will connect and he'll glare at me. This is hands down the most awkward meal I've ever experienced.

Drake

I've said it before and I will probably say it again and again, life's got away of totally fucking with me. When I walked through Mrs. Field's front door, that's exactly what happened—life fucked with me. There is no other explanation for how Zoe—the girl who's been in the forefront of my mind—is standing in front of me. I don't know who this girl is, but lately, she's been showing up at every place I find peaceful. She's interrupting my peace, and it's pissing me off.

After dinner, Mrs. Fields plays with Mia in the living room while Zoe and I are left cleaning up the mess. I still can't shake this feeling about her, and I hate that she's here. This is my place of solace. I feel like, when I'm here, I can just be and the evil of everything outside of this door is

104

gone, but now that's destroyed. Zoe is related to Mrs. Fields, and there's nothing I can do or say to get her away from here. Then to top it all off, Zoe works for my brother at the bar where I like to escape on Saturday nights.

We say nothing as we rinse the dishes off and place them in the dishwasher. Zoe scrapes the leftover food into a container and places it in the fridge. I catch her staring at me every so often, and it's making me uncomfortable.

I can't hold my tongue any longer. I peek my head around the wall to make sure Mia is distracted then I snap my glare back to her. "Do you mind?"

"What?" she snaps back then firmly shuts the fridge door.

"You keep looking at me, and it's really pissing me off." I sound childish, I know, but this is very uncomfortable. I saw this woman in the bar, and for some unknown reason, she has made me look up. There's something about her that angers me, yet more than that, there's something about her that terrifies me.

"Get over yourself, would ya? I was just trying to figure out why fate would do this to me, but luckily for you, I'll be gone as soon as I make enough money." With that, she sets the dish towel down and moves to the living room to accompany the ladies, which leaves me to stew by myself, trying to figure out why her last statement pisses me off so much.

***

In the late afternoon, I decide to let Mia have another short nap before we head back home. She's getting rather cranky and needs a little catnap to be in better spirits for the rest of the day. After I put her down, Mrs. Fields is trying to keep the conversation between Zoe and me alive by asking us boring, mundane questions. I find it annoying, however I refuse to say anything.

"So, Zoe, where do you work?" she asks.

Zoe clears her throat and glances at me briefly. "Ummm...I bartend at *The Slab* on the weekends." Mrs. Fields looks over to me then back to Zoe. Then she starts to chuckle. We both look at her and back to each other. What the hell? "What's so funny, Aunt Connie?"

"It's just that I knew you guys recognized each other when he walked in." She points to me then wipes the tears from her eyes. I didn't think it was that funny. "The looks on your faces were priceless. I may be old, but that doesn't mean I don't notice things."

Zoe smiles in return and then looks at me. She is quite striking when she smiles; it lights up her entire face. "It was busy last night, and it was a surprise to see him here, to say the least."

"Why? Did something happen last night?" Mrs. Fields looks to me and I can't deny the truth on my face. She knows the trouble with my anger. She's never seen it, but I've told her in weaker moments about how I harbor so much rage toward my brother. After I attacked the first guy, Mrs. Fields was the only person I talked to about it. She knows me well and she is aware that I fought last night.

I look up at her, ashamed, and then back down to my hands. "Yeah...the same thing as before." When I connect my eyes with Zoe's, she tilts her head slightly, curiosity peaking just below the surface.

"I see." It's all Mrs. Fields says because she's suddenly interrupted by an onslaught of coughing. It hits her fast, and then she is coughing so hard that she can hardly catch her breath. I look to Zoe and she looks back to me, both of us confused. Zoe jumps from the couch and gets a glass of water then, when Mrs. Fields pulls her hand away from her mouth, blood is covering her palm. I'm no doctor, but I do know coughing up blood is not a good thing. Not at all.

Zoe returns with a glass of water and sees the blood in her hand. She lets out a gasp and looks to my confused expression. "Aunt Connie, what's this?" Zoe snaps as she stares at her hand.

"Mrs. Fields?" I say, just as inquisitively.

"Connie, please, Drake." She lets out a big breath and looks to both of us. Then she stands and moves to the kitchen with Zoe and I following close behind her. She begins to wash her hands and is trying to hold back the tears. "It's really no big deal."

"Coughing up blood *is* a really big deal," I firmly debate. "Tell me what's going on."

She looks to me, tears streaming down her face. I can't help but feel the heartache resurfacing again because her eyes are telling me something I don't want to know. Not yet. Not today. Not ever.

"I didn't want you to know this. God knows I was trying to find a way to tell you, but I couldn't find it in me to tell you this, especially after everything that's happened. But...I'm dying, Drake."

Chapter 12
Zoe

I was in the middle of stewing over Drake and his onslaught of anger toward me when Aunt Connie starts coughing. They are short little coughs at first then she struggles to get her breath, wheezing and gasping for air. All the anger I've had bubbling inside of me evaporates as I shift gears. I jump from the couch and get Aunt Connie a glass of water then I see her hand as I come back. The palm of her hand is red, blood red, and her eyes are leaking water. What the hell?

Now I'm angry again, but for other reasons. I'm not sure what those reasons are, but it annoys me all the same. I follow Aunt Connie into the kitchen and demand answers, but she doesn't give them to me. She looks to Drake, heart break in her eyes and tells him she's dying. The look on his face is one I will never forget. His golden caramel complexion turns ghostly white, and he looks like someone's just sucked all the life from his body.

"What?" he manages to whisper, still shocked where he stands. "Why…why didn't you say something sooner?" Drake grabs a hold of the counter to keep himself upright, and I'm soon baffled by his reaction. Why is this so devastating to him? Granted, I'm sad and she's my family and all, but Drake looks like he's losing a battle with life itself. Why is he having this kind of reaction?

Aunt Connie moves from the kitchen and sits back on the sofa, wiping the tears from her eyes. "Initially, I wasn't sure it was anything, but after I wasn't feeling better, I went to the doctor. That was about six months ago. I was diagnosed with stage four lung cancer. There isn't much they can do for me considering it has spread to both my lungs and trachea. And I don't want to do treatments when there's really no point. So now they'll just keep me comfortable. I was doing well until recently. Then last week I started to feel really poor and was told my disease is progressing quickly. My specialist has given me three months to live. He suggested I stop watching Mia full time and get reacquainted with my family." She looks over to me, the tears soaking her eyes, and I feel them filling mine. "And I'm so glad you're here, honey."

Drake stands straight on his feet; the sadness is gone and replaced with anger. I feel like I'm in an episode of the Twilight Zone. I'm present in the room, however the majority of the conversation does not involve me at all. There is something between the two of them, a connection I cannot put my finger on, but I know it exists. I can feel it present in the air.

"Why would you not tell me about this?" Drake begins to pace the room, running his hands through the dark hair on his head. "You've been caring for my baby when you should have been taking care of yourself."

"I know, but…I just didn't want this to be your burden. You've had your fair share of troubles, Drake." Aunt Connie shuffles her feet, cutting off Drake and stops him from pacing. He looks down at her with sadness and hurt, not anger…just pain. "I will be okay, Drake. I'm an old woman; this is what we're supposed to do."

Drake wraps his arms around her weary body and holds her tightly. She comforts him with motherly arms, and it's a sight that brings tears to my eyes. I will miss my Aunt Connie. No one deserves to die the way she's dying, but I can't help but feel overwhelmed for Drake. For the first time since meeting him, I don't think he's a psychopath or a serial killer; he's a man with a broken soul. For reasons beyond me, I have to know what has broken him in the first place.

Drake

I was so sure seeing Zoe today at Mrs. Fields's was going to be the worst part of the day, but when Mrs. Fields reveals to me that she is dying, all the wind gets sucked out of my body. We've gotten so close over the last year or so, and whenever I've been really struggling with life, Mrs. Fields has been that comforting person that I needed. She is my rock and the only motherly figure I've had in my life. Now she's dying. *Dying.*

When I arrive at my house sometime later, I pull Mia from the back seat. We've stayed longer than intended after her revelation, and now it's after ten o'clock at night. Mia is exhausted and needs her sleep. When I walk in the house, Darcie and Reggie are snuggled up on the couch watching a movie. I stand in the entryway to the living room and stare at them. It takes a moment, but Darcie meets my eyes and stands to her feet.

"What…what is it?"

I clear my throat and readjust my sleeping child in my arms. "Mrs. Fields has cancer." The words feel like poison in my mouth and I can barely get them out. "She's got three months to live."

I can feel the emotions start to surface and I quickly turn on my heels, heading to Mia's room. I lay her down in her bed and quietly close the door. When I turn around, Darcie is standing behind me, waiting for me to elaborate. I push past her and walk into the bathroom, shutting the door behind me, instead deciding to start the shower and wash away the events of the day.

***

The next morning I'm not able to avoid Darcie when she corners me in the kitchen. I tell her all I know about the situation and ask her if she can watch Mia while I go in search for new daycare. I call in sick to my job, knowing I won't be able to do it for long. I've never had to look for daycare; I've been lucky to have people in my life willing to help watch Mia.

The first place I go smells horribly of dirty diapers and mildew, then when I get a good look at the toddler room where Mia would be, it is disgusting. I am in the place a total of three minutes before I flee out of it like a bat out of hell. Next, I go to a daycare that is a little more expensive and looks nice on the outside, but when I walk in the front door, it is the same as the first; filled with a disgusting smell and inadequate conditions. This will not be acceptable.

The final daycare seems nice on the outside, the toys look taken care of and the yard has been maintained. When I walk inside, I notice it smells clean. I look around the lobby, seeing it appears well kept. So far so good. Then I visit the toddler room. It is exactly what I've pictured a daycare to be. The teachers are on the floor, playing with the kids, the room is clean and the children appear to be really happy. They also have a webcam installed so I can watch whenever I want to. That is the selling point right there.

I sign her up thirty minutes later and fill out all the appropriate paperwork. Tomorrow will be Mia's first day, and hopefully, she will like it.

When I drive home, I can't help but think about why I have to do this. Mrs. Fields is dying—before the year is over, she will be gone. I'm not sure which is worse, knowing when someone will die or them being ripped from your life unexpectedly. Granted, Presley's death was torturous, yet how I'm feeling now does feels eerily similar. Mrs. Fields is like a mother to me, someone I can count on for the advice I seek. I've been looking forward to her watching Mia grow into a young woman, but now all of that will be gone. By this time next year, she will be gone. I will miss her so much. This right here is the reason why I don't want to get close with anyone. It hurts too much when they leave, and there is nothing I can do about it. There never is, and it's infuriating.

When I arrive home, Mia is up from her nap and is keeping Reggie busy. I stand in the threshold of the door, observing Mia interacting with her uncle.

"Uncie Edgey…no." She shakes her head and takes the doll brush from his hand. Reggie just chuckles out loud and shakes his head.

"Okay, princess. Then you tell me what I need to do," he says back, trying to be stern with her.

Mia hands Reggie the doll and shows him how to

brush her hair. "Like dis, Uncie." She starts combing the doll's hair, slightly ripping it out, but insists she's doing it right. "Now hers pretty." Mia turns the doll and stuffs it in Reggie's face. "See?"

"Yes, Mia, I see. She's very pretty." Reggie notices me and smiles. Then Mia sees me and comes running to my arms.

She looks precious as usual with her hair combed into a cute little braid and short outfit. I lift her in my arms and give her a hug. She wraps her arms around my neck and quickly rests her head on my shoulder. It melts my heart, as it always does.

"Hi, Dada!"

"Hi, sweet girl. Are you having fun with Uncle Reggie?" I ask as she fiddles with my cheeks.

"Yeah! He likes my baby." Mia holds up her doll and shoves her right in my face. I push the doll away and nod my head. The look on her face is puzzling as she creases her brows and studies something beyond my sight. When she connects back with me, Mia practically throws me off guard. "Dada, what's douchie bag? Uncie said his team was douchie bags and yelled at the TV."

Reggie sputters a laugh and begins to gag while trying to hold back the laughter. I look at her and I'm dumbfounded. Awestruck. I don't know what to say.

I glare over to Reggie as he makes it to his feet, holding up his hands. "Don't look at me, man. You know who says that phrase around here."

"Damn, Jake," I mutter under my breath.

"Damn, Uncie Jake," Mia repeats and smiles her big, dazzling smile. Shit, she's repeating everything I'm saying.

The timing couldn't be worse because she's starting daycare tomorrow and I don't want her cursing at the teacher on the first day.

"Now, Mia, those are grownup words, okay? You don't say those words," I scold her.

She looks at me like I took away her favorite toy and crushed it under my boot. The tears fill in her eyes just before she lets them fall down her cheeks. Her bottom lip begins to tremble and then the onslaught of sobs soon follows. Fuck! Now I feel like a douche bag and the world's worst dad.

Reggie again tries to stifle a laugh because he knows I feel like a fucking jerk right now, but as long as *he's* in good graces with Mia then it's all good. As much as I want to tell her I'm sorry, I know I need to hold strong. She needs to know her limits, but what that fucker in the books neglects to tell you is how tormenting the guilt can be.

"Dada, m-m-ad at me!" Mia wails and I start to sway back and forth, rubbing her back to calm her down.

"Mia," I say, pulling her back to look at me. "Dada is not mad at you. You just can't say those words."

She snuggles up to my chest and rests her head on my shoulder. I continue to rock her back and forth, humming the lullaby song she loves, and before I know it, Mia's asleep in my arms. Crisis averted for now. But next, I need to call Jake and explain for the millionth time that cursing in front of a two-year-old is not a good idea.

***

I pull up to the daycare and park the Chevelle. All morning I've been talking to Mia about going to school and making new friends. She seems to be okay with it, but in all

114

honesty, I don't think she really understands anything that is happening.

When I pull her from the car, Mia has a smile on her face as we walk through the front door. I like it that you have to have a special card to be able to enter the building and you can't get into the classrooms unless someone from the inside lets you in or you have a key. The security in this place is perfect, plus with the webcam, I think it couldn't get any better. It will be expensive sending her here, but my daughter's happiness and safety is worth it.

The director escorts us back to Mia's room and opens the door with a key. The children are sitting around a very small table with tiny chairs eating breakfast. I set Mia down and let her get acclimated to her new surroundings. The teachers introduce themselves to me again and reassure me everything will be fine. I can't help the aching feeling I have in my gut about leaving her behind, however it's what needs to be done.

I bend down and Mia comes running into my arms, showing me a toy she's holding. "Dada, look."

"That's nice, sweet girl, but Daddy's got to go to work now. Be a good girl and I will be back soon." Mia looks over at me with a confused expression on her face.

"Nanny? Go to Nanny's house, Dada." She's so smart and very observant—it's definitely a quality she will need in the future, I just wish it wouldn't pop up now.

I stand with her in my arms and kiss the top of her head. "Remember, Nanny's sick. You can't see her today." Mia looks like she's about to cry, and if she does, I'm sure that I will quit my job here and now just so she doesn't feel alone again.

The teacher recognizes what's going on with Mia and intercedes. "Mia, would you like to have breakfast with your friends?" She points to the table with the kids sitting around munching on cereal. The teacher then holds out her hands. Mia looks to me and I nod, letting her know it's okay. She bends down and allows the teacher to hold her. "Say bye to Daddy."

Mia squirms from the teacher's arms and runs to me. I squat down and give her a swift hug. She rests her head on my shoulder then stands up. "Bye Dada!" She runs back to the table and joins her friends. Yeah, she's going to be fine here. My baby girl will be just fine.

Chapter 13
Zoe ~ One Month Later

Life in Sulfur Heights is not what I've expected when I moved here over a month ago. I never would have predicted that I would see my aunt, let alone take care of her now that she's dying. I never would've thought I'd find a job I enjoy going to every weekend, and Lord knows I've never expected to make friends, yet I've done exactly that.

After my first weekend working at *The Slab*, Darcie, Gavin and I have a blast. We work really well together and they both know how to make me laugh. We don't have too much time to joke around when we're working, but as soon as the bar closes, we blast the music, take some shots and clean up. There have been a couple of nights I've had to sleep in my car because I had a little too much fun after work.

Reggie is really cool as well, but he tends to be a little uptight. Actually, he's the complete opposite of Darcie. He's always worried about things and rarely does he let loose. However, I will catch him staring at his wife, and in those moments, he has peace and contentment written all over his face.

Since my aunt has told me she is dying of lung cancer, I've made it a point to take care of her by checking in every day. The day after she broke the news to me, she told me that her own daughter doesn't even care what's wrong with her. Aunt Connie called her daughter, Rebecca, when she found out she was sick and that woman has yet to visit or even check up on her condition. The thought disgusts me and makes me wonder what happened to turn her against her own mother.

Then there's Sophia, Aunt Connie's granddaughter; my cousin and former best friend. She's just graduated from college with a degree in teaching, is dating someone special and she too has yet to check up on her grandmother.

And my own mother... well, her absence doesn't even surprise me. She's never been one to care for someone who isn't going to do something for her in return. She's selfish and greedy and nothing has proved this more than the night she kicked me out of her life. She chose her asshole boyfriend over her own child. My mother chose to believe the lie he fed her, and when I refused to back down this time, she figured I was eighteen and it was time for me to leave the house permanently.

I think about that day all the time. It was the day my life changed forever, and part of me thanks my mother for being so selfish because I wouldn't be where I am now if she had believed me. Nevertheless, it always hurts reflecting on the choice she made.

Fred had been her live-in boyfriend for my entire senior year of high school. He was creepy, to say the least, but he was good to my mother—and by good I mean rich. She was happy. I mostly ignored him until there was one day where I couldn't avoid him. It's hard to ignore someone who's trying to force his dick into your body after he's tied you to the bed.

Luckily for me, I wasn't a virgin and hadn't been for three years. Yes, I was a little loose in high school. I loved and still love sex. I love the attention I get from men, but it always has to be a mutual exchange. I said no. I bucked, thrashed and kicked as I was telling him no. He tried to rape me and didn't give it a second thought. He did it knowing my mother wouldn't believe me. No one believed me because I was a whore. And when I told my mother, Rebecca and Sophia what happened, they were appalled at *my* behavior. My mother took Fred's side, and that very night, two days after graduation, she threw me out.

I spent the remainder of the night crying and confused when reality of what she'd just done sunk in. She chose herself over her daughter. My mind started to recall all the times she'd done that in the past. I had known right then and there that she would always choose herself. I would be second to her continuously and that wasn't the life I was willing to live. The next morning, I walked to the bank, withdrew all the cash I had received from graduation as well as saved, then headed to the bus station with the Rocky Mountains in sight.

So when I think about my family, excluding my Aunt Connie, only one word comes into mind, selfish. They will only do something if it benefits them and them only. At first, I was exactly like them, however over the course of time, since I've been on my own, I know now how to survive this life and it's by avoiding relationships. That way, no one is disappointed. I fell off the wagon with Terrance and learned my lesson when he called me a cunt and slammed his fist into my head. Yet, since coming here, I'm forming relationships left and right—it's impossible to avoid. First with my Aunt Connie the day I ran into her at the store and she invited me to her apartment. Then with the people I work with. I can truly say I will be sad to leave them when I'm ready to move on.

The one relationship I have yet to form but can't stop thinking about is Drake. I am fascinated by him. I haven't seen him since that day at the apartment because he hasn't been back to the bar or Connie's place, but I want to see him.

At night, I lie awake and imagine what it would be like to feel him on top of me. My mind drives me crazy with erotic thoughts. I often find my hands in the waistband of my panties, pleasuring myself with images of Drake. I chalk this up to being starved for sex, considering it's been at least three months—the longest I've gone in ages.

I love sex. I find it a perfect way to express myself, live through fantasies in my head, and completely lose myself in another world. It took me a couple of years to perfect my style, yet by the time I was seventeen, I had my first orgasm. It was amazing, and I've been hooked since.

I'm not a dominatrix type of woman. Yes, I do like to have control in my life, but the one place I want to be completely controlled is in the bedroom. I want the man to push my inhibitions and I want to be completely his. Terrance was amazing at this, and to date, he is the only man who's ever pushed me to feel the intensity sex possesses. There's something about Drake, though. I can feel the vibe radiating off him. He has this pent up energy and it's dying to get out.

Drake

It's been a long time since I've gone to the bar, and

120

I'm ready for a night away from my reality. Delilah and Jake have volunteered to watch Mia tonight so I can go have a drink. There's a part of me debating if I should go to *The Slab* or not. I really don't want to sit in a different bar, filled with different people because there will be no Reggie if I snap again, but I know Zoe will be there.

That girl bothers me. She's been in my mind more than I care to admit and it angers me because I feel like I'm pushing Presley out. I know I need to move on eventually, but if I do, does that mean I can't have Presley in my life? Will I replace her with someone else? If that's the case, then I don't want to move on because I refuse to replace her or forget about her. I love her and I always will, but my body is aching to touch a woman. Ever since Zoe came to Sulfur Heights, my dick has awoken from its long slumber and it's coming back with a vengeance.

I pull in the parking lot of *The Slab* and turn off the engine. I can do this. I will do what I always do and keep my head down. I will have a few drinks then I will go home and pass out. I step from the car and walk through the back entrance. The bar is slower than normal, although it's still keeping the bartenders busy.

When I step to the bar, Reggie comes to my side. He puts his hand on my shoulder and gives me his classic look. "You okay to be here?"

Inwardly, I roll my eyes, but I think better of actually doing it. "Yeah, I'm not planning on being here long." My attention then goes to the long legged vixen behind the bar. Zoe looks incredibly sexy tonight. She's wearing tight black jeans and her designated *Slab* t-shirt. However, she's tied a knot in the back, making the fabric ride high and baring her midriff. Zoe's long, brown hair has been tied on top of her head, giving me another view of her long, sexy neck.

I haven't even realized Darcie has poured me a beer until she clears her throat, smiling a wicked smile. "You okay, Drake?"

I look to Darcie and begin to chug down my beer before nodding my head."Yep, I'm okay."

"All right, just checking." Darcie snickers then goes back to helping the customers.

I keep my head down, refusing to look up at her or anyone else. This has been my life for the last year and a half, and it has to continue. I have got to fight the desires I have to feel Zoe underneath my body. Everything she represents in my life is nothing I need at this point. I still have a lot to work out.

Since the incident of choking Jake, I've been doing a better job managing my anger. I can recognize it coming on, and instead of holding it in, I will seek out Reggie's advice. I will talk to him, just as I've always done. I look up to my brother even though I know he really has no idea what to tell me to make me feel better, but I think just talking to someone is all that I've needed. Yet, I only talk to him when I feel the need to explode. So basically, I'm still harboring my anger. I just defuse it before I unleash it on someone else.

Mia and I still visit Mrs. Fields once a week. I will call her throughout the week to check on her, but Thursday nights are our nights. We will go over for supper, cooked or bought by me, and then we will hang out like we used to.

Why Thursdays? Because I know Zoe won't be

there—she works at the bar on Thursdays—and I won't have to contend with my unwanted feelings toward her.

Each week, I think Mrs. Fields gets a little thinner and seems to be a little sicker. I'm not sure if this is because I know what's going on with her or if she's just finally unable to fight her disease, but I notice it nonetheless. She doesn't talk much about her family and it makes me wonder what kind of relationship she has with them. I finish chugging down the last of my beer, refusing the whiskey Darcie offers. I'm not looking to get wasted, just enough to take the edge off and relax a bit. I start my second beer when a phone rings from behind the bar. I look up at the sound, and see Zoe pulling her phone from her pocket. She's pressing her phone to her right ear while her other hand is covering her open ear. I can't help but stare at her and study her reaction. She looks scared, terrified even, and I'm mesmerized. Then she looks up and connects her eyes with mine. My heart accelerates in my chest, causing it to beat wildly into my ribs. I can feel the adrenaline building through my veins. When she's done with her phone call, Zoe is instantly by my side.

"That was the hospital calling. Aunt Connie is in ICU."

Without a word, I stand to my feet and follow Zoe out the back door. When the early autumn wind collides against my body, I'd normally be chilled, however now I'm anything but. We make it to our cars and I now solve the mystery of who drives the red Chevelle like mine. Fucking hell. This woman is going to be the death of me, I swear. Because, as she climbs in the driver's seat, I can feel my reaction to her as her sexy body sits behind the wheel of a car with so much power.

She looks over to me and sees me getting into my Chevelle and smiles slightly. "I'll follow you," she says then she fires the car to life and I do as well.

Five minutes later, we pull into the parking lot at the hospital and I'm immediately brought back to the night Presley overdosed. It was the last time I had been here and what I thought was the worse night of my life. I'm feeling nauseous, but I push it down because I need to see what's going on with Mrs. Fields.

Zoe runs to the reception desk and we get ushered to the ICU section of the hospital. When we arrive, the area is deafly quiet with only the faint sound of the waiting room television audible in the background. Zoe and I request to see Mrs. Fields, and as soon as we tell them we're her family, we're ushered into a small room by the nurse and doctor.

Zoe's leg is shaking wildly under the table and she's fidgeting with her fingers resting in her lap. I, too, am freaking out, knowing the news won't be good, but I try to keep on a strong front for Zoe.

"Hi, I'm Dr. Burgess and I've been treating Connie for the past year. You're her family?" A short older man with white hair and glasses appears through the door, instantly getting our attention.

"Yes, I'm her niece and I've been caring for her lately," Zoe replies softly.

"Zoe, I assume. Connie has been talking about you a lot." The doctor smiles as he takes a seat and we follow his lead. Zoe looks like she's going to be sick.

"Well, as you already know, Connie is fighting with her illness. Tonight, she's had a major setback, and unfortunately, she will need to stay here until we can get her stabilized again." The doctor starts running through her symptoms as Zoe sits quietly, taking in the overwhelming information. From the moment he's said Mrs. Fields will have the maximum of a couple of months left to live, I tune the conversation out. I don't want to think about her dying.

"How did she get here?"Zoe asks, her voice is still as quiet as night. "I mean, she was home alone and I was at work. How did you know she needed help?"

"Connie was able to dial 911 before she collapsed. They were able to trace her location and the paramedic found her unconscious on the floor." The doctor clears his throat and continues, "This is the time for you to keep Connie as content as possible. I'd make the calls to other family members and friends because they won't have long with her." Zoe gasps slightly then nods as the doctor continues. "She woke up momentarily when she arrived at ICU and told me she wanted to go home to be with her family. And we can help you with that. We can set up home healthcare to make her as comfortable as possible for her final transition. I just wanted to let you know, so you're prepared to handle this kind of request. Here is the information for home healthcare." He hands her several brochures and business cards."And as soon as she's stable enough, we can have her moved."

Zoe says nothing, just nods to the doctor. He stands and shakes both our hands before exiting the room. Zoe gets to her feet, tucking the information in her pocket. She's trying to be strong.

When I stand to meet her gaze, her brave front disintegrates. Her hands come to her face as she cries into them. Her body is racking from the sobs and my heart aches to comfort her. I don't think; I only act. Before I can stop myself, I pull Zoe against my chest. I pull her in tightly, and for the first time since Presley's death, I get the nerve to hold a woman in my arms.

Chapter 14
Zoe

The room is dark and quiet. There's a slight glow coming off the machines hooked up to Aunt Connie's body, faint beeps echoing throughout the room, tracking her vital signs. I stand at the threshold of the room, stunned and shocked at the sight of her lying in the hospital bed. She looks like she did when I left her this afternoon, but now she has tubes coming out of her body.

The room is small with only a recliner type chair in the corner and a TV mounted on the wall. Drake stands behind me. He has not let me go since I broke down after we talked to the doctor. The pained look on his face was unnerving, but when he pulled me close to his chest, I felt the warmth of his body and let the comfort of his arms soothe me. Drake didn't move; he only held me tighter as he rubbed small circles in my back with one hand and cupped the base of my head with the other. I wrapped my arms around his waist and held him to me, relishing in how good it felt to have him here.

When we left the room, Drake kept one arm around my shoulders as he led me past the nurses' station and into Aunt Connie's room. Now, we both stand at the threshold, his hands resting on my shoulders as I summon the nerve to walk closer to her sleeping body.

I'm about to take a step when Drake's phone vibrates in his pocket, successfully pulling me out of my trance.

"It's Darcie," Drake whispers and I nod my head to him before he leaves the room for a moment to take the phone call.

I finally step inside the room and move to the chair next to her bed. She looks so normal, almost like she's sleeping. I go back to what the doctor has said about notifying other family members and how much I don't want to do this, but I have to. I owe it to Aunt Connie to tell her daughter and granddaughter about her current situation. It's on them if they come to see her before she dies. However, I have reservations about calling my own mother, Aunt Connie's sister. I don't want to speak to her or see her, and if she's still with Fred—that's the last person I ever want to lay my eyes on again. I'm not sure I can face her or any of them.

I pick up Aunt Connie's hand and hold it between my own. Her skin is warm and soft inside of my hands. I feel the tears resurface when I look at her sleeping face.

"For you, Aunt Connie. I will see them for you," I whisper to her, knowing the grief my family will put me through the moment I speak to them.

Drake comes back to the room and moves silently to my side. He hesitates momentarily then places his hand on my shoulder again. We spend the rest of the evening staring at the woman we love as a mother, who is battling to stay alive.

***

Four days later, with the help of home healthcare, I am able to get Connie home and comfortable. Drake has been visiting the hospital after work to check up on us, and every night, he's brought me something to eat, knowing I haven't had the opportunity to consume much. The very gesture is heartwarming, but it scares me as well. It terrifies me how much I enjoy him being around and helping me. What frightens me the most is how I feel when he's not around—I actually miss him. So much so that he's always on my mind.

Drake meets me at Connie's apartment when the paramedics transport her back to her apartment. I've never seen her so happy. She loves this little place. It's her peace, and if that's all she wants in the remaining days of her life, then I will grant that to her.

I pull the blankets over her body and get things situated in her room. I pull the table over closer to her and organize magazines and her medicine.

"Drake and Reggie are coming over to hang your TV in here," I say as I finish straightening her things. "They were supposed to come over yesterday, but things got busy at the bar. Are you okay with them doing that?"

"Yes, that will be fine." Aunt Connie readjusts herself in bed to sit up a little straighter. I move to her side and help hold up her frail body so I can adjust the pillows behind her back. "Zoe," her voice is quiet and a little sad; it breaks my heart.

"Yeah?'

"I don't know where I'd be if you weren't here, honey. You're the only family who wants me in their life. If it weren't for you and Drake, I probably would have died years ago." She's holding back her tears, trying to stay brave for me, but now it's my turn to be the strong one. It's my turn to care for her.

"Do you mind me asking what happened between you and Rebecca?"

Connie clears her throat and struggles to find the words. "Well…" She clears her throat again and I hand her a glass of water. She takes a quick drink and continues. "About a month after you and Sophia graduated high school, I went to Wisconsin to visit. We planned a shopping trip to purchase things for you two to have in your dorms. When I arrived there, I asked where you were and noticed they were avoiding telling me something." Connie takes another sip of water and clears her throat again. "Your mother proceeded to tell me about you and Fred being involved in a sexual relationship." All the blood leaves my body. The very mention of his name sends chills down my spine, making me want to run and hide. I hate that man, but worse yet, I hate my mother. "Then Rebecca and Sophia proceeded to tell me about your past…you know, with gentlemen.

"I was appalled at their behavior and the callous way they could treat you. Virginia told me she kicked you out of the house, and when I tried to defend you, they…well, it hasn't been the same since." She finishes her glass of water and I take it from her, placing it on her bedside table.

"You…you defended me?" My head is flooded with confusion as to why she felt the need to stand up for me.

"Because no one bothered to really question Fred as to what happened. Virginia just took his word for it and swept the whole thing under the rug like she does with all of her problems. They never considered the fact that you've never had a reason to lie. You're a very honest person, and they

130

refused to take that into account. That's what I said to them and neither your mother nor my daughter agreed with me. You know them; they're always sticking up for one another, have been since they lived with me. And Sophia, well, she just does what they say." She relaxes back into her pillow and closes her eyes. Moments later, Aunt Connie's asleep.

I move from the room and start cleaning up the kitchen. I'm in emotional overload right now. How Rebecca, Connie's own daughter, would mistreat her because she was sticking up for me... It sickens me how crude they can be to someone who's shown them nothing but kindness their entire lives.

I start taking my anger out on the kitchen floor. After sweeping it, I pull a bucket from under the sink and fill it with soap. I fall to my hands and knees then begin to scrub. I scour the linoleum as hard as I can just to extract the fury my mother has always instilled in me. The water is hot, but I let it singe my skin as I dip the rag in the water and slop it onto the floor. I scrub away all the pain, anger and dishonesty my mother hemorrhages from me. I scrub it away until my arms burn from overexertion.

I didn't even hear them come in, but when I stand up, Reggie and Drake are standing in the living room unhooking the TV. They both nod to me as they trail down to the bedroom and place the TV onto the wooden stand. Next, they both lean behind the TV, hooking up the cords in their proper place. Before I know it, Connie has a working TV in her room. Sounds from the kitchen cause me to exit the bedroom to find Darcie and Delilah stuffing food in the fridge.

"Hi, guys. What are you doing here?" I ask as I watch them empty bags.

"Drake told us what's happening with Mrs. Fields and we decided to help out a little," Darcie says as she hands Delilah some fresh fruits and vegetables.

"You guys didn't hav—"

"Stop it," Delilah demands, holding up her hand and interrupting me. "This is the least we could do. We love Drake and Mia, and we know how important she is to him. We're a family. This is what a family does." Delilah comes to my side and pats me on the arm. "Just let us know what we can do and we will help as much as we can."

I nod in acceptance as words get strangled in my throat. We move in silence together as we finish putting the groceries away. Delilah chops up some vegetables and puts together a quick salad for me. I am blown away by the generosity of this family. I hardly know these people. Yes, we've spent some fun, drunken nights together, but they know very little about me and I, them.

I didn't even know people like the Evans exist. The people I have been raised by and the people I've surrounded myself with over the last four years have never shown me this kind of love. The thought terrifies me because I can see myself falling in love with this entire family. And that's dangerous for me. It's been four years since I detached myself from my own family, and if I get close, the possibility for rejection is inevitable. Breaking away from them may be harder than it was when I left my real family.

After finishing my salad, I head to the bedroom to check on Connie and thank Reggie for moving the TV. I

132

stand just outside the door and listen to Drake and Connie's conversation.

"…Mia is fine. She likes her new daycare a lot." Drake is sitting on the bed with his back turned to the door. His body is blocking Connie's view of the doorway, giving me a better ability to eavesdrop. "Don't worry about us. We will be fine." His voice is very quiet, and it's hard to understand what he's saying.

"Well…that's not going to happen. From the moment I met Presley, I've done nothing but worry about you and Mia." Aunt Connie's hand moves and I think she's holding his, but it's hard to see from this angle. They don't say anything more so I make my way into the room to see if Aunt Connie needs anything.

Drake stands from the bed and moves to my side. Since the night at the hospital, he has no problem being around me and is comfortable talking to me. Every once and a while he will even pull me in for a hug or sling his arm around my shoulder.

"Well, I should go and check on Mia. I left her alone with Jake. God knows what curse words she'll be speaking by the time I pick her up." Connie chuckles to herself and watches as Drake comes to my side.

"Call me if you need anything, okay?" he says to me, and before I realize he's doing it, Drake pulls me into his strong, warm arms and wraps me in a hug. I close my eyes and inhale his comforting smell. He lets me go and leaves, his family following behind him.

I forget Aunt Connie is in the room until her voice breaks my trance. "I see you and Drake have gotten close."

I turn on my heels and move to the chair beside her

bed. Her tired eyes meet mine and the faint smile on her face makes me smile in return. Her skin is ghostly and her hair is thinning, however she looks peaceful and content. "Not really. We just became friendly when you were admitted to the hospital."

"Has he told you...about his family?" Connie asks.

"I've met them working at the bar. They seem like a pretty nice group of people. Darcie and Delilah were here putting groceries in the fridge."

"Yes, you wouldn't think it by looking at them or even hearing them speak to one another, however, they are an extraordinary family. But I was referring to Mia's mother. Has Drake talked to you about her?" I am thrown completely off guard. He's mentioned nothing about his family. Actually, he rarely talks to me about anything. I can't really recall having a conversation that has been more than a handful of words. I look back to Connie and shake my head no. "Well...I don't expect him to speak so freely about that." She takes a deep breath and rolls to her side, losing her battle with tiredness. "That boy's been through a lot. More than any young person should have to ever live through." As she speaks, Aunt Connie's eyes close and she falls to sleep almost as soon as the last word has left her mouth.

I sit back in the chair and stare at the TV, not really watching it at all. I think about what my aunt has just shared with me. When I first arrived, Gavin told me there was an incident in Drake's life, something that changed him. Now, Connie talks about Mia's mother and Drake having a rough life. It peaks my curiosity so much so that I move from my chair and pull my laptop from my bag.

Drake

"Daddy! Uncie Jake told me not to say douchie bag anymore," Mia shouts as she comes barreling toward me. I scoop her up in my arms and kiss her on the cheek. "Uncie Jake says d-bag is okay, Daddy?"

I turn my glare to Jake, who has just come into the room. Our relationship has improved since I've attacked him. We have yet to discuss it and I don't think we ever will. He knows where all my anger stems from. Although I have a better handle on my rage lately, I can honestly say that I have no idea how I will react when the day comes for Jeremy to be released. I still hold a lot of discontent toward my brother, and I'm not sure when or if it will ever leave.

"Don't give me that look. Axl knows not to say douche bag anymore. I helped her find a proper way of talking about people she doesn't like," Jake states as he moves closer to us. "Right, Axl?"

"Right, Uncie Jake," Mia agrees, and I deem this conversation a lost cause. When will he ever understand what is appropriate to say around a very impressionable two-year-old? Her newly formed vocabularies are on repeat and speak back.

"Mia, Uncle Jake needs to remember how much you like to repeat what he says," I say to her as she turns to look at me.

"But, I wuv Uncie Jake." Mia looks over to Jake and his face lights up with joy. My little girl has a way of making my brothers and me melt like putty in her hands. All she needs to do is look at us, and we turn into puddles of goo.

When Jake snatches Mia out of my arms and twirls her

around the room, she giggles with delight as he spins her around. When he stops, she sits up in his arms and smiles. "Uncie Jake loves you, too, Axl." Jake kisses her cheek then gives her a toss in the air, making her erupt in laughter.

It's moments like this that fill my life with purpose. I was in a very dark place after Presley died, and in those tender moments, I struggled with my own reason to live, but when I thought of my daughter and the life I'd be missing out on, I couldn't do it. I couldn't let my little girl grow up without me. Seeing her laugh now, proves I've made the right choice.

Chapter 15
Drake

Halloween has come and gone as we begin the start of November. Life has shifted for me greatly since I found out Mrs. Fields is sick. Initially, it was hard to know someone I love isn't going to be around anymore and dealing with death again has been a major trigger for my rage. Somehow, though, I manage to work through it. My family has been big supporters of me and my decisions since I've been old enough to make them, and when I told them about Mrs. Fields, they stepped in to help where they could.

Mia and I still visit on Thursday nights with Mrs. Fields, and when Zoe can, she will stop by to have supper with us before she heads over to the bar. Mia seems to understand a little about her nanny being sick. She will cuddle up in bed with Mrs. Fields and watch Mickey Mouse or they will read books. Mia knows something is wrong, and whenever she's around her Nanny, she knows to be careful.

Zoe lives with Mrs. Fields pretty much full time now. She stays over on the nights she's not working at the bar, knowing she cannot be left alone in her condition. When she does have to work, a home healthcare nurse stays with her throughout the night until Zoe comes back the next morning. The arrangement is tiring for Zoe, I can tell by the exhaustion on her face, but she has yet to complain. She does it without expecting anything in return, either.

I am impressed by her willingness to help out. I know Zoe has a rocky relationship with her family—it's obvious by what little she has let slip out—but that hasn't stopped her from swallowing her pride to help someone in need. It only proves she's got a strong character and is a dependable person. Nowadays, those types of people are impossible to find. People you've trusted your entire life can end up being the worst kind of people to be around. Nothing has proved this more than the night Jeremy was arrested.

I am discovering that, whenever she's around, I've become captivated by her presence. My body reacts to the nearness of hers, and it's getting impossible to ignore. The only thing that keeps me in check is the devotion I have to Presley. I refuse to let her memory be trumped by someone I barely know, however it's getting harder and harder to fight the physical desire I have to be with Zoe. I am yearning to be with a woman. Even before Presley and I met, I never went without the touch of a woman, and since her death, I have never craved it so much in my life as I have the last few months.

It's Saturday night and the bar is unusually slow. There are hardly any people drinking, only a few regulars and myself. I've finished my second beer when Zoe strides up in front of me. She fills a shot glass with tequila and passes me the lime wedges. I look at her and see she's poured one for herself.

"I want to get drunk tonight. How about you?" she asks as she holds up the shot.

"I'm in the drinking mood." I hold up my shot of

tequila and join her as she toasts.

"To getting drunk tonight," she pledges.

"To getting drunk tonight," I repeat and we clink the glasses together then down the liquid. It burns on the way down, yet it goes down better than I've expected. Zoe pours another shot for both of us and we tip them back again.

"Drink on your own time, Zoe!" Darcie shouts from the other side of the bar.

"Do you care if I call it a night so I can get drunk? This place is dead and I need to get out of here," Zoe shouts back to Darcie.

They've become pretty close over the last couple of months. They don't spend too much time outside of work with each other, but they're friendly enough, nonetheless. I remember a day when Darcie would refuse to be friendly with anyone. Man, she used to be such a bitch.

"No, that's cool," Darcie agrees and begins to wipe down the bar top as Gavin repeatedly flips through the sports channels.

As Zoe grabs her stuff from behind the bar and comes back over to me, she has a big grin on her face that makes me wonder if she's already feeling pretty drunk. "So, you wanna go to my place and get drunk? I've got tequila," she singsongs to me. I can't remember ever seeing her so hyped up. The grin on her face is huge, and I'm finding it impossible to look away from her.

I nod as she pulls me off the stool and we head out the back door. The cold winter air hits my face, sending a chill down my spine. Snow has lightly started to fall, dusting the ground with a white, shimmery powder. We both brush the snow off our cars, and I look over to Zoe. She looks happy, maybe *too* happy.

"Are you okay to drive?"

"Please...I've had two shots. I'm good. Follow me and try to keep up." Zoe falls into her Chevelle, and I get into mine. She peels out of the parking lot and fishtails onto the highway. I start to regret letting her drive, not really knowing how she will be able to handle liquor or driving on the snow covered roads.

It only takes a few minutes to get to her apartment, and I'm relieved we haven't had to go further. She pulls into a garage and I find an empty parking space in front of her apartment building. She meets me on the sidewalk and I follow her up the stairs to her apartment.

With each step she takes, I get hypnotized by the sway she has in her hips and the round curve of her ass. Zoe's long legs are wrapped in denim and I'm aching inside my own jeans to take her out of hers.

As we finish walking up the stairs, I start to get the feeling that I should leave. I know what will happen if I allow it. My body is dying to feel a woman again, but all that will be left in the morning is the guilt and pain for what I might do. There is too much attraction with this girl and it can only lead me down the wrong road.

Zoe

After my conversation with Aunt Connie, I decided that I needed to know more about this man. I needed to find out what happened in his past. When I pulled up Google on my laptop, though, I froze. I was scared to know what the real truth was. Right now, we are passing as friends, and if I find out more about his past, that may cause me to turn and run, or worse. Maybe I will want to stay.

140

Although, I can't leave yet—not until Aunt Connie has passed away—I don't want to have any other reason to stay. Or do I? The last thing I want to do is make him a reason to keep myself from running.

The Saturday night crowd has been moving at a snail's pace. I've been feeling guilty about leaving my aunt with the home healthcare nurse even though I've done it several times before, but today, she has been really bad. She has been barely awake and her heart rate has been getting weaker over the last couple of days. I know it won't be long before she will be gone. So when Drake walks through the door, I take a long look at him and know I need to let loose. Unbeknownst to him, he is going to be the source of my good night.

He looks very sexy in his dark jeans and long sleeved, gray shirt. From the first time I've laid eyes on him I've been craving to see his muscles. I can tell he's very trim underneath his shirt and I'm aching to touch his skin.

Channeling my inner whore, I concoct a plan to get out of the bar to my house. What guy doesn't want to get drunk at a random girl's house with the promise of a good time? Well, I can't think of one, and I am dying to see if Drake will follow along. To my surprise, he does.

After leaving the bar and driving home, I open the door to my studio apartment and toss my keys on the counter. "Welcome to my one room palace," I say as I spread my arms like a spokesmodel on a game show. I bend down and remove my boots then walk into the kitchen.

Drake moves into the apartment and removes his boots as well then stands and looks around. He is taking in my empty apartment, studying the small space as I move to the cupboard and pull out the tequila.

All the apartment holds is my air mattress, which is taking up the space in the middle of the living slash bedroom. My laptop and small stereo sit next to the mattress on the floor. I have my clothes hanging in the closet and my tiny microwave sitting on the kitchen counter.

"This is all you have?" Drake's deep voice questions as he looks over my apartment.

"This is all I need," I correct as I hand him the bottle of tequila. "I don't have glasses or a lime, so we'll have to drink it out of the bottle and choke it down without the lime."

When Drake takes the bottle from my hand and tips his head back, the fire in my belly ignites. I watch his lips curve around the bottle and his Adam's apple bob when he swallows the amber fluid. He's got the sexiest lips I've ever laid eyes on. I can't wait to taste them—to feel them all over my body.

Drake moves to the air mattress and looks confused whether or not he should sit on it. When I pull on his arm and flop down on the bed, he comes down with me, and we both laugh. Then, I lean over and turn on the music. I've been heavily into blues lately, and I allow Etta James to sound through the apartment.

I take a sip of tequila and then another and another. I'm starting to experience the numbing effects, and it feels good. Drake follows suit and takes a few sips from the bottle. Then we sit in silence for a moment without looking at each other, waiting for the other to speak.

"So," Drake says as he takes another drink. "Tell me

about yourself, Zoe."

Ugh, the dreaded filler conversation. I neither have the patience for, nor the desire to share. I just want him. My body is aching and has been since I first saw him. I am not going to kill my buzz and his good mood by drudging up my past ghosts. I don't talk about my past with anyone because that means I'm getting too comfortable, and I refuse to get comfortable here.

"Nope, we're not doing that."

"Doing what?" Drake questions.

"I don't want to talk about my past any more than you do." I look over to him, seeing the pain and anger in his eyes. Something dark is clouding him, but tonight's not the night to know what that something is. "Drake, tonight is about having fun, not walking down some fucked-up memory lane." I pull another sip from the bottle and soak in the burn.

"Fair enough, but you have to tell me one thing." I snap my glare to him, not wanting to spoil the night and my chances of finally having him in my bed. "Tell me what the hell we're listening to."

Drake

When I step into her apartment, I am shocked at the little amount of stuff she has. Just an air mattress, computer and small stereo—that's it. She's been living here for a while, so I guess I've been expecting to see a real bed or maybe a picture or two, however there is nothing. She has no roots here or anywhere. It makes me feel sad for her and appreciative of the family I do have.

Although we've had our troubles in the past, I know I'm better off being with my family than being alone. After

143

Presley died, it took me a little while to realize that, but I'm so glad I have. Jeremy aside because he's not my family anymore, and when I think of my family today, my mind excludes him.

I'm glad she has told me she doesn't want to exchange our past stories because I have no intention of telling her mine and have decided to change the mood to something lighter. Zoe seems offended when I ask about her music, and it causes her to pop up from the air mattress.

"This…" She points to the stereo. Her speech is slurred slightly and I know she's feeling a little drunk. I'm actually feeling pretty good myself, though I'm not quite as bad as she's appearing to be. "…is Etta James." I give her an incredulous look and she rolls her eyes then falls to the floor, attempting to change the song.

The sound of bluesy guitar riffs start to flood the apartment and a woman with a sultry, deep voice pipes through the speakers. Her passion is electrifying as she sings about watching the love of her life walk away with someone else. It gets me thinking about what Zoe's past could be. Has she been burned by someone she loved? Has she had to watch the love of her life walk away from her?

Before I get too much time to think, Zoe gets up and pulls me with her, standing in front of me with our bodies very close together. She grabs my arms and wraps them around her waist then trails her hands up my torso and chest, wrapping her arms around my neck.

"Dance with me?" she questions.

As I start to move, her hips sway slowly to the music as the song changes to Otis Redding's "These Arms of Mine", and I'm proud I actually know this song. We say nothing as we circle slowly around the room, holding each other as well as our broken hearts. I feel the guilt starting to build, but in my intoxicated state, I find it easy to push it away. I find it effortless to simply enjoy this moment before my guilt overshadows what I want to do with her.

Zoe

I allow the music to take over my body and I completely immerse myself in the heartbreak of it. Although I have never been walked away from by a man, I know what it's like to be betrayed by someone I love. And whenever I listen to blues music, I'm transported back in time and reacquainted with those feelings of hurt.

Drake says nothing as we move around the room, holding each other, feeling each other's pain. I rest my head on his shoulder and completely fall into him. I'm comfortable in his arms, protected even, and I don't want this feeling to end. I've never experienced this kind of contentment with a man before. I thought Terrance was someone I was in love with, but after the limited time I've spent around people who are truly in love, I know it could have never been love. What Terrance and my relationship was, wasn't love—it was a joke.

One of Drake's hands slowly starts to trail up my back, sending tingles up my spine. He then leans down and plants a kiss to the top of my head. I'm taken off guard by his actions, but I want nothing more than to feel his body on top of mine.

I break away from him and look into his eyes. They mirror mine—broken by someone we love, and now—in this moment—we can take each other's pain away.

Bravely, I move my hands down his chest and to the

145

bottom of his shirt, keeping my eyes planted on his. Then the pads of my fingers connect with his naked skin. I inch them up from his waistband and rest them on top of his very tight abdomen muscles. Drake closes his eyes, taking pleasure in my touch. I can feel how much he wants me as his erection pushes into and rubs against my body. When he opens his eyes again, his dark, broken pools are lit with a fire. I fall helplessly into him. I know in this moment that nothing else matters except him and me. We are all that matters right now, and I want nothing more than to feel him on top of me and inside of me.

"Drake…" I whisper, trying to find the right words without begging.

"I can't give you anything more," he says as the brokenness slowly starts to trickle back into his eyes. I look him over, still struggling once again to find the right thing to say, when Drake sighs deeply and faintly whispers, "This is all I can give you because I'm nothing but a shell. You have to understand, I no longer have anything left inside of me to give." And I fully understand. He's been burned—scorched by someone he loves—and there is no need for an explanation.

Truthfully, I let my own pain form into words and float out into the air. I look honestly into his eyes as I let him understand that we've come together through our pain. "Me, neither."

Drake

I am having a battle inside myself. This woman's had me in a tailspin since she walked into the bar. My body has craved to feel her pressed up against me.

Acting on a whim, I kiss the top of her head. I'm

letting her know something, but I don't know what that something is quite yet. She takes my cue and touches my skin. It's been so long since I've felt a touch like hers and it burns. My skins lights on fire as I crave to feel hers in return. I want this. I want to feel a woman again, if only for a few hours. I want to know what it's like to be with someone in that way again. I just want her.

"Me, neither," Zoe whispers back and sparks my desires to full-on lust.

I grab a hold of the back of my shirt and rip it over my head. She has no time to react when I then yank her shirt off along with mine. The carnal beast inside of me has taken over my body, and there is only one thing on its mind.

Zoe reaches around and unclasps her bra, freeing her breasts. She stands on her tiptoes to kiss my lips, but I avoid them like the plague, taking an old rule from Jake's book. I want to avoid any move that can spark emotions in the other person. Instead, I plant my mouth on her jaw and trail my lips down her long, swan-like neck. It's so beautiful and her skin is so soft. My tongue slips from my mouth as I taste and nip my way down to her collarbone then over to the other side.

Zoe lets out a sensual moan, and I can hear the desire as it escapes her throat. I break myself free from her neck then push her back at arm's length. She only stares, bewildered at what I'm going to do. I take her by surprise, pushing her down on the air mattress, before I fall down on top of her, kissing my way over to her breast and suckling her nipple.

As I put it into my mouth, her nipple becomes taut and

hard; it buds under my lips. Zoe is writhing underneath me, grinding herself against my dick. I move over to her other breast and continue the onslaught with her other nipple. She's moaning and quivering, ready to feel me inside of her.

Before I allow anything to stop me, I sit up on my knees and unfasten her jeans. She lifts her hips slightly, allowing me to pull them over her ass, down her thighs and over her knees. I toss them to the floor and look at her lying under me, wearing nothing but a black, lace thong.

I move down her body with my lips, kissing and biting her hot, slick skin until I find my way to the hem of her panties. I pull them off her body before I stand, undoing my own jeans and sliding them down. Zoe sits up on her knees with her eyes glazed over, oozing sex, and then grabs my dick in her hand.

She strokes it slowly from the tip down to the base and then back up. Her mouth comes forward and I feel her soft, supple lips wrap around my cock. Heat and pleasure erupt inside my body. It's been so long since I've felt comfortable to even touch myself that to now have Zoe's mouth sucking my dick… makes me want to live in this moment forever.

She strokes my cock as she starts to quickly pump it in and out of her mouth. I can feel I'm close, but I don't want completion this way. I pull her from me and push her back on the bed. I settle myself between her legs, and before another thought surfaces in my brain, I shove my dick inside her body and shudder. Her entrance is tight and warm, sucking me in deeper as I hold myself still inside her.

Zoe releases another moan, and it awakens my sleeping libido. I push hard, slow and deep. She screams, her voice mirroring the aching vocals coming from the stereo. I pull back, hold myself still, then push hard once again, knowing she's about to unravel around me. I slightly lift my hips, grab her long, sexy legs and hook them over my shoulders. When I return my hands to the mattress, I lean down, putting her face close to mine as I fold her in half. She comes instantly as her body starts to quiver uncontrollably and she screams my name. The sounds coming from her body are intoxicating. I can feel my balls getting heavy and my thighs burning for my own release.

I pull her legs down and start to move, fast. I thrust my body in and out of her, so quick and hard. Zoe handles my movement, meeting me thrust for thrust. I can feel the familiar build and its then I realize I'm not wearing a condom. Fuck! I'm not going to last too much longer and I'm not going to blow my load inside of her.

"Zoe..." I say through faint breaths. "I'm gonna...I'm gonna come."

"It's okay. Here." She pushes me off her and I make it to my feet. She sits up swiftly to her knees and sucks my throbbing, hard dick back into her mouth. Zoe wildly sucks my dick until I can no longer hold it back. My head falls back out of sheer, unadulterated pleasure. When I tip my head forward, I grab the back of her neck, grasping her hair in my hand as I start to fuck her mouth.

I pump my hips rapidly until the warmth of my come pours from my body and down her throat. She sucks every last drop, savoring my taste. When I'm finally done, I fall to the air mattress, pulling her down with me. I am spent, drained. My energy is gone as I lie back and fall fast asleep.

Chapter 16
Zoe

I awaken a couple hours later from the most incredible sex I've ever had. Drake is passed out next to me, completely naked and sprawled across my king size air mattress. The only light in my apartment is glowing from my stereo, but it provides enough light to look at him. He is a really beautiful man with his rock hard chest, well defined abdomen muscles, and the ever present V trailing down to his wonderful cock. I can't take my eyes off it, and it's not like I haven't seen a man naked before, yet Drake's cock is perfect. From the base where it extends from his body to the tip, it's the perfect size and length to fit inside me—it is unbelievable.

I can't help myself, I need to touch it. I want him to be hard because I need to feel his dick inside of me again. I keep my eyes on his sleeping face as I slowly move my hand over to his body and put him in my hand. It only takes a couple of long, slow strokes to have it hard in my hand. It's as hard as stone yet as soft and smooth as the finest silk.

I keep my hand on him, slowly bringing it to life. I move my face close to his. His lips are full and very sexy, and I want to feel them against mine. As I lean forward, I get within a centimeter when Drake's eyes fly open. They are angry, maybe scared, or confused. It's hard to tell, but I know they are not happy.

He rolls over on top of me, pinning my shoulders down to the mattress. My hand releases his dick and lies lifeless to my side. It's then I get to look into his eyes. They are molten and angry. I start to feel scared. I know he has a history of rage-filled outbursts and I've been so sure they were gone, but now I can see the fury that lies underneath.

"Don't..." he whispers, putting his face so close to mine. "Don't ever try to kiss me." The tone coming from him is low and dark. He climbs off me and stands to his feet then reaches for his jeans.

I know I shouldn't, but I can't help it. I have to know why he is so against kissing.

I grab his jeans from his hands and toss them back to the floor. I get to my feet and stand tall, so I can confront this angry man. I know it's wrong, however I'm just stupid enough to follow through with it.

"Tell me why," I demand.

"Because it doesn't belong to you." He bends to get his jeans again, but I kick them out of his reach. Drake's eyes ignite as he turns fully to me. The muscles in his arms are rock hard and the tension I've seen when we first met is back.

"What the fuck does that mean?" I'm walking on unsteady ground, brushing my way to his edge, and one wrong move will topple me over the side.

Drake steps close to me, putting no distance between us. He lifts his hands, cupping my cheeks and it's then I think he's going to kiss me, but he doesn't. Instead, he walks me back to the wall and pushes me against it. It's a little painful, but I'm too overwhelmed to stop him from whatever he's going to do.

Drake leans forward, our foreheads touching. Then his eyes transform back into the broken pieces of black glass I'm used to seeing. He glances to my lips and back up to my eyes. "Because kissing falls in the category of *more*, and I will never be able to give you that."His breath is hot against my lips. He's so close we are practically kissing with the air we expel from our lungs.

As his hands leave my cheeks and slowly brush down my arms, I begin to feel the tingling excitement at the apex of my thighs. Drake bends down, grips my ass, and lifts me up with his powerful arms, holding me pressed against the wall. I wrap my legs around his waist.

"But I can give you this," he whispers, and before another word forms, Drake reaches down between our bodies and joins us. I feel his cock enter my body and everything stops as pleasure takes over.

Drake grinds against me, slamming his body into mine. It doesn't take long to feel the heat building in my core, and before any other thought can register, I come—hard. The shivering is present when the pleasure erupts and channels its way through my entire body.

He pumps into me a couple more times then drops me onto the bed, coming down on top of me. When I open my eyes, I see his semen fall from his dick and onto my breasts. Beads of his white fluid pool and trail across my breasts, and I'm mesmerized. Seeing his face become completely overtaken by the pleasure I was giving him is enough to make me want to come again. I can feel the heat beating at the heart of my core.

I take my finger and trace it down my body, dipping it into his juices resting on my breast then put my finger in my mouth, tasting his saltiness. I move my hand between our bodies landing it on my clit. Drake looks back at me with want and lust. I start to move my fingers in circles on my small, sweet spot.

With my other hand, I push Drake off of me so he's kneeling on the floor, giving him an up close and personal view of my show. He sits back on his heels, his face captivated as I deeply run circles over my clit. The intensity is growing and my fingers are complying with my body's needs. I keep moving them around, faster and faster with every second. Drake hasn't looked away. He gazes between my legs as I start to quiver. His eyes meet mine and he watches me as I unravel for him.

I let the pleasurable feeling comedown a bit, and then I sit up so our faces are close once again. I desire to kiss him, yet I respect his inability to have more and say, "And I can give you this."

Drake

After fucking Zoe for the third time, she has fallen into a deep, deep sleep. I, on the other hand, am completely awake. The tequila in my system has burned off hours ago, and as I lie next to this beautiful woman, guilt is all that my body feels now. Being with her has been amazing and I've never expected it to be as intense as it was, but what have I really done? I'm confused because one part of me really likes what Zoe and I have together, but the other part of me feels like I've just cheated on Presley.

I really don't remember too much of what sex was like before I met Presley. With her, it was always gentle and soft. Sometimes she'd get a little wild, but never what I've experienced with Zoe. I never really wanted to go too crazy with Presley, thinking I could hurt her or take her back to a dark place she had experienced with Robert.

Zoe, on the other hand...well, I think she can take it. She's not as fragile as Presley was, and I have a feeling her past has made her that way. She liked it when I came in her mouth and on her breasts. She liked touching herself, knowing I was watching. I don't think any of that was an act. Zoe truly liked what she was doing, and the terrifying part is that I really liked what she was doing, too.

I look over and see light starting to come through the window. It's time for me to go. I roll off the bed and quickly dress. After I put on my boots, I give another look to Zoe who is lying on her stomach with the sheet pulled down, just barely covering her ass, and I feel guilty again. She has told me that she couldn't give me more, and I really hope she is serious. Because I know I can't.

I pull open the door and walk out into the cold, winter morning. I let the Chevelle warm up for a couple of minutes while I scrape the windows then drive away from her apartment and to my house, dragging my guilt with me.

155

Chapter 17
Drake

When Mia and I go over to Mrs. Fields for our Thursday night supper, this is the worst I've ever seen her. She is lying in her bed while the nurse is sitting in the chair beside her. Mrs. Fields is barely able to keep her eyes open. She is still coherent, which the nurse tells me is a good sign, however it won't be long before she will not be awake at all because she will be gone. Like Presley, gone.

Mia is watching Mickey Mouse while snuggling up with Mrs. Fields as I nervously start to think, pacing the room, when her faint voice stops me in my tracks. "Drake...can you do something for me?"

I fall to her side, holding her hand. "Of course. Whatever you need."

"I know it won't be long now..." My heart falls to the floor, knowing what she saying is the brutal truth I do not want to hear. "I want to have Thanksgiving dinner." Confused, I'm thinking she wants me to run up to Francine's, the local diner, and ask for their version of Thanksgiving dinner, but I stand corrected. "I want you and your family to come over here on Sunday. I want all of us to have Thanksgiving dinner. I know I won't...won't make it 'til then."

Tears start to fill my eyes and I nod at her request. It is

the least I could do for the years of love and support she's shown me. "Consider it done."

***

Sunday rolls around quicker than expected. Mia is settled in her car seat as I finish loading the groceries in the trunk. My entire family has jumped all in when I told them about Mrs. Fields's request. Delilah and Darcie went shopping for the groceries and started making some of the food ahead of time yesterday. Reggie and I loaded Big Mike's truck with a long table and chairs from the bar yesterday and set them up in the apartment.

Zoe has said she'll take care of the decorations and help with the cooking. We have not really talked since the night we had sex. I snuck out of her apartment like a coward because I was too afraid to confront the new emotions she's starting to make me feel. Before we had sex, we were friendly with one another. There were times where she'd tell a wildly inappropriate joke, making me laugh, but we'd never been on a level of intimacy. Once we had sex, all of that changed.

There is something hidden behind her eyes. She's fighting with something, but what?

A week later, the guilty feelings of being with her have not gone away. I really enjoyed the night we spent with one another, but what did I do to the memory of Presley? Am I starting to replace her because I'm feeling something new for someone else?

After I left her apartment that night, I drove home, wanting to turn back. I didn't want to leave like that—I wanted to be with her one more time. However, I knew reality would always be chasing me, and I have a devotion

157

to myself and to Presley that she'll be the only woman in my life.

I pull into the apartment parking lot and pull my Chevelle next to Zoe's. I take Mia from the back then make my way to the door. When I walk in, Zoe has pushed all the living room furniture to the walls to make more room for the table Reggie set up yesterday. She's draped a Thanksgiving themed tablecloth over the table and has a paper cornucopia sitting as a center piece.

I set Mia down and she goes running into Zoe's arms, demanding to be picked up. Zoe obliges my daughter and smiles. "Zoooooeeee!"Mia shouts then puts her arms around her neck. Zoe looks to me and is slightly confused, considering this is the most affection Mia has shown her, but she doesn't say anything, just hugs Mia back. "Go see Nanny?" Mia asks and squirms down from her arms.

"Sure," Zoe says and then follows Mia down the hall and into Mrs. Fields's room.

I head down to the car and start hauling up the groceries as the rest of my family pulls into the parking lot. Jake is carrying the electric roaster with the turkey, Reggie has his arms full of other covered dishes and Darcie and Delilah have sacks of stuff. We all set the items where we can find the space and then the girls get to work, finishing up the meal.

Reggie, Jake and I set the chairs around the table then sit in silence. The reason why we are here is a little awkward for us, knowing this will be the last Thanksgiving meal Mrs. Fields will have. And from now on, I won't be able to get through a Thanksgiving dinner without thinking of her. The day is going to be bittersweet, but it's important nonetheless.

Zoe

I was really nervous this morning at knowing I would see Drake for the first time since last Saturday night. It was one of the best nights of my life, though when I woke up to an empty bed, I didn't feel great at all. I actually felt lonely—a feeling that hasn't surfaced in years. I've always been okay on my own and really enjoyed it, yet after that night, loneliness is all I've been feeling. It's scary.

Two days ago, I finally got the nerve to call Connie's daughter to tell her about her mother's condition. I knew their relationship was rocky, but I wasn't expecting to get the cold-hearted comments coming through on the other end.

"The prodigal whore returns. So what do you want, Zoe? Money for a VD treatment?" I couldn't believe what I was hearing. Granted, she's called me a whore before, but it's been years since we've spoken and this is how she's going to treat me?

"Well, I can see nothing's changed," I snap back.

"I know all about you, Zoe. Sophia enlightened me and your mother when you left four years ago and I'm ashamed you're related to me." I can hear Rebecca's disdain in her voice. It pisses me off even more with how Sophia would talk about me behind my back.

"I just called to tell you that your mother is not well. She's not expected to live through the month and I thought you'd like to know." I swallow down the anger burning inside of me, knowing my aunt is a few feet away from me.

"How do you know about my mom?"

"Because I've been caring for her for the last few

159

months."

"What! How did—"

"It doesn't matter, Rebecca. I just wanted you to know that you could pay your respects and repent for your soul or whatever it is an evil witch needs to do to ask for a person's forgiveness." I can feel my blood pump wildly as the adrenaline storms inside of me. "Feel free to pass this information to Virginia as I won't be calling her.

"Aunt Connie has been moved to her apartment where she will live out her final days. Call this number if you're planning on visiting." With that, I disconnected the call and slammed my cell phone on the table. Luckily for me, it didn't break, but damn I wish it would have because I really wanted to break something right then.

I push the angry feelings from the memory of that phone call out of my way so I can properly care for my aunt. I step into her room and check her monitors. The home healthcare system has been working closely with me and teaching me how to take care of her. They've shown me how to properly bathe her, how to read the machines and change the catheter bag. I do it all, just so she will be comfortable and loved in her final days.

When I moved here, this was the last thing I expected to be doing. According to my initial plan, I would have been gone weeks ago.

I help dress her in a new nightgown I've purchased for her and then she falls asleep again. I am concerned she won't make it through the dinner, and I know she won't eat the meal. Right now she's only surviving on what's in her IV bags and that's it.

Drake and Mia come through the door, bringing in the

cold November air with them. I hold Mia in my arms as she requests to go see her nanny. When we walk in the room, Connie is sleeping again and I instruct Mia to be quiet as I turn the TV on low.

I then walk back to the kitchen and see the rest of the family has made it. I start pulling items out of bags and setting them on the counter. Delilah comes to my side and puts her arm around my waist, pulling me in for a hug. She's a lot shorter than me, then again, girls typically are when you're almost six foot tall. As Delilah is hugging me, I bend down and rest my head on top of hers. She takes my other hand in hers and just holds me, knowing today is going to be very hard.

"What can I help you with?" I ask as I break away from the embrace.

"Will you peel potatoes?" Delilah hands me a large sack of potatoes and a knife.

I get started as I grab a potato in my hand and start taking the skin off. I'm standing at the kitchen counter, but I can see the living room clearly. I get lost in my thoughts while I watch Drake interacting with his brothers. They are all very close and completely different from one another. When Mia comes running into the room, it doesn't take long before she's controlling the conversation and demanding all of their attention. She is a darling and as sweet as she can be.

Delilah moves to my side and starts peeling along with me. We stand there in silence until she breaks up my wandering thoughts. "He's a lot happier now."

"I'm sorry?" I ask, not understanding who the *he* is that she's talking about.

"Drake. Since you've came into town, I've seen him smile more. It's nice." Delilah's voice is quiet. I can't think of anything to say. Drake and I haven't really spent a whole lot of time alone together. We will randomly talk at the bar or text one another about Connie's condition, but that's it. Well with the exception of last weekend. "He hasn't been happy for a long time. It's nice to see him smile."

Curiosity gets the better of me as I look out to Drake, wondering what has caused him to be so sad. "What happened to him?"

Delilah expels a deep breath and chokes back tears of her own. "It's not my story to share, Zoe, but just know it wasn't good. It still isn't good." This gets my attention and I now need to know what I'm getting into. I have to know what has caused him to break and not feel what I feel when I look at him. Wait…wait? How do I feel? Is it different? Is it the dreaded feeling of love?

As the questions zigzag around my brain, I focus once again on my sack of potatoes and ignore any other thought.

**

It's four o'clock when dinner is done. As Darcie and Delilah put the food on the table, Reggie and Jake move the recliner to the head of the table for Aunt Connie to sit in. Drake and I walk down the hall toward her bedroom when he pulls me into the bathroom and then shuts the door.

I look at him confused, but before I can say anything, Drake wraps me up in his arms, crushing me to his body.

"I'm sorry," he whispers. "I'm sorry I left the way I did, but I'm just…"

"It's okay. Let's just make it through today," I plead, knowing today will be impossible.

162

He gently pushes me away from his body and looks deeply in my eyes. He's debating with something, and I hope it's his decision to kiss me. Drake leans down and plants a kiss to the top of my head. It's friendly and stays away from the *more* he thinks he can't have, though.

We quickly exit the bathroom and I wipe the loose tears from my cheeks as we walk into Aunt Connie's room. She's awake and smiling.

"So, how should we do this?" Drake asks.

"Here." I start to push the equipment forward. "It's all portable. I can move this, but we'll have to get her the wheelchair—"

Drake stops me mid-sentence as he leans down and picks up Aunt Connie, cradling her in his arms. She's so thin, and practically weighs nothing. "I'll carry her and you can follow behind me." I nod and start pushing the IV bag and heart monitor machine behind Drake as he carries my dying aunt to the Thanksgiving table.

Drake gently sets her in the plush recliner as Reggie and Jake assist in pushing it up to the table. Delilah helps me move the equipment next to her and Darcie gets a blanket to drape over her legs.

"Hi, Nanny!" Mia says from her chair seated next to my aunt.

"Hi, sweetheart." Her voice is breathless and weak. "The food smells so good. Thank you for doing this." She takes another deep breath as she continues to speak. The rest of us remain quiet, allowing her final words to be heard. "In the tradition of Thanksgiving I want to tell everyone what I'm thankful for." I sit next to her and hold her hand in mine. I look across the table and Drake is seated on the other side of Mia, putting jam on a warm dinner roll. "This is the best Thanksgiving I've had in years, despite the fact it will be my last." Tears from Delilah are heard and my own start to leak from my eyes. "Now, don't cry, ladies. This is a good day."

I look around the table, overwhelmed by this family. I barely know these people, yet they've done so much for me and my aunt in the little time we've been acquainted. Then there is Drake. He is someone I wasn't expecting to meet. When I recall all the small gestures over the last few months—the care he has for my family, his family and me—I finally understand the emotions I'm feeling. I think I am falling in love with him. What else would explain the loneliness I've felt, or my constant smile when he walks into the room, or the undeniable connection we've had from the moment our eyes met. It's only been a few months, but I don't need any more time. I am in love with Drake Evans.

"I just want to say how grateful I am for this little angel," Aunt Connie says, nodding over to Mia, who is quietly snacking on a roll, getting jam all over her face. "I am so thankful Drake and Presley moved in next door to me a couple of years ago I miss her every day. She was such a precious soul." I can't help noticing she said *was*, meaning in the past. I soon come to the conclusion she is no longer living. Now, all the random comments are starting to blend together. Before I can run away with it, Connie squeezes my hand and whispers, "Then there's you. I know forgiving family isn't easy, but you must have your peace with your mother before the regrets takeover." I nod. "And thank you to the rest of you for making this day special."

With that, we all begin to scoop up our food and start the traditional Thanksgiving dinner conversation, which consists of the boys discussing football, forcing us ladies to listen. As we sit around the table, I realize the moment is perfect for Connie. I'm happy we could do this for her.

Chapter 18
Zoe

The house is quiet again now that the Thanksgiving dinner is over and our company has left. Drake and I put Connie back in her room shortly after we began eating and she's been asleep since. It feels good that we were able to give her what she wanted before she passes away. Not too many people get that option, so I was glad I could do it for her.

I pull the blankets from the hall closet and make a pallet on the couch then sit in the dark, feeling overwhelmed with two pieces of information. One, I am in love with Drake. And two, he will never love me until he allows himself to move past Presley's death.

My mind is boggled with scenarios as to how she died. Was she in a car accident? Was she ill? Did she kill herself? As the questions float around in my brain, I know there is only one way for me to find out.

I pull my laptop off the side table and hook up my portable internet device. Google is flashing on my screen, staring me in the face. I place my fingers on the key pad and hesitate for a moment then I begin to type. I first start by typing *Drake Evans Sulfur Heights, MI* in the search bar. Links start to pop up and I soon find records of adoption with his name on it along with Jake and Jeremy

Evans, the documentation stating that Reggie has primary guardianship for the boys. After I do the math, I figure out that Drake was seven or eight-years-old when that happened. This means something happened to their parents to give Reggie guardianship of all the boys.

I study the document and come across a name I've only heard once, but the reaction his name has exuded from Drake leads me to my next search. I type *Jeremy Evans Sulfur Heights, MI* and soon it's flooded with newspaper stories. I click on the top link and see the headline *Drug Ring Busted with Evans's Arrest.*

What the hell?

> *"This afternoon, authorities with the Drug Enforcement Agency's office arrested twenty-two-year-old Jeremy Evans after 450 ounces of heroin was found in his possession. The long time investigation came together when a tip came from Evans's accomplice, Carter Brown. Brown is currently housed in I-Max prison in Ionia, MI after he plead guilty to the lesser charge of man slaughter for the murder of Presley Quinn. Brown turned state's evidence against Evans in exchanged for the lesser charge and is currently serving a ten year sentence. Evans..."*

The article goes on, but I push my laptop off my legs, astonished.

Murder?

I stand from the couch and grab a soda from the fridge. I crack it open and chug down the contents. This explains the rage Drake has inside of himself. The mother of his child was murdered by someone affiliated with his brother. I am lost as to what I am supposed to do with this information, though.

Last week when I started to look up Drake's past I was worried the information would make me want to run, but after reading what I just have, it makes me want to stay. I don't want to leave him, or his family, or Mia. I want to be with him and help him mend his aching heart. I know he has it in him because of how he's been with me. Every ounce of the newly founded love I have for him makes me want to try and help him.

Drake

I am awoken abruptly out of sleep from the ringing of my cell phone. I sit up quickly in bed and answer it. "Zoe…are you okay?"

She is sniffling on the other end and my heart starts to beat wildly in my chest. She doesn't even need to say it because I know the day we've been dreading for the last few months has finally arrived. It's time to say goodbye to a friend.

As she's trying to get the words out, I quickly get to my feet and start pulling my clothes on. "Sh…she's close, Drake."

"I will be there in ten minutes. I will be right there."

She disconnects the phone and I go into robot mode. I don't want to think about the emotions that will come when I get to Mrs. Fields's apartment or how I will react to them. I just want to get there and be there for Zoe. I know she's hurting right now, so I will myself to be brave for her. I have to be brave. I have to keep myself together. Later, in the quiet of my room, I can fall apart—when it's over.

I drive quickly to Mrs. Fields's apartment, and when I walk in, the space is dark and solemn. Associates with hospice care are gathered in the living room having a private conversation. One older woman looks at me with pity in her eyes.

I can feel myself starting to breakdown, but I don't. I swallow the hurt and choke down the looming pain. The feelings arising in my gut are killing me. I can't ignore them and I can't overlook the similarities to when Presley died. Although, we've known for some time that she was not going to make it through the year, the pain of losing someone you love never lessens. I swallow deeply again, trying to get the large baseball to go back down that's rising up my throat and eliminating my ability to breathe.

As I walk back to Mrs. Fields's bedroom, I see Zoe sitting in the chair, holding her hand. Tears are streaming down her face, and she is holding back from sobbing. Her knee is bouncing wildly up and down, and she looks like she's barely hanging on. I know how she feels more than she could possibly understand. I've been looking like that for well over a year now.

I enter the room and walk to her side, resting my hand on her shoulder. She grabs it immediately as we listen in silence to the faint beeps of the machines. My eyes affix on the numbers as I slowly watch her blood pressure drop and her heart rate decrease. It's agonizing to know it won't be long now.

"I'm going to miss her," Zoe whispers to me. I squeeze her shoulder and nod.

At that point, two hospice staff enter the room and we

all wait. At two thirty-eight a.m., Mrs. Fields's body finally gives out and she's gone.

Zoe bends down, kisses her hand and quickly exits the room.

I take the opportunity to say something to Mrs. Fields. I bend down and kiss her forehead. "I love you. You were like a mother to Presley and I, and a grandmother to Mia. I will never forget you." Then I step from the room, allowing the hospice workers to do their job.

Zoe is trapped in the bathroom, refusing to let me in when I knock. "Zoe, open the door," I plead from the other side.

"Just go away, Drake!" she screams through the door. It's pointless to talk to her now, I should know. Out of respect, I leave her in the bathroom to grieve because, again, I know exactly how she feels.

I sit in the living room and think about what's to come. I will have to cross the threshold of a funeral home again and relive the biggest nightmare of my life. The reality of what I've experienced with Presley is still too raw, even after almost two years, and now I have to do it all again with Mrs. Fields. How will I manage to make it through? I just know the moment I walk into the funeral home, it will be like walking through a torture chamber. I will have to grieve yet again for someone I've lost.

The very thought pisses me off. My entire existence can be summed up with people always coming into my life and then leaving shortly after they arrive, gone forever. It's like I don't get a chance to really know someone because time and fucking God take them away from me. I can feel the familiar rage boiling under my skin. This I why I hate

God—because, if he wanted me to praise him, he'd keep the people I love around for longer than a few years. I'm always losing someone. I can't get close to anyone because before I turn around they will be gone and it's His fault.

I take deep breaths in and out, trying to suppress the desire to slam my fist into something. My skin is hot and stinging with rage. My feet begin to pace like a caged animal and my shoulders start to tense. It won't be long before I will start scaring the shit out of all these people, yet I can't contain my feelings.

I start to head for the front door to at least attempt to cool off with the bitter, cold winter air when Zoe emerges from the bathroom. Her eyes are swollen and red. She looks completely devastated. Before I realize it, my rage completely evaporates. I take a glance into her broken eyes and am immediately aware that she needs me to comfort her, to ease some of the pain I know she's feeling.

I meet her halfway up the short hallway and pull her into my arms. She stiffens for a moment then falls into my body. She doesn't wrap her arms around me—she's too weary for that. She only leans in to my frame, using my body to keep her from collapsing.

I guide her in the kitchen as the hospice staff finish tending to Mrs. Fields. The sounds of the equipment and her body being transported from the apartment sound through the air, the noise is sickening. I hold Zoe tighter, swaying back and forth until the apartment is empty and the noises have ceased.

Several minutes go by before Zoe speaks. "I want to go home. I can't be here anymore."

"Okay, I'll take you."

She only nods then grabs her coat and laptop bag.

We walk to my car in silence. She's sitting in the passenger seat staring off into space as I move around the windows, scraping the frost off the glass. When I'm done, I get into my car and drive the short distance to her apartment. Zoe's breathing becomes normal again, but every so often she will take a deep breath to suppress the onslaught of emotion trying to escape. I recognize all the signs—I've been doing them every day since Presley's death.

I pull into the parking lot and shut off the engine, but Zoe just sits there, refusing to get out. Her body is shivering from the cold and heartache as a few tears leak from her eyes. I exit the car and swiftly walk to her side. Opening the door, I pull her out and lift her into my arms. She rests her body next to mine as I carry her into her apartment. I step in the door and set her down where she pulls off her boots and tosses her things on the floor next to the door.

"I'm going to take a shower. Thanks for…for…bringing me home and…" Her words trail off as she heads for the bathroom, shutting herself inside.

I stand in the entryway of her apartment, debating with myself. When it was me, I didn't want anyone to be there for me. I didn't want to hear the words spoken from my family that everything was going to be okay. I wanted to be by myself and fall apart. I'm debating with myself on whether to give this to Zoe. Should I leave her here alone to grieve? Or should I stay?

Before I can think about it too much, I remove my coat and boots then toss them on the floor next to Zoe's stuff. I walk to the bathroom, hearing the shower sounding from the other side, however it's the faint crying that captures my attention.

I start undressing myself, pulling my shirt over the back of my head, sliding my jeans and boxers down, and then slipping off my socks. I open the door and find Zoe in the shower, holding her face in her hands as her shoulders bob up and down. When I slide open the shower door and step in with her, her head snaps up then she falls apart as she falls into me. I catch her before she tumbles to the shower floor and hold her up against my body to allow her the time to simply cry.

Minutes pass before she is able to look up at me. I look back at her and feel her pain. It's as familiar to me as an extension of my own body. I wipe her loose strands of hair away from her face, gently caressing her soft, wet skin with my palm.

"You stayed." Her voice is hoarse from crying and barely audible.

"I couldn't leave," I whisper back.

"Thank you," she whispers to me and releases her hands from around my waist, sliding them up my torso and to my chest. The look in her eyes is different now. She needs something, something to suppress the pain, and I know exactly what that something is. She stands on her tiptoes, attempting to press her lips to mine, but I turn my face so she kisses my cheek instead.

The disappointment floods back in her eyes. I can see the pain restoring in her eyes, too. However, I don't want it to be there. I want to take her pain away.

I cup her cheek in my palms, raising her face with my

hands. I want to do it. I want to press my lips to hers, but I can't and I won't. Presley is the only woman I should ever be kissing, so I stop myself then plant a kiss on her forehead instead. Zoe releases a deep breath.

The feeling of her naked, wet body pressed against mine makes me come alive. I want nothing more than to feel her from the inside. I want to take her pain away, and if I can't kiss it away, then I will fuck it away.

When I glide my hands under her ass and lift her up, she instantly wraps her long legs around my waist as I turn around and press her against the wall. Putting my hand between us, I begin to rub her clit. I slowly move my fingers around her swollen, sweet spot, feeling her ignite at my touch.

Zoe's head falls back against the shower wall as I expertly extract her orgasm from her. When I recognize she's close, I move my fingers faster and let her fall apart on my hand. Her body begins to quiver and my body begins to ache.

I trail my hand down between us again and grab my dick in my hand. I start to stroke it slowly, getting ready to put it inside of her. Zoe adjusts her hips just enough so I can slide my cock into her body.

It feels incredible the way we fit together. We connect in a way that I've never felt before, something that has been present from the moment I've laid eyes on her. The connection is intense yet scary and not something I need in my life. It's currently everything I want, though.

Zoe's body wraps around my cock tightly, sucking me deeper inside of her. Then I begin to move. Slow at first, savoring the feel of her warm, tight body fastened to mine.

Zoe releases a moan from her throat and the sound is intoxicating, pushing me to drive harder and faster into her.

I push her hard into the wall as I begin to pick up the pace, fucking her as quickly as I can. Zoe leans forward, wrapping her lips around my earlobe and biting down. The twinge of pain sets me ablaze as I pull myself from her body and allow the beads to drip from my dick and onto the shower floor. I come so hard that my legs feel weak, and that, at any moment, I will fall down to the ground.

I slowly set Zoe down and we shut off the water then exit the shower. She hands me a towel then grabs one for herself and dries off while I do the same.

"Can you stay?" Zoe asks as she's running a brush through her hair.

"Darcie and Reggie know I'm with you. They said they'd watch Mia until I get back, so yes, if you need me to stay, I will," I reply, knowing how much I want to stay, though I'm feeling like it's the wrong thing to do. I struggle with my affections toward this woman. I know I shouldn't feel them…I can't feel them because of Presley. I can't lose her memory and if I allow the feelings I have for Zoe to move in, what will happen to my feelings for Presley?

Zoe takes my wet towel, tossing it to the floor and then tugs on my hand, pulling me from the bathroom. She leads me to the air mattress blown up in the middle of the room and lays me down. She then climbs on top of me, her knees on either side of my hips. Her hand strokes my dick, getting it hard with each deliberate movement.

"Drake, do that to me again," she pleads. She sits up enough to place me inside of her. The slow onslaught of pleasure lights the fire in my body as I watch her take me into hers. She begins to move and I fall victim to this woman's body as she rides me, sending me to a blissful world of peace.

Chapter 19
Zoe

Drake and I have another marathon of sex, similar to what we did the first night we were together, only this time my feelings toward him are different. I care for him deeply and I'm brave enough to admit to myself that I may love him. Nothing has proved this more than when he refused to leave me alone, knowing I was falling apart bit by bit. Drake stayed and held me.

He's been my rock through this entire agonizing process, and I know he cares about me. I can feel it from him, but because of his past, he won't allow himself to acknowledge that he has feelings for me. He's scared and rightfully so, however I'm scared, too. I've never felt like this toward a man. I've never wanted to be with someone so much in my life. Not in the physical way, either; although that is earth shattering. No, I want to be with him in every emotional way possible. The feelings came on so strong. He's like a beacon of light to an incoming ship, guiding me to him and eliciting feelings I never knew I could have.

We lie in silence after the third round of incredible sex and I can tell he's tired, but I can't sleep knowing what I know about him. I want him to be certain that it's okay to feel something for someone else, and I want that someone else to be me. However, if I'm asking him to make a bold move, then I need to make those moves as well. I need to be open about my past in hopes that he feels that he can be open about his.

"Did my aunt ever tell you why I haven't talked to my family in four years?" I ask, attempting to get the conversation started.

"No, she didn't." Drake rolls to his side and I roll to mine. I tuck my hands under my cheeks as I stare into his black eyes, falling completely in. We are lying very close. I can feel the heat we generate between us even though our bodies don't touch.

"I have a history of being with men. I guess the technical term is promiscuous or nymphomaniac. It all started when I was fifteen; I just wanted to see what all the fuss was about, so I had sex with my boyfriend. Then after two years of figuring out what to do with my body and what I could do to his body, I really started to enjoy having sex." Drake's face doesn't change. He doesn't cringe when I openly admit I'm a whore and how much I like having sex.

"When we broke up, I spent the next year or so having sex with a lot of guys. It didn't matter if I was drunk or high or completely sober, I just loved the feeling of it. I love sex. A couple days after I graduated, my mother's boyfriend decided that, since I was a whore, it was okay to tie me up and try to have sex with me," Drake closes his eyes, expelling a deep breath, and when he reopens them, they are angry. "but I was able to fight him off me.

"That same day, I told my mother—Aunt Connie's daughter, Rebecca—and my cousin, Sophia; but none of them believed me. Then, when Fred came home, he said I came onto him and he was the one who denied me. They chose to believe him and my mother banished me from her life. I was exiled from my family, just like that and not a single one of them showed any remorse. Sophia was my best friend for hell's sake, and she wanted nothing to do with me. When it comes to Sophia, the part that kills me is that she acts so above me when she's exactly the same." I look down at my hands, feeling the hurt of their betrayal in my heart. It's been a long time since I've allowed these feelings to live inside of me. "Anyway, it's been four years, and I've been on my own ever since."

"What have you been doing since you left Wisconsin?" Drake's hand brushes a loose strand of hair away from my eyes. I slightly lean into his hand, enjoying his delicate touch.

"I've been living from place to place. Once I got my car, I pulled out a map and let the fate of a dime dictate where I'd land next."

"What?" Drake's brows crinkle in confusion and the sight makes me smile. Finally, a smile.

"I will lay a map across the hood of my car and toss the dime. Wherever it lands is where I go next. It's stupid, I know." I cover my face with my hands, embarrassed by my vagabond way of living.

"Stop. It's not stupid. It's kind of cool. And that's how you came to Sulfur Heights, from a toss of a dime?" I nod and he smiles. "So where have you lived?"

"All over, really. I tried to stay away from the Midwest, but I started running out of different states to live in and I had to get out of Louisiana."

"Why?"

I lift my bangs, exposing the fresh scar Terrance gave me after he punched me in the head. "Terrance. He's the closest I've ever come to having a relationship, and that was a mistake." Drake's jaw tightens as he closes his eyes, suppressing his anger. It makes me happy knowing he's angry because someone tried to hurt me. This proves he cares for me. How deeply? Well, that's yet to be determined.

Drake's hand moves from his side and comes around to my waist. He pulls me close to his body, his forehead pressing against mine. He then leans up and kisses the scar on my head and I want so badly to kiss his lips, but I stay still. I hope he takes that leap and kisses me, though.

"I know how betrayal feels, more than you will ever know." Drake pulls away and I know he's thinking about telling me his story, yet he says nothing more.

The quietness is killing me, so I say something to break it. "I never told anyone that."

Drake clears his throat then asks, "Did Mrs. Fields know what happened to you?"

"Yes, she did. And unlike them, she chose not to believe the lie," I whisper, thinking about the conversation we had not so long ago.

I texted Rebecca when Aunt Connie took a turn for the worse. She never responded back. I dread to think of the reality for her if it wasn't for Drake and me—my aunt would've had no one to care for her in the final months of her life. She would have been left alone.

An uneasy feeling settles over me when I suddenly realize living a life as a gypsy is the last thing I want. If I refuse to establish myself somewhere—anywhere—then, when the time comes, I will die alone.

Then, before I can stop them, the tears trickle down from my cheeks and fall onto his chest. Drake pulls my head back and I fall again into is black eyes. His hands come to my face as he wipes away my tears with the pads of his thumbs. We get lost yet again in each other's bodies, but this time I'm not just having sex with him. I'm making love to him even though I can't kiss him. I can still make love to him.

***

My aunt has made all her arrangements before she passed. I'm assuming when she found out she was sick, she took care of it all because there is very little I need to pay for. I dress in the only black dress I own, which is more suitable for a dance club than a funeral. I snatch a black cardigan from my closet and pull it over my shoulders. I apply a little eye shadow, liner and lip gloss then tie my hair up on top of my head. I look as good as I possibly can when my insides feel like their dying. The winter air bites when I step from my apartment and walk to my car. I fall into the driver seat and head toward the funeral home.

Drake has been with me every step of the way, helping me deal with the aftermath of my aunt's death. He's been attentive as we've spent the past few nights together in my apartment. He will come over late, after Mia is put to bed, and then leaves before she'll wake up. When I've asked him about work, he told me they gave him the week off for the funeral and he doesn't need to be back until Tuesday. I am grateful he's here to help me, but in the back of my mind, I'm scared that once this is all over, so are we.

He's made it clear on more than one occasion that he can't give me more and I've never pushed, even though I know he's capable of give me so much more. But how do I convey that to him? What is the right thing to say when it's someone's heart at stake?

I pull into the funeral home parking lot and walk in the building. My stomach is pained, making it harder to move inside the door. The Evans family is standing in the lobby area, but I cannot see Drake. Everyone is here but him.

"Darcie, where's Drake?" I ask. She points to his Chevelle. I can see him sitting behind the wheel, the tension is on his face and he looks like he's battling with the demons he's had since Presley died.

I turn to the door and open it, faintly hearing Darcie say, "I wouldn't," but I choose to ignore her and walk to Drake.

I open the passenger side door and fall into the seat. He doesn't look at me. He simply glares at the funeral home, killing it with his eyes, and his hands are gripped around the steering wheel so hard his knuckles are white.

I move as close to him as I can and put my hand on his forearm. His skin is hot and slick with sweat. "Drake," I whisper. "Tell me what's wrong?"

"Just go inside, Zoe, please." The tone of his voice is low and deep, mirroring the tone he used when I first heard him speak.

Boldly, I say, "I can't, Drake."

When he turns and faces me, his eyes are pits of tar as they ignite on fire, blazing me with every second. "I said, GO!" he screams at me and then loses all control, punching the steer wheel and scaring away all the anxiety in me of

182

going to my aunt's funeral.

"NO!" I shout, struggling to find my voice. I won't let him hide in the car. He needs to be able to move on. When people fall apart, they somehow manage to get back to their feet, and it's his turn. I will help him. "I can't do this without you." My voice becomes soft and pleading.

Drake turns to me, finally looking into my eyes. His breathing is rapid when he starts taking deep breaths in and out, calming himself enough to function. Finally, I can see the anger start to melt away. His hands release from the steering wheel and fall onto his lap, but they are still balled into hard fists.

I slide my hand to his and cup his raging fist in my hands. "Please...I need you."

Drake nods his head up and down then exits the car. I meet him on the sidewalk and we stand face to face, both scared to walk into the funeral home, though we're scared for two very different reasons.

He doesn't know I've researched what happened to Presley and his brother, but I won't let him suffer anymore. He needs to know that, no matter what, I won't let him fall. We have to keep each other upright.

"Just hold my hand, okay? Please don't let go of my hand and I won't let go of yours," I plead. He looks at me quizzically. Now is not the time to divulge to him that I know his secret. That can wait for another day. Right now, this day will be easier for both of us if I stay silent and we hold onto each other.

Drake

The entire drive to the funeral home I am slowly building myself up, and by the time I get there, I am far too angry to be around anyone. I can feel the looming pain as I flashed back to the last time I walked through those doors. I can see her lying in the black casket, her hands folded across her lap, holding the picture of our daughter. I can feel her cold body when I collapsed on her and when I kiss her for the very last time. The thoughts have been in my head from that day forward, slowly torturing me every time I've closed my eyes.

I'm debating on leaving. I have the keys in the ignition and the engine running when the other door pops open, Zoe getting into the passenger seat. I refuse to look at her. The familiar rage-filled feelings are right there on the brink of exploding out of my body, and I can't stand the feeling. She needs to leave. She doesn't need to see my fucked-up-ness.

I beg her to go inside, to leave me with my pain, but this woman is defiant and chooses not to listen. She wants to know more, but I don't want her to. I don't ever want to speak to her about why I can't have more. She will never know. Her presence and my anxiety are too much to bear without adding that in the mix.

Then I explode. Red fades into my line of sight and I begin to punch the steering wheel, taking out all of my anger on my car, but she doesn't leave. Zoe only sits there, scared yet brave. She knows what I'm capable of; she's seen me lose it before and she's still here. I don't want her here. I want her just to go and leave me to drown in my misery. I've been doing it for so long that it's all I know how to do.

I hear her words, pleading with me to get out of the car. I can see how terrified she is when my eyes connect with hers. I ignore the fact that she's probably frightened because I just freaked out with her in the car. Then again, she refused to leave and I can't say no. She needs me and I need to be there for her.

"Just hold my hand, okay? Please don't let go of my hand and I won't let go of yours." Zoe tightly grips my hand and I get an unsuspecting feeling that she's talking about something completely unrelated to her aunt's funeral. I shake off the eerie feeling as we walk hand in hand to the funeral home.

As we step through the door, I help Zoe out of her coat and hang it on the coat rack. Her back is exposed as the sweater she's wearing to cover her arms falls off when I removed her coat. The curve of her spine is long and sensual, like her neck. Her milky white skin is flawless. I've touched her body so many times, but I've never actually taken the time to study it.

Zoe looks over her shoulder at me and gives me a faint, blushing smile as she slides her sweater up on her shoulders. The black dress is hugging her curves, and without the sweater, it looks like a dress a girl would wear for a night out, not a funeral. She looks beautiful nonetheless. Her long legs are covered in black, sheer nylons. Every part of her body looks flawless. I can't take my eyes off her, and I really don't want to. I would rather be here, lost in her body than face the reality of Mrs. Fields's death.

When I walk deeper into the funeral home, I see Mrs. Fields's casket at the front of the room and all those feelings come flooding back like a huge, giant wave. It crashes into my body and nearly knocks me off my feet.

The casket looks the same as well as the flowers. The lighting in the room and the smell of the cinnamon air fresheners are all the same, taking me back to the last time I saw Presley.

I'm frozen. I can't move into the room. I can't walk up to the front and look inside that fucking box. I can't move. I don't want to move. I feel sick and suffocated and the air in my lungs is escaping too quickly out of my mouth. My muscles became as taut and ridged as they were moments ago when I was sitting in my car. I just can't do this.

I squeeze Zoe's hand and lean in to tell her, attempting to tell her I'm leaving. She has a look of great sadness and it tears at my heart because I'm making this about me and my stupid fears. What else am I supposed to do? This is a fear I cannot face—I don't want to face—yet I'm being confronted with it.

Zoe pulls me to her side and leans in. She rests her head on my shoulder and just stands beside me. We remain stock still in the back of the room while everyone else is sitting and waiting for the service to start. Zoe doesn't ask me questions, she just remains by my side and I remain by hers. We are both grieving for her aunt, but saying goodbye to her is not my problem. I've made my peace with her death the night she died.

It's Presley and the fact I cannot make peace with anything when it involves her. She was everything to me. I don't know where I should go in life without her.

The officiator starts the service while Zoe and I stay in the back, standing against the wall, listening. Every once in a while she will lift a tissue and dab tears off her cheek, and I will swallow the giant lump in my throat.

Shortly after the service starts, three woman walk through the door, disrupting everything as they stumble in. When Zoe's body hardens at my side, I turn to look over at her, seeing she looks surprised, angry and scared. I know immediately these are the women who have been so cruel to her, banishing Zoe from their lives. Two of them are older, in their forties I'd guess, and the other one looks to be our age.

When they walk deeper into the room, all their eyes connect with Zoe's. The tension is palpable.

Zoe

I don't say anything to Drake when we get into the funeral home. Even though he's never told me about his girlfriend's murder, I know this is the source of all his anger and hesitation today. I want to help him get better, to have acceptance.

If I've learned one thing from my aunt, it's to face your problems head on. She's said it to me for as long as I can remember, but it hasn't been until recently that the advice has finally sunk in. The only way to move forward in life is to accept your past, work through it and walk forward.

I know I have to stand up to my mother. I have to tell her how I really felt when she chose to believe Fred's lie instead of me.

I could have told myself that all day until the side door opens and in walks my mother, Rebecca and Sophia. My heart rate skyrockets as it beats wildly in my chest. I'm forced now to deal with my past as I say goodbye to the one person from my family who has given a shit about me. Our eyes meet and they say nothing. They find a place to sit and listen to the man talk about my aunt.

***

Drake refuses to go to the cemetery. He never tells me why, but I soon realize Presley's grave is right next to the plot my aunt shares with her deceased husband. It makes me wonder how many times he has come out here, or if he comes at all.

I walk back to my car once the cemetery service is over. The snow is numbing my feet by the time I get back into my car. I quickly fire it to life and crank on the heater. When I look back, Darcie and Delilah are standing by Presley's grave. They appear to be crying with their men standing strongly behind them. Reggie and Jake have their girls wrapped tightly in their arms then Delilah lays a bundle of colorful flowers in front of her grave.

None of them talk about her when I'm around, but I would like to know more. I want to know about her and what has happened to her. I really do like these people and being around them. I want to understand what makes them click together as a family.

Watching how Reggie and Jake comfort Darcie and Delilah makes me yearn to have that with a man. I want someone who will be in my corner when the weight of the world gets to be too much. I want unconventional Thanksgiving dinners, wild nights at the bar, and I want so much to have a family again. I miss it. I miss my family, but I know we will never be what we once were.

What I want more than anything is to have all of that with Drake. I want to be that woman in his life, and I want to help him care for his daughter. I know I could never replace her mother; I just want to be the woman who she looks up to as a mother figure. I want to be a family.

Before I can stop it, the sobs break free from inside my chest. I fold myself forward and then lean into the cold steering wheel. I cry for the family I've lost and the family I'd love to have. Can I have all of that with Drake? Am I strong enough to be that for him?

A loud knock on the glass shakes me out of my internal rant, and when I roll down the window, Sophia is standing next to my car.

"We all need to talk to you." Her face is turned up in a wicked smile. The same smile she dawned when she told my mother and hers about my past with men. The same smile she had when I was forced to leave my family home, and was left to figure out the world on my own.

"I will meet you at her apartment. Do you know how to get there?" I ask, masking my anger just enough to get the words out.

As Sophia nods and leaves, I roll up the window and pull out my cell phone. I want to text him. I could use him right now. I need that rock to lean into, but he's already been through enough today. There's no sense in piling my troubles on his already weighted down shoulders. I tuck the phone back in my purse and dread the entire conversation I'm about to have.

I unlock the apartment and take a moment to clean up. The home healthcare staff has taken the last of the equipment and any traces that someone died in the house days ago. I remove my sweater and sling it over a dining room chair as I wash a couple of dishes in the sink. Rebecca doesn't even knock when she opens the door and the three of them come storming in.

God, I don't want to do this. I don't want to see my mother—or any of them. I just want this all to go away.

"It smells disgusting in here. This is how you take care of my sick mother?" Rebecca sneers.

"Well, at least someone was here to take care of her, don't you agree?" I snap back. The nerve of this woman astounds me. She's never once cared about her mother or the sacrifices she's made to make her happy. I never really saw it until I was away from their poisonous minds. "So what do you want?"

My mother steps to Rebecca's side. She looks a little older from the last time I've seen her. She has more wrinkles around her eyes and a little more weight around the middle, but she's still beautiful. I'm similar to my mother in a way because of my height and dark brown hair, however she has this old, Hollywood star glam look that is breathtaking. I've never had that glamorous look, just simplistic and natural.

"My sister has an estate and I need to see the paperwork to get it over to my attorney. Do you know where she'd keep that stuff?" Her voice is condescending and crude.

"Of course that's what this visit is about, Connie's money." I cross my arms over my chest and lean against the counter. She doesn't care that her sister, the woman who raised her, has just died. Oh, no. She cares about getting her greedy little hands on Connie's money.

"It's not only her money, Zoe. It's my money, too. Our parents' estate was left to her when they died and I am entitled to it." The vein pops from her forehead and her wrinkles deepen as she intently stares me down.

190

"Well, I don't know what to tell you. She never mentioned money to me so I have no idea where she keeps her papers."

Rebecca walks to the backroom and stops in her tracks. She's standing at the threshold of the spare room, staring at the child's toys and bed. "What is this? Did your whoring finally catch up with you?"

Before I can get the words out of my mouth, the front door opens and Drake is walking into the apartment with Mia in his hands.

"Zoe?" I hear him say, and then Mia comes running down the hallway.

I bend down to pick her up and she giggles. "Hi!"

"Hi, Mia. How are you?" I ask when she gives me a little hug.

"Fine!" She squirms from my arms and runs by Rebecca standing in front of her room. Mia starts getting toys from the box and begins to play.

We make our way back up the hall as Drake sets their coats on the back of the couch. He's still wearing his black jeans and dark gray shirt, but the look of devastation is no longer on his face. It's bewilderment instead.

"Drake, this is my mother, Virginia." I turn and point to the others. "And this is Connie's daughter, Rebecca, and her granddaughter, Sophia." As I introduce them, I notice Sophia practically loses herself when she looks at Drake. She stands a little taller and pushes out her chest. Her eyes slant slightly as she puts on her sex kitten face. Yeah, and they call me the whore.

Drake holds out his hand and they all shake it. Sophia is panting like a dog in heat when she touches him. It's disgusting. We are all standing there in silence and I'm praying they leave soon, now that Drake is here, but that doesn't stop my mother from getting what she wants. She wants her money, and until she gets it, she will be a complete nightmare.

"Where does Connie keep her lockbox?" she asks, her harsh glaze is penetrating into my eyes.

"I told you; I don't know," I snap back.

"Fine, I will look for it myself." Rebecca starts to move through the apartment, the sound of closet doors opening and closing in the background. She is disrespectfully going through her mother's things, leaving a mess in her wake.

"Rebecca, stop! Your mother just died. Why is that the only thing you care about right now?" She is a shameless bitch and I can't believe I ever looked up to her when I was younger. She and my mother were Sophia and my role models. Until I was kicked out of their lives, I idolized them.

I walk back toward the room, but she meets me just outside the bedroom door, a small lockbox in her hand. "Found it," she gloats.

Rebecca sets the metal lockbox on the table and slams it down with a loud thump. The three of them collect around the dining room table, discussing amongst themselves on how they will open the safe.

"We could call a locksmith…" Sophia suggests.

"No, they will want proof that we live here before they will open the safe. How about a knife? Do you think a knife will pop it open?" Rebecca asks.

"It would have to be a small one," my mother chimes

in. As they continue to chatter about breaking into Connie's privacy, it infuriates me. My skin begins to heat. I am boiling with rage.

"Stop it," I say, moving toward the box. I refuse to let these horrible women disrespect my dead aunt. I will not allow them to tear through her things all for the sake of money. They are disgusting and the worst kind of human beings. "Give me the box!" I shout then step toward the table. My mother snatches it closer to her body, glaring at me to get back.

"This is none of your business, Zoe!" my mother shouts back.

"Don't you have a venereal disease to treat, slut," Sophia snaps.

"Fuck you, Sophia!" I shout and she stands, meeting me face to face.

"Are you mad at me because I speak the truth about your dirty crotch?"I roll my shoulders and then back slap her across her face. I am so distracted by their presence and my anger, I forget Drake and Mia are here until I feel his strong arms wrap around my waist, holding me firmly against his body.

He leans down to my ear and whispers, "Just blow her off."

The anger inside of me starts to dissipate slowly as his arms tighten around my body. Drake holds me to his tight frame, protecting me from doing something I'll regret.

"Who's this, Zoe? Another John?" Sophia is such a stupid, jealous bitch—she wishes she could be with someone as amazing as Drake.

I glare at her, trying to ignore her comment. However,

I can't ignore how she appears whenever she talks. She looks constipated when she opens her mouth. The more I glower at her, the more I want to rip her head off.

I can feel my body tense once again, but Drake holds me firmly and whispers in my ear. "Ignore her. She's trying to get a rise out of you on purpose. Just blow her off."

"Excuse me, but who are you again?" My mother stands next to Sophia, the accusatory tone laced through her voice.

Drake stands up straighter and I can feel his body become rigid. "I'm Zoe's and your sister's friend, and I think it's time for you to leave." Drake's voice commands attention and respect as he looks my mother over with his deep, black eyes.

He moves from behind me to stand by my side, keeping his arm tightly wrapped around my waist. It feels like home here, wrapped in Drake's protective arms. I've never really felt like I was home anywhere until I came to Sulfur Heights, even when I was younger and had these women as my family. I know *now* what has been missing.

Maybe that's why I've found comfort in other people's beds—because I never really felt I belonged anywhere. I have always been an outcast. Yet when I moved here, every other place felt wrong. This is exactly where I need to be— where I should be. Having Drake here by my side only proves that what I've had before has been inconsequential. All of it was false, a fake sense of a family. I can't believe I'm just figuring that out now, but damn it, I'm glad I have.

When I was straightening up Connie's room, I remember seeing a small key taped to the inside of her top dresser drawer. That has to be the key to the lockbox.

Maybe if I give them what they want, they will leave. I really don't care about her money; I just want them to leave.

I abandon Drake's side, heading toward my aunt's bedroom, when I hear Mia. She's building a tower with her blocks, perfectly content and happy. She looks in my direction, and a large smile spreads across her face as she comes scampering to my arms. I bend down and pick her up, captivated by her eyes. They are a beautiful, golden honey color that sparkle in the light.

"Hi, Zoe!" Mia wraps her arms around my neck and gives me a hug. My heart fills with joy at her generous touch. Mia is a sweet little girl and so full of life. It's hard not to fall in love with her.

I walk out of the room and move to my aunt's, carrying Mia with me. "Hi, Mia. How are you?" I ask as I rest the toddler on my hip and open the top dresser drawer in search of the key.

"Auntie D says Nanny's in Heaven with Mommy." I freeze. Mia is so matter of fact about the entire situation, but I'm ill prepared for these types of comments. How am I supposed to react to this? What do I say? I didn't know her mother obliviously, but the statement throws me completely off guard.

"Yes, that's right," I barely choke out as I open the drawer and find the key for Connie's lockbox taped to the side. As I pull it from the drawer, my hand is shaking and I'm trying to get it under control before I go back out there.

I can feel Mia's finger on my earring. She's twisting the diamond stud in my ear, fascinated by the sparkle. They're the only thing of value I took when I left my family four years ago. They were a graduation present from Connie and they've been in my ears ever since.

"Pretty." Mia smiles as she turns the stud in my ear.

"Nanny gave those to me."

"I wuv Nanny," Mia says sadly, bringing water to my eyes.

"I love her, too," I say then walk from the room with the key in one hand and Mia in the other. I hope this will be enough and they will be satisfied. I hope whatever we find in that lockbox will be enough to keep them away and enough for Drake to want me to stay. I…hope.

Chapter 20
Drake

Zoe turns on her heels, heading down the hallway toward the bedrooms. I watch her as she walks away and see out of the corner of my eye she's holding Mia. When I focus my attention back on Zoe's family, I can understand why she has been so hesitant to be around them again. Her mother is cold, frozen in time, and refuses to see what she will be missing in the future if she continues to shut Zoe out. She's already lost four years of her daughter's life, you'd think she would want to salvage that. She doesn't, though. Restoring their relationship is the last thing on her mind; her mother is blinded by money.

Then there's Sophia. She hasn't taken her eyes off me since I came into the apartment. Her eyes are icy blue, but have a sense of creepiness about them. As soon as she opened her mouth, throwing insults at Zoe, I began to loathe her. She's catty and weak, knowing she can pry on someone's despair. Rebecca is sitting next to Sophia and is s spitting image of a young Mrs. Fields. She has the same small frame, light brown hair and blue eyes. However, she doesn't look sweet and endearing, that is definitely not a trait she got from her mother. Rebecca is the complete opposite—a cold hearted bitch.

I refuse to say anything to them, pretending to be

distracted by my phone when I hear Virginia ask, "So is the child hers?"

My eyes pop immediately from my phone, anger ever present behind them. "What business is it of yours?"

"Well, being she could be my grandchild, I would say it's all my business. I presume you're her father?" I say nothing because I'm trying to swallow down the boiling rage that's risen to the top of my throat. "Well, just a word of warning. Zoe isn't who you might think she is. I'm not sure if she's told you about her past, but she has problems keeping her legs closed. Which is why it doesn't surprise me that she's had a child, but you'll want to make sure it's yours if she asks you for money."

I tuck my phone in my pocket and step closer to Virginia. She immediately takes in my size and how I tower over her. "I will warn you now," I swallow again, doing what I can to not blow up on this woman, "say one more word about Zoe or *my* daughter and I will throw your ass out the door. Got it?"

"She sure knows how to pick em', doesn't she?" Sophia says to Virginia, coming to her side. "She clearly has no taste or regard for a real man."

Zoe comes strolling from the back, holding Mia on her hip and a small silver key in the other hand. "Here." She hands the key to her mother and a wicked gleam comes onto Virginia's face.

The three women gather back around the table, all whispering about what they might find when they get in the lockbox. Virginia pops the lid and starts pulling out papers. Nothing really of interest has captured their attention as they intently stare at each piece of paper until Rebecca's voice breaks through.

"What! I can't believe this!"

They all gather around the documents Rebecca is holding and gasp in disbelief. Zoe and I share curious glances as we watch the dismay unfold right before our eyes.

Virginia snatches the papers out of Rebecca's hand. "I can't believe this! Who the fuck are these people? Why would she leave half her inheritance to..." She snaps her head back to Zoe and eyes Mia, glaring at my child. I instantly go into protective mode, stepping in front of Zoe. "What is that child's name?"Virginia asks, practically foaming at the mouth.

"Mia!" My daughter shouts from behind me, always willing to participate in conversations now that she's an avid talker.

"Unbelievable...and you're Drake *Evans*, I suppose?" I nod my head, still trying to cap the anger this woman extracts from me. "My sister left half her inheritance to you, someone who's not even related to her."

"Who's the other half left to?" Sophia asks with hope in her voice.

"A bunch of different charities." Virginia's voice is low and angry. She knows there is nothing she can do about it.

She pushes the paperwork into my hand and its right there in black and white. Mrs. Fields's will states Mia and I will receive the funds in her two trust accounts with the amount totaling one hundred and forty thousand dollars. I practically fall to my knees, trying to fully understand what I'm reading. This means I won't have to worry about Mia's college. I could buy a house or take a vacation. I won't have to worry about how I will be able to feed my daughter the next day. I've never had serious money problems, but knowing I have this will keep my mind at peace. Mrs. Fields has made sure Mia will be taken care of, and it's a gesture I will never be able to repay.

"What a complete waste of our time." Rebecca storms from the apartment with Sophia hot on her heels.

Zoe's mom just looks us up and down then stares intently at Mia again. I stand directly in her line of sight, unsure what she's planning to do. "Well…at least she looks like you, but if you're smart, you'd take my advice and get a test. Like I told you before, my daughter is shameless."

I can feel Zoe's defeat sink into my back as her mother cuts her down once again. She is a heartless woman and I hope I will never have to see her again. "Virginia, Zoe may be all the things you say she is, but at least she's true to herself. She doesn't have to pretend to be something she's not. Unlike you, who is willing to believe a rapist and pig instead of their own daughter. And all to ensure that you'll never have to abandon your comfortable lifestyle."

Without a word in response, Virginia storms from the apartment, slamming the door in her wake.

I take Mia from Zoe's arms. I can tell at any moment she's about to break down. Who wouldn't after someone that vile has said something just as vile to her?

"She mean, Daddy," Mia states out into the open. "She mean to Zoe."

I kiss her on the head and reply, "I know, baby. She was not a nice person. Why don't you go play with your puzzles so Daddy can talk to Zoe?" I set her down on the floor and Mia goes running down the hallway toward her toys.

As soon as Mia is out of sight, the tears begin to fall and Zoe breaks down again. When I pull her into my arms and pick her up, she nestles into my chest, crying her broken heart into my shirt. Her body is trembling and I want to take all her pain away. I know firsthand what it's like to be abandoned by your parent. It's a pain you can never get rid of. It's always there, lingering in your heart, and in weak moments, that pain resurfaces, leaving destruction in its wake.

I walk to the couch and sit with Zoe on my lap, letting her finish her rant of tears. Moments later, she sits up, wiping the tears off her cheeks. The whites surrounding her blue eyes are bloodshot and the skin surrounding them is red and puffy. Even in her emotional state, she is still beautiful.

"Well, it looks like I've got an apartment to clean out. I'm not sure where to begin."

I'm stunned momentarily.

Initially, the major attraction to Zoe was the fact that she was never going to be a permanent fixture in Sulfur Heights. She specifically told me she was going to leave after a couple of months. But now, I don't know how I really feel about her leaving. Over the time she's spent here, we've grown to be friends. I feel comfortable with her, something I haven't felt since Presley's death.

For the first time since meeting her, I'm beginning to realize how much I think about Zoe and how beautiful she really is—inside and out. From the day our eyes met, I knew she is unique, but there has been something behind her eyes that attracted me to her, and now, whatever I felt that night is starting to take over some of my painful thoughts. We've spent a lot of time together, and the more time I spend with her, the more I feel that attraction—an attraction beyond the physical.

I want to be her friend. I don't want her to leave, but if she stays, will she want *more*? Can I give the *more* she deserves to have? The answer scares me, knowing I will never have it in me. Eventually, I will lose her just like I've lost everyone else I've gotten close to in my life. Soon, it will be time to cut those ties and it has to be done before the *more* finally settles in.

Zoe shifts on my lap, taking me out of my trance. I nod to her question, however I'm overcome once again by the feeling of loss.

Zoe

I feel like I've been put through the spin cycle of a washing machine, watching my reality spin out of control when my mother finally leaves.

I was stupid to hold on to the sliver of hope that my mother might want to reconcile our pasts. When she left, I finally grieved for the relationship I will never have back. Now that Connie is gone, there's no reason for her to see me again. As it turns out, she didn't care about Connie, either, only her money.

Drake recognizes my breakdown brewing, that it's on the brink of exploding, and acts quickly so I don't have to upset Mia. As soon as she's out of sight, I fall apart, landing in his arms. This wouldn't have been possible to go through without him, and I will never be able to repay him for the strength he's given me since I've been here.

When I finally calm down enough to think, I realize I am responsible for taking care of Connie's property, but I don't know what I will do with it. I could probably sell it or take it to Goodwill, but the thought of doing either is sickening. When I speak out loud my concerns, Drake vanishes from the conversation, withdrawing inside himself as he tends to do so often. However, it's been awhile since I've had to see it.

"Are you okay?" I ask, taking in the pained look on his face.

Drake shakes his head and looks into my eyes. "Yes, I was just thinking." He picks me up slightly, removing me from his lap, and then stands to his feet.

I'm not sure what he's thinking, but I'm dying to know. I would love to spend a day in his head to understand what makes him work and why he acts the way he does. I want to understand how he copes with everything he's been through, which I still haven't disclosed that I know about.

"You could sell it or if you need to get rid of it quickly, you could put it on the curb. People around here would have her stuff gone in seconds."

Get rid of it quickly, the words are floating in the air and its then that I realize he wants nothing more from our relationship. I knew this. I knew the moment Connie passed he would be done with our friendship, if you could even call it that, and close himself off. He's said from the first time we had sex, he could never give me *more,* and until this very moment, I never believed his words were true.

Defeated, I respond, "Yeah, I guess you're right. I will keep what I can and get rid of the rest." My heart is filling with pain once again. I just want to be alone to wallow in it. "I'm going to lie down for a little bit. You can stay if you want."

"Nah, I won't bother you. Mia's probably ready for dinner anyway. Do you want me to bring you anything?" Drake sits back down on the couch next to me, only this time he's a couch cushion away.

I shake my head no and look down at my hands, trying like hell to hold back the tears. I feel his arms wrap around me as Drake pulls me into his side. "You know, Zoe, I know what it feels like to be in your shoes."

"You know what it's like to lose a loved one?" I ask, hoping he will finally come clean about what's happened to Presley. I want him to tell me, to wrestle it out of himself, then maybe he will finally be free of his emotional prison and be able to move forward with his life—with me.

"Yes, but that's not what I'm talking about." I lean back and look into his black eyes as they travel back to the past. "My mother didn't want me, either. If you haven't been able to tell, I'm not blood related to my brothers." I nod my head, realizing just then how different he looks from the rest of them. For one, his skin is darker and it's clear he's bi-racial, but his actual features look nothing like the rest of them. "My mother decided drugs were more important than her child. She basically traded me for heroin to my brother's mom. She discarded me like a piece of trash, not thinking twice about what she was doing."

I am stunned speechless sitting next to him. I'm glad he is telling me something about himself, however I'm shocked at what I am hearing. "I was taken in by Mrs. Evans, but it was Reggie who raised me. She was a horrid woman and overdosed a few years after I lived there. Reggie was eighteen and adopted me and then became all of our legal guardians. I am grateful for what my brother has done. I wouldn't change it for anything, but I still feel the loss of my mother. Until I met Mrs. Fields, I never really had that."

I say nothing. I don't dare interrupt because he's talking and maybe it will lead to the major issues he's battling. I only sit next to him and listen, nodding every once in a while so he knows I'm still paying attention to him. Drake takes a deep breath and I can feel the conversation moving toward Presley and the loss he's experienced.

"She's been there for me since...sin—" Drake abruptly stops. He doesn't go any further and I know from experience to not pry. Once he's ready, he'll spill it. I wonder if I'll still be around when that day comes. "Look, Zoe, you don't have to leave. I know that was your original plan when you moved here, but you don't have to go. Not right away, anyway."

A small smile surfaces at the corner of my mouth, knowing that he's just given me a little bit of his more without actually realizing it.

Chapter 21
Drake ~ Three Months Later

We've successfully made it through the holidays, and the New Year has come and gone. Nothing much has really changed since the night after Mrs. Fields's funeral.

I clearly remember the feeling of loss, knowing Zoe was going to be leaving. Why wouldn't she? So I asked her to stay in a roundabout way. The thoughts were raging inside of me and I was trying to convince myself she needed to go for her own good and mine, but when she started talking about cleaning out Mrs. Fields apartment, I didn't want her to go. I took one look at her broken state, her feeling of abandonment, and I caved.

I will never be able to give her more. I can't give her that emotional part of me, but I can be her friend. Well, friend with benefits. The relationship seems to be working for us.

Zoe spent Thanksgiving with us as well as Christmas. Putting her ingrained southern hospitality to use, Delilah wanted to host Christmas dinner at her and Jake's new place. Zoe got a small glimpse of the Evans family when we had Thanksgiving with Mrs. Fields, but my brothers and Darcie were on their best behavior then. When actual Thanksgiving came around, she was baptized by fire, so to speak, when she had dinner with us. All of us together can be overwhelming, to say the least. Zoe sat quietly, observing and soaking up the various personalities that make us unique. However, it wasn't until Christmas dinner where Zoe was welcomed to the chaos, Evans family style.

I was cringing because Zoe and I are not a couple and I was worried they would bring up Presley. I'm never going to be ready to address that with her. Needless to say, I was in a constant state of paranoia. Delilah spent hours getting the meal prepared and her house decorated. It looked like we were attending a formal dinner, only we were all wearing jeans, hoodies and sneakers except Delilah. She was wearing a dress similar to how she used to look. Her hair was all done up and she looked the opposite of how we all did. From the time we walked through the door, Zoe, Mia and I could hear Jake and Delilah going at it, and not in *that* way.

"...you could at least wear a shirt without grease on it!" She was nowhere to be seen, however Delilah was heard all throughout the apartment. Jake was standing in the kitchen, twisting the cap off an aged bottle of Irish whiskey he received for Christmas from Reggie while rolling his eyes.

"Tell her she's crazy, Drake. She wants me to fucking dress up? Really? Are you kidding me right now? That woman pisses me off like no—"

Delilah hadn't realized we were standing in the kitchen as she yelled back at Jake. "Jake! For the love of God you could dress decent one day in your life!"

"We've...what! I'm not changing my fucking shirt, cupcake. Now get over it!" Jake poured a glass of whiskey and then poured me one as well. I took the drink, sipping small mouthfuls and trying to ease my stress.

After Darcie and Reggie arrived, I thought it was going be fine. Everyone was talking about normal, random things, like work, drunks, racing, etc…but no such luck. Jake and Reggie were tying one on and they were completely obnoxious. Once each of them shared half the bottle of whiskey, their alter egos took over. I was mortified.

Jake started in. "So Zoe, what's going on with you and my bro here?" He slapped me in the chest and I returned it with a rather hard punch to the arm. "Ow, calm the fuck down. I think the family has a right to know what's going on with you guys. Axl, here…" Jake tapped Mia on her head and she returned his smile with one covered in jam.

"Kiss, Uncie Jake!" Mia demanded as she distracted Jake from his thought and leaned forward. He complied, kissing my child's jelly covered face.

Delilah wiped the trace of jelly from Jake's face then he licked it off her finger. I was getting grossed out, but he picked up right where he left off. "Where was I? Oh, yeah…if she's going to be around Axl, I guess I'd like to know—well, we'd all like to know what the fuck is going on between you two."

Darcie then chimed in, only to stir things up—she's infamous for that. "Oh, I agree with Jake. Your relationship seems a bit interesting, to say the least." She took a bite of her mashed potatoes, smirking the entire time. I wanted to punch the shit out of Jake at that point. I had no idea where the conversation was heading, but my gut was telling me it was going downhill fast.

"Yeah." Zoe kept as cool as she could and glanced over at Reggie with the look of indifference on her face. "What's with you and my brother?" He crossed his arms over his chest, scolding her like he would one of us. "As his eldest brother."

"Eldest is right," I jabbed, in hopes to distract his drunken mind from its original thought. However, I got awarded with his classic scowl and then shut my mouth.

"Anyway, I need to know what your intentions are with him."

"What am I, twelve? You guys are completely out of your mind." I turned to Zoe. "You don't have to answer them. They're just drunk." I was fuming mad at this point and ready to start whooping ass.

Zoe grabbed my arm, smiled and then zeroed in on Reggie. "Well, I think it's pretty clear what my intentions are with your brother, Reggie." She set down her fork and wiped the corners of her mouth with a Christmas themed napkin. Her glare was serious, intense. I had nothing to say. What could I have said? It was a slow moving train wreck anyway you looked at it. "It's not like we've been hiding it and I must say his intentions are very, *very* generous, if you know what I mean." She winked to him and went back to scooping up her food. I, on the other hand, began to choke on my dinner roll, trying to capture my breath after Zoe's rather blunt comment. I pounded my fist against my chest as all eyes looked to me in bewilderment.

Jake let out a huge laugh. "Holy shit, dude. I like her. She will definitely fit in here."

"ZZZZOOOOEEEE!" Mia screamed from out of the blue and we all busted up laughing. Needless to say, the

209

night got better by the minute and she handled my brothers perfectly.

When New Year's came around we rang it in at *The Slab*. No kissing was exchanged, but later we had a quickie in the back of my Chevelle. I haven't had sex in a car since I was fifteen, long before Presley and I were together. It was pretty amazing. Actually, I don't remember car sex being amazing at all. Back in the day, it was hard to find places to put your limbs, and if the girl wasn't good at rocking her hips, it was all on the guy to get it done. I got it done, you can believe that, but it was difficult to get there. However, Zoe and me in the front seat of my Chevelle… yeah, she knew exactly what she was doing right down to the denim skirt and the sexy way she moved her hips. I came in no time, as did she.

Zoe, Darcie and Delilah have formed a bond with one another. Darcie and Zoe especially. They spend a lot of time at the bar, working of course, but Darcie and she have been hanging out at our house as well. It was strange at first, seeing them together, knowing it was once Presley and Darcie sitting on the couch and watching movies. I'd be lying if I said the sight didn't pain me a little.

I was concerned at first that the girls were going to tell Zoe about Presley. I never wanted her to know about her during the short time we've had together because that means I would have to face the pity and heartache I've been trying to avoid.

I pulled Darcie and Delilah both aside right before Christmas, knowing they were all going shopping together. The conversation was on my mind for a long time before I could fight it. We were standing in the kitchen of Jake and

Delilah's apartment as the girls were making their shopping lists and arguing about a gift. Zoe went to use the bathroom so I took the opportunity to share my feelings.

"Don't say anything to Zoe about…" I trailed off. Both Delilah and Darcie looked up from the piece of paper and waited for me to elaborate, but it wasn't needed. They knew exactly what I was referring to.

"Drake, we would never disclose anything that was rightfully yours to share," Delilah whispered. "But she will want to know eventually, don't you think?"

I shake my head, knowing she understands where I stand on the *more* factor. "We have an understanding and she doesn't pry, but if you start talking about *her* or the past, she will catch on. I can't answer those questions." I stood tall, getting irritated as they looked at me with judgmental eyes. "I will never answer those questions. Do you understand?"

"Drake, she's not an idiot. She'll want to know sooner or later," Darcie hissed.

"Well, that's something that will never happen, so don't raise her curiosity."

Zoe exited the bathroom and we finished our conversation. I know it was probably an unreasonable request in their eyes, but Darcie and Delilah don't have to live through the pain like I do. They didn't feel the blood on their hands and watch helplessly as the love of their life breathed her last breath.

Sure they've lost a friend, but it's very different from my end. I'm faced with the horror of what I've lost every day when I look into my daughter's eyes. I see Presley, and every time I'm reminded she's no longer here.

Later tonight, Zoe and I will spend the evening in her bed. I have finally convinced her to at least get a bed to sleep on instead of that blow up air mattress. After a night of a hardcore sex-fest, we popped the air mattress, and when she went to buy another, I told her to get an actual bed instead. She purchased a mattress—no box spring—and told me she'd have to leave it behind when that time comes. I remember the thought of her leaving angering me, yet I'm still unsure if it's because I care so much that she's still thinking of leaving or at the thought of her physically being gone.

I walk up the stairs to Jake and Delilah's apartment with Mia in my arms. She's going to be three in a couple of months and her vocabulary has tripled. She says so much now; it's unreal how much she sounds like a person instead of a baby.

I open the door into their kitchen to find Jake standing shirtless, digging in the fridge. I swear he never wears a shirt unless he has to, but I think it's also because Delilah can't help herself. He's added to his collection of tattoos and now his back is covered with much of the same shit that's on his arms. He's becoming a walking work of art. I will never understand nor have the desire to, but as long as Delilah likes it, that's all that matters.

When I shut the door, Mia wiggles out of my arms and runs to Jake. "Uncie Jake!"

Jake picks her up and gives her a toss into the air. Mia laughs loudly and Jake does it again. "Axl, you're getting so big. Pretty soon, Uncle won't be able to toss you up in the air."

"Where's Auntie D? I want her to see my fingers." Mia

holds up her fingernails that have been recently painted a bubble gum pink with glitter.

"She's in the bedroom," Jake informs her and Mia shoots from the kitchen like a rocket. That's another thing, she only has one speed nowadays and that speed is run. She runs everywhere.

Jake cracks open a can of soda, taking a large swig. "So, are you and Zoe hanging out tonight?" He wags his eyebrows up and down, insinuating that he already knows what we do when we are alone. I just return his comment with an eye roll. "You know, it's okay to be happy with her." His statement comes from left field and rocks me off my axis.

"What's that supposed to mean?" I'm irritated instantly.

"It means, it's okay to move on. You of all people deserve to be happy, so just...be." Jake finishes his soda and tosses the can into the trash. He then rubs his belly and releases a huge burp. "Zoe's cool and she's good with Axl. I think she's exactly what you need, but the question is, are you smart enough to realize that?"

I'm taking relationship advice from the one man who has avoided it at all costs. Now that he and Delilah are exclusive, he thinks it gives him a right to council me. Give me a fucking break.

"I'm not having this conversation," I say, trying to suppress my anger as I hear Delilah and Mia walking into the kitchen.

I plant a smile on my face then lean forward, kissing my daughter goodbye.

"Bye, Daddy! Auntie D has finger paint, too!" She's

very excited to show me Delilah's nails are also painted pink and the site of her happiness is impossible to ignore. I give her another swift kiss and walk from the kitchen.

As the cold air hits my skin, an unsettling feeling starts to flood in. I can't shake what my brother has just advised me to do. What does he know anyway? He's only been in one relationship and that person is alive and well, sleeping in his bed. She's not six feet under and didn't leave you abandoned with a child to raise alone. Nevertheless, it's impossible to ignore his comments.

Is it okay to really be happy with Zoe? I mean, I'm happier now than I have been in almost two years, but is what I have enough?

Jake gets my mind thinking about a place I know I can't go, but it's a place I will soon have to face if I want to keep Zoe in my life. And right now, I don't have the ability to give her the part of myself she deserves to have.

The sickening reality is cutting me deep, knowing our days are numbered. I should have let her leave sooner. I should have never told her it was okay to stay. I should have...I can't even complete a thought, it's too overwhelming.

Zoe

I'm finishing getting ready for Drake to come over, and I can't stop the excitement. Every time he comes over, my heart flutters and my knees get weak. I am head over heels in love with this man, but I have yet to tell him. I've been waiting patiently to disclose my true feelings, knowing it will be impossible to keep them inside for much longer. However, I'm afraid. I don't know how he will react. We've never had that conversation of *more* since the first time we were together. I've avoided it like the plague. The day I reveal my heart is coming soon, as I feel it living just below the surface. I only wish he'd be as open to my love as I am to his.

Two hours later, Drake finally stumbles up the stairs to my apartment and bangs on the door. When I open it up, he is barely standing while holding a half empty bottle of Jack Daniels—completely drunk out of his mind.

"Hey, ZOOOOEEEE," he emphasizes my name in long, loud syllables. He's so drunk he can no longer control the level of his voice. Well, it looks like I will be babysitting a drunk tonight, so much for anything else.

I open the door wider and invite him to come in. He's barely holding himself up, using the wall as a brace, however that ends up moving on him and down he goes. His backside hits with a hard thud and the bottle of Jack crashes to the floor, shattering into a thousand tiny pieces.

"Jesus, Drake!" I scold and am secretly thankful the below neighbors moved out last week.

"Oops." He begins to laugh then momentarily gets angry at himself. "Fuck!" Drake punches the carpeted floor hard. Great, whiskey drunks are the hardest. It makes people so mean and hard to deal with. Hopefully, I don't have too many problems with him.

After sweeping up the shards of glass and wiping up the booze, Drake starts to pass out on the floor. I bend down and grab his boot in my hand. "Here," I say as I untie the strings and carefully slip them both off. I stand to my feet and extend my hand. I glance at him to take my outstretched hand so I can help him up, which he gladly does. I manage to get him to his feet, just enough to help

215

him over to the bed in the middle of my living room.

I move to the kitchen and get a glass of water and two Advil, knowing he will need this sooner rather than later. "Here." I drop the pills into his hand and pass over the glass of water. Drake chugs it down and wipes off the wandering dribbles of water that have fallen onto his chin. I kneel in front of him and his eyes light up with delight— yeah, that's not going to happen. "Not right now, cowboy. You need to sleep for a while first."

"I've never had whiskey dick...ever. So let's do this, Zoe." Drake grabs the crotch of his pants, clasping onto his manhood. I am turned on slightly, but I cannot have sex with someone—well, Drake—when he may not remember it in the morning.

"Just sleep for a couple of hours and I promise you I will take care of that rather big situation." I'm good at stroking the egos of drunks—hell, I'm a bartender; I do it for a living.

He smiles wickedly and then lifts his arms. I remove his shirt, and when he lays back, I unbutton his pants and slip them off. Drake rolls to his side and mumbles incoherently. Seconds later, he's passed out, snoring.

This is not the night I've envisioned for us, but hopefully we can salvage something positive before he has to leave in the morning. I stand, stripping to my bra and panties then slip under the covers next to him. I turn on the small stereo, allowing the blues-filled voices to take me away as I fall fast asleep.

Drake

I crack my eyes open when the sound of quiet music begins to stir my consciousness. My stomach is queasy and my head is aching. I open my eyes fully to a dark apartment, and when I roll to my side, Zoe is passed out next to me. The faint blue light from the stereo is illuminating her face just enough for me to see her. She looks beautiful, as she always does.

I slide out of bed, noticing I'm stripped to my boxers, and walk to the bathroom. My bladder is dying right now and my mouth feels like it's full of cotton. I was angry at Jake's and my conversation, which prompted me to drive to the liquor store and buy a bottle of whiskey. Two hours later, I was drunk in Zoe's parking lot and willing myself to go upstairs. That's the last I remember. I must have talked myself into it, considering I'm pissing in her toilet right now.

I flush, wash my hands and splash cold water on my face. The coolness wakes me up a little and takes me out of my drunken state. Next, I bend over and take huge drinks from the faucet, saturating my dry throat. It feels like the best drink of water I've ever had. I open up her cabinet and squirt some toothpaste in my mouth, using my finger as a brush. When I'm done, I feel a little more human as I quietly walk back to the bed. Zoe is sitting up, wearing her bra and panties, arousing my dick instantly.

"Are you okay? Do you need more medicine?" she asks with a look of general concern on her face. I feel like a douche knowing she's had to babysit my drunken ass.

"No, I'm fine. Um, sorry about showing up wasted. I never meant to do that," As I apologize, I lie down next to her on the bed. She scoots closer to me and snuggles into my arms. "Jake and I had a discussion and it pissed me off."

"Do you want to talk about it?" Her fingers are tracing the lines of my stomach and coming dangerously close to the waistband of my boxers. Suddenly, I have no idea why I was mad in the first place. She's distracted me just enough.

I roll on top of her, settling myself between her legs. She looks up at me with hooded eyes and then they glance down to my lips. We've been hanging out for a while now, but I still I haven't kissed her. I would be lying if I said I haven't thought of it, yet I just don't know if I can give her that part of myself. I'm too big of a pussy to give up what I had with Presley to possibly have something similar with Zoe.

"Kiss me, Drake." Zoe's voice is barely above a whisper, however the desperation is evident in her tone. Her eyes are pleading and lust-filled all in one. Her lips…they beg me to touch them with mine, yet her eyes look scared to know what it will truly mean when they do touch. I don't ever want to discover that. I can't give that part of me up. I don't think I ever will.

"I…I…can't, Zoe. You know I can't." The guilt slices me up one side and down the other when her blue eyes flash the hurt. It kills me knowing I'm the reason the brokenness is there.

She releases a deep breath. "I know."

I lean down and kiss the side of her face, coming very close to her lips. The heat from her breath is tickling my cheek as I hold my lips to the corner of her mouth, just outside the reach of her lips. She holds me tighter with her arms, crushing me into her body. We need to get lost in each other. This is how we can erase all the fucked-up-ness we have in our lives and find a piece of solace. We find it here, together.

I start to kiss Zoe down her neck, sucking her earlobe into my mouth before I travel my way down to the base of her neck. As she lets out a moan, it only encourages me to kiss her more, to kiss every inch of her body. So that's what I do. I take my time trailing down her body, spending time on her breasts, the valley of her stomach and finally down to her waistline. I pull her panties down and toss them to the floor. Then I kiss my way back up her legs until my lips are touching hers at the peak of her thighs.

Soon, I'm grazing her delicately swollen clit. I take my time caressing her body with my tongue, tasting her sweet juices and savoring in the pleasure I am giving her. Zoe clenches and shakes as her orgasm rips through her body like a ramped tidal wave. She's quaking and trembling, overtaken by the indulgence of our passion.

I keep placing faint kisses to the insides of her thighs and the rumble of her quaking vibrates my face. I inch my hand down my torso and wrap my fingers firmly around my dick. I start at the base then slowly move my hand the length of my cock. It's as hard as a piece of steel and the slight upward motion feels insanely good. I am so fucking turned on as I watch Zoe come down from the intense orgasm.

I want her to know what she does to me. I lean up on my knees, just as she opens her eyes and they immediately affix to my dick. I start to move my hand slightly faster, watching her fall victim to me yet again with every stroke I give.

I've never been so brazen with sex as I am with her.

I've never jerked off with a woman in the room, let alone allowed them to watch. With Zoe, though, all my inhibitions are gone. She brings out this sexual beast I never knew existed, and I like it. I like it probably too much. Even with the girls before Presley, I was never so forward. With Presley, yeah, we had hot nights I cherished, but she was far too fragile to get creative with. I would've never been able to slap her ass when I'm riding her from behind, or slam her into the wall. I could never pin her arms above her head and have her completely submit to me, especially after what she experienced with Robert. It was sweet and slow; never...this.

A small drop of come moistens the tip of my finger and I know exactly what I should do with that. I swipe my finger over the head of my dick, collecting the drop on the pad of my finger then nod my head up to Zoe. She watches closely as my finger gets closer to her mouth. "Open," I demand and she complies. Her lips wrap around my finger and she slowly starts to suck the white pearl. I become ravenous.

I fall down on top of Zoe, crushing her with my weight then snag her wrists up into my hand. Securing her hands above her head, I use my other hand to guide my dick inside of her. Zoe sucks in a deep breath through her teeth; she's tight and I fill up her small opening. I dip my face down to hers. Out of a moment of weakness, I lean down, planting a faint kiss to the outside of her lips.

I want to kiss them badly right now. I want to have a night of love making and not just sex or fucking. I want a night like I used to have with Presley. Now, I want that in this moment with Zoe.

I succumb to the overpowering feelings and release her wrists. I put my elbows on either side of her head, and I begin to move my hips. I push myself in deep, hold my body still then pull back out. I continue this slow tortuous movement, bringing Zoe closer to the brink each and every time. I lean down and touch my forehead to hers. Our lips are close, so close I can feel the heat of her breath against mine, but I don't move closer. I just keep moving in and out of her. Our eyes connect and we hold each other's gaze while we make love to each other for the first time.

Zoe lifts her legs and wraps them around my body. She elevates her hips to match each movement of mine. Her hands find my face, palming my cheeks, yet her gaze stays affixed to mine as we move in unison.

The sensation of being with Zoe is overpowering me. I am feeling something new that's been building for quite some time. And here it is. I am standing at the edge of the bridge. It's right there for me to cross, and if I do, I will tell Zoe I want her to be mine. However, as I make love to her, holding her in my arms, I can't will myself to take that giant step. The possibility of losing Presley in my thoughts holds me back from being with Zoe in life.

The heat from her hands on my face warms the ice I've packed around my heart. She's been melting my icy existence from the moment I saw her. And now, I'm right there with her, the last piece of ice is starting to crumble, but it holds strong. It holds on to me, reminding me of Presley. I can't allow that piece to disintegrate. I have to hold onto it. I have to protect the memory of Presley.

I start to quickly move inside of her, suddenly feeling the need to get this over with. My emotions are distracting me, and I need to break free from this treacherous prison. I clear all the thoughts from my head and focus on one thing, making her come again.

I push myself into her hard and deep. She accepts me when her hands release my face and come around to my ass, instructing me to push harder and deeper. Then she starts to cry out as her orgasm hits her like a crashing wave against a cliff. As I sit up on my knees and drive myself into her hard, she shakes and trembles then arches her back from the mattress. I become possessed by the pleasure she's feeling. I ram into her a few more times and feel my release explode inside of her. It causes my own body to go weak and I collapse on top of her, fighting to find my breath.

We are lying face to face, forehead to forehead, and the feelings I've been trying so hard to suppress start colliding with my heart. I can feel myself wanting to give Zoe the more she deserves. It's right at the tip of my tongue, but my past still holds me back. It has a choke hold on me and I don't think it will ever release me. I'm not sure I want it to.

Fuck! I'm so confused.

That's when the anguishing vocals of Billy Holiday's "Gloomy Sunday" connect with my eardrums and I feel myself fall back into the pain of loss and emptiness. I'm instantly transported to the night Presley overdosed—hearing the suicidal lyrics, not knowing what I would find on the other end of the door. I'm transported back to the months just after her death, playing this song over and over and over as I mourned the loss of my love.

My body tenses immediately and the choke hold my past has around my heart is now sucking the air out of my lungs. I need to leave. I have to get out of here.

"Drake, what's wrong?" Zoe's voice slices into my raging thoughts.

I sit up on my knees and start sucking in deep breaths of air. How could I do this to her? I'm lying naked with a woman I just got done making love to when the woman I vowed to love for the rest of my life comes alive through the haunting lyrics.

"I…need to go," is all I can say.

I fall off the bed, stumbling to my feet and looking for my clothes. Where the fuck are my clothes?

"Angels have no thought of ever returning you…" The words are killing me, cutting my will to breathe. *"Gloomy is Sunday with shadows I spend it all. My heart and I have decided to end it all…"* I scramble to find my clothes, spinning in a circle when I spot my boxers at the foot of the bed. I pull them on, but all I can see is her blood. The blood on my hands—her blood on my hands. I can feel the wetness of the crimson poison. I am spinning around and I can't find my anything. Nothing is there. *"Death is no dream, for in death I'm caressing you…"* I need to escape this song…I need to escape her. I need to escape Zoe.

Her warm palm grabs my forearm, snapping me back to where I am. "Drake, what's wrong?" She is standing next to me, the sheet wrapped tightly around her body like a makeshift toga. "Please talk to me."

"This fucking song," I squeeze the words out of my strangled throat.

"What about this song?" She moves her hand around my back and is pulling my body to hers.

"Get your hands off of me." I am shaking. The rage

223

and anger floods back in as my heart bleeds from the loss of Presley. I can't believe I've done this to her. I can't believe I've been spending my nights with Zoe when Presley is still so fresh in my mind. I hate myself. I should have never looked up. I should have just disconnected myself fully.

My hands start to ball up as I disconnect myself from Zoe—both physically and mentally. I need to get away from her. I am recognizing the signs, and I need to move away from her immediately. The red is seeping in and at any moment the floodgates of my anger will burst. She doesn't need to experience this.

This fucking song. It's blinding my sanity as the lyrics keep me in the dreaded past—as they keep me in the pool of blood. I walk over to the stereo. I need to shut this off. When I bend down, Zoe snatches my hand up in hers, preventing me from turning it off.

"No." Her voice is stern yet curious. I hate it. Curiosity arises questions; questions I never want to address. "Tell me about this song."

"Zoe, I'm warning you now…shut the fucking stereo off!" I can't hide the hatred in my voice. I can't do anything except keep my anger from exploding.

"Does this have to do with Presley?" My eyes widen then snap to hers. The boiling anger is uncapped as the explosion of rage leaves my body. I've hit the brink. It's the point of no return as everything goes red and life as I know it changes.

Chapter 22
Zoe

Everything was perfect. From the moment he stepped into my life, Drake has been perfect—broken, yet perfect. He's my kind of perfect. I was attracted to his edginess and mystery initially, but as I got to know him, I just wanted to know the real Drake. I wanted to hear it from his mouth what makes him so withdrawn and held back. I wanted to know more about Presley and the love he had for her. I wanted him to know it's okay to hurt, but it's also okay to move on, and to love again.

Although Drake was two hours late and drunk when he showed up, I still couldn't have been any happier in that moment. I fell asleep, snuggled next to his body, only to be awoken to the best sexual experience of my life. It wasn't the best because of the act itself. No, it was the emotion we shared through our love making which had me falling harder into him. I was irrevocably his until the sight of him ripping the stereo cord from the socket and the sound of shattering as I watched the radio crash as it hit the wall.

Soon, I'm plummeted back to the past and the pain he will always have, but I have to push him through it. I can't give up on him, even though I'm so scared for what I will see once he finally lets me in.

His icy glare freezes my body instantly when I look

into his cold, black eyes. The sound of Presley's name leaving my mouth has transformed him into a man I haven't seen since we met. The anger he's held onto is encasing him, and there's nothing that will penetrate his fury. I have never been so scared in my life. He is unpredictable.

Before I can summon another thought, Drake crosses the room in two steps, grabs my shoulders, and slams me into the wall. My head connects with the drywall and a shooting pain travels down my neck and back. I'm momentarily stunned but keep my wits and stand tall. If this is what it takes to get him to speak to me, then so be it. I will push him until he cracks or until I break myself.

"What did you say?" A low, menacing growl passes through his lips. His face is an inch from mine and the grip he has on my arms is making them scream in pain.

"Does this song…remind you of Presley?" I'm scared to ask again, but I have to know.

"What do you know about her? Who told you about Presley?" The volume of his voice has heightened to where he's practically yelling at me. When he speaks her name, he squeezes harder on my arms. I keep my lips closed. I don't want him to know how I know. I just want him to start talking. "Tell me!" Drake pulls me close to him and then slams me back against the wall, jarring my body yet again.

"I overheard a conversation you and Connie were having. Then at dinner, when she was giving her thanks, she spoke of Presley," I admit.

"But she never said what happened to her, so how do you know anything happened at all?" His questions are loud and irrational.

"After you left that night, I did an internet search and found out how she died." He is stricken speechless. I can still feel his hands on my arms, but the tension is gone and all that's left is his shell. It's like he disappears from my sight, yet he's still right in front of me. "I read about her and what happened to your brother, Jeremy." I take a deep breath, trying to break myself through this wall of pain and hurt he's strategically built around himself. "It's okay, Drake. It's okay to be mad and to miss her."

Drake's eyes come back to life at the mere mention of my suggestion. "What do you know about it, Zoe? Have you ever held someone you love and watched them die in your arms?" His hands are squeezing my arms again and the volume of his voice reaches a high decibel with every spoken word. "Do you know what the blood feels like when it's caked all over your hands, all over your clothes? Do you know what it's like to look in your daughter's eyes every single fucking day only to be reminded of the love you lost?" The tears start to well up from his pain and mine, but I choke them back. I can't allow them to fall. "No, you fucking DON'T! You don't know shit. Do don't know that every night, when I close my eyes, all I see is her dying face? All I can feel is her limp body in my hands. So don't presume you can sympathize with my situation because you have no FUCKING CLUE!"

"I've lost people, too, Drake! I was thrown out on the street when my own mother chose to believe a rapist instead of her own daughter. I lost my mother and my best friend that day because they chose to believe a lie. I was left ALONE without a purpose or direction. I was abandoned! Now, don't talk to me about pain because I've been there, too!" I scream back. "It may not be the same thing, but I know what it feels like to experience loss. Why do you think it's so easy for us to be together? Because we know...we...*know* how much life can fuck with everything." I'm fighting my way through his wall. I want him to understand through our situations we can come together. We can be there for each other.

Drake releases my arms and they instantly throb when the blood starts to circulate back into my limbs. He walks the length of the apartment, stalking, fueled with anger.

I wipe the tears away from my eyes and roll my shoulders back. The last thing he wants to see is someone's weakness and pity. He needs to see strength in me, so he can finally have the strength to let go of some of the heartache—to let go of his hatred. I swallow down the lump rising up from my stomach and shake off my apprehension. I need to be his rock right now. No, I *will* be his rock right now.

He starts searching for his clothes until he spots them folded on the kitchen counter. He yanks them off the counter and begins to get dressed. The sheet wrapped around my body falls to the floor as I make a mad dash to him dressing. I don't care that I'm naked. He won't do this. I won't let him. I will help him face this. We will do it together.

"No!" I shout. "You're not leaving!" I snatch his jeans from his hands and toss them across the apartment. "I'm not letting you run from this. You have to face it sooner or later, Drake! Otherwise, it will always own you!"

"What exactly do I need to face, Zoe? This pain will always own me because that's what keeps her alive!" he shouts, his voice loud and laced with fury. Then he runs his hands roughly over his head, getting angrier by the second; angry because he's finally starting to let me in.

That's it. He thinks that if he keeps himself in misery that she will always be with him, but what he ceases to understand is that she will always be with him regardless. His chest is heaving and his frame is taut. When Drake leans down to get close to my face, the black in his eyes mirrors the evil and misery living in his heart.

I stand tall. I stand strong. I don't back down to his intimidation."She's dead, Drake!"

It's like I hit him in the gut with a sledge hammer, the pain buckles him at the knees as he falls to the floor and shatters. The strong façade and the wall built around him have finally crumbled. I've broken him. And now, I will put him back together. As long as it takes, I will be there to put him back together. I can't leave or tolerate an existence without him when he has so much life left to live. A life I want him to coexist with me.

Indescribable sounds of agony blanket the air and rip through my body. I fall to him. My heart breaking for the man I love, the man I want to mend. Drake wraps his arms securely around my waist, pulls me into him, and then lays his head onto my lap. The tears are finally unleashed, and I can feel their saltiness saturating my skin. I bend myself forward to rest my head on top of his. The pads of my fingers trace small, soothing circles on the skin of his back. I don't say anything more. I allow him to feel his pain and remember the love he once had for Presley.

Drake

The room is spinning and my body feels like it's

breaking in half. I'm lying on the floor of Zoe's apartment, finally letting her see the unearthed agony that lives inside of me. Her soothing touch is stroking my back, comforting me with every movement. She says nothing as I allow my misery to take over and flood from my heart onto her lap. My body is shaking with hurt as the torture leaves my chest.

This is a pain I've never wanted to experience again. I have done everything possible to not feel this kind of hurt once more. I've masked it with my anger. I've fought my brother and isolated those I love because I don't want to deal with the constant feeling of loss. It has been bottled up inside, always boiling just under the surface, and tonight, all that has changed. I've finally realized that Zoe has come into my life for a reason—I knew there was something wonderful about her. Now, I know she is meant to be by my side, just as I've been by hers.

Finally, I'm ready to sit up and look into her eyes. I have always hated the look of pity in everyone's eyes; it's the part I've disliked most about being around my family, seeing their fucking eyes full of misfortune. I swallow the junk that has made its way up my throat and slowly pull my head off her lap. She doesn't speak or move. She only sits as still as a statue, waiting for me to say or do something more.

I lean up and meet her eyes, however I stand corrected. Her eyes are not looking at me with pity inside of them, only understanding. She understands my pain and that is all I can see when I look into her eyes—she understands. Relief washes over me, and for the first time in years, I feel some of the weight lift off my shoulders. She understands, and it makes me appreciate her that much more.

Zoe raises her hand and cups my cheek in her palm. Her thumb sweeps under my eye and wipes away the wetness of my tears. I look into her water blue eyes and fall head first into her. She has stood her ground. Zoe has fought for me, knowing I was drowning in my own despair, and she has pulled me out. She has pulled me away from the brink. She has gotten me to look up and see the world around me, and it's all because she's refused to give up on me.

Small, finger sized bruises are now formed on her arms and I feel like a piece of shit.

While controlled by my fury, I pushed her into a wall because I was blinded by my own rage. I was fighting the onslaught of feelings that I knew would eventually break me down.

Her arms have paid the price.

"I'm sorry, Zoe. You know I never meant to hurt you."

"It's fine. Are you okay?" I nod slightly and look deeply at her again.

I recognize the feelings that have been growing toward her, but I'm not sure what I should do about them. I'm not sure if I should have them at all. There is still something unsettled in my life, and that's Presley. Before I can move forward in my life with Zoe, I need to deal with my emotions for Presley. I need to accept that she is truly gone before my heart will allow me to feel anything for Zoe.

I stand to my feet and help Zoe up from the floor. Holding her hand, I lead her over to the bed and pull her down with me. She never says a word, only follows my every action and waits for me to say something. Only this time, I do want to say more. For the first time in almost two years, I want to talk about Presley—I want to do that with Zoe. I want her to know why it's hard for me to fully give myself to her when I have yet to let go of Presley.

"She was beautiful," I whisper as Zoe settles by my side. She nestles her head on my chest and covers us with the blanket. I clutch her in my arms and hold her to me tightly. "The moment I met Presley, I knew there was something special about her. There was a light that surrounded her and you couldn't help but be attracted to it. The night she died, I felt like I was living someone else's life." I expel a deep breath, knowing I need to free my thoughts. "The reality of what happened didn't seem possible, like I was watching a horror movie instead of living it." Zoe's hand comes to my stomach and slowly sides back and forth in a soothing motion.

"The day was like any normal day. I got up, kissed my family goodbye, and went to work. When I got home, all hell broke loose, and the next thing I know, that fucker was pulling a gun on me." I close my eyes tight, reliving the horrifying images in my head. "Then she was there and covered in blood. It all happened so fast, it was impossible to comprehend." My jaw tightens when I see Carter's face as he pulls his gun. I only hope his life is long, agonizing and filled with pain. I want him to suffer for what he's done and I want it to hurt.

"She was strong, though. Presley held on for several minutes before she died, and I got to tell her I loved her. She was finally at peace." A tear balls up and rolls from my eyes as another grips onto my eyelashes, threatening to fall.

"And the song… it was playing the night she suffered

a drug overdose and almost died. It continuously looped over and over while I tried to get in the bathroom to help her. For days after her funeral, I'd listen to that song and fight with myself to keep breathing."

"It's okay to miss her, Drake." Zoe sits up and looks into my eyes, conveying the seriousness in her tone. "I don't want you to think you can't talk about her or mourn for her. I understand. I want you to tell me about her. I want to know more about your life and she was a big part of that."

Nothing can express the appreciation I have for this woman. She has walked into my life at the worst possible moment and stayed around through it all. Zoe has put up with my moods, anger and emotional distance because she has known that's what I've needed. She's what I need, and I can finally see that. I can finally see her and accept how I feel about her.

I turn my body to face Zoe. When I sit up alongside her, she looks at me with surprise. Hell, I've even surprised myself. I'm not sure what I'm doing, but I'm tired of thinking about it. I want to follow my gut and I want to be near her. I slowly move my hands up her arms, up over her shoulders and finally palm her cheeks. She is absolutely beautiful—an angel in disguise.

"I love you," Zoe blurts out. That takes me off guard for a moment, however it makes me smile. She always makes me smile and that feels good. Being happy feels good.

"I know you do because no one would put up with me otherwise. And I...I..." I'm fumbling with my words, but I want to get them out. I want her to know. "I feel something for you, too. Something powerful. It's almost indescribable, but I don't think I'm ready to name it yet."

Zoe smiles again and nods her head, still resting in my hands. "It is powerful, isn't it?"

I look into her eyes then down to her lips. She freezes, not knowing what I'm going to do. I can feel her ramped up heartbeat pounding from her neck. Slowly, I lean forward and put my lips to hers. I hold them there, reveling in the overpowering feelings she evokes in me. Her lips are soft and full. They are a cushion of desire and they bring me back to life. The moment our lips touch, I feel my body come to life.

I pull my lips off of hers and lightly push them onto hers again, trying to see if the electricity is still there, and it is. The feeling is intense, and soon, I press my lips to hers again and again and again. I'm lost in her lips. I stroke them with mine. Zoe wraps her arms around my back, pulling me closer to her naked body. This time, with each tender kiss, the action itself gets deeper and more connected until, finally, I feel her tongue on mine and they begin to tango. Then, like everything I've ever had with Zoe, my feelings overwhelm me. I'm completely lost in her.

I reach my hand around to the base of her neck and pull her closer to me. I'm addicted to this woman's kiss already, I can feel it. I can feel what I'm ready to have with her and once I've let go of Presley—gained the acceptance—Zoe will fully be mine, and I will completely be hers. With each stroke of our tongues and dance of our lips, I can feel myself becoming hers and her becoming mine. Our connection is finally sealed, and we've done it with one kiss.

Tears are falling from her eyes; I can feel them resting on my cheeks. As I pull my lips from hers and study her face, Zoe smiles her big, electrifying smile and so do I.

"More?" she whispers through her tears.

I nod my head, knowing what I want. For the first time in a long time I know what I want, and that is Zoe. "More."

She pulls me down to lie on top of her and we get lost in each other. Our lips, our bodies, our feelings blend and meld when we become more than our excruciating pasts. We become united. We become blissful. We are finally connected, and soon, we will be free of the pain because we've faced it together.

Chapter 23
Zoe ~ Two Months Later

The air is crisp and clean, refreshed from a spring rain. The grass is gleaming with drops of water as it's been brought back to life by a simple drink. The winter has gone, the snow has finally melted, and now all that remains is the life a new season can bring. My life mirrors this.

It's been a couple of months since Drake was ready for more, and since that day, the emotions surrounding his heart have thawed, just like the cold Michigan winter. It's slowly begun to melt and he is fully exposed to his feelings—ready to begin anew. Our relationship is now like the grass, we've been brought back to life as we thrive and grow. And it feels good.

With Drake by my side, I've come to forgive my mother and her horrible choice to disown me. I know we will never gain back what we've lost or could ever have in the future, but I've forgiven her anyway. My aunt told me it's better to forgive than live with the pain of not, so I have. I wrote the words in a notebook and filed the letter away. I forgave my mother, and each day that passes, it gets better and better. With Drake by my side, it all seems to get better. Besides, I couldn't possibly tell Drake to move on with his life if I don't do the same.

The weight of my past has been lifted, and whenever I

feel the sadness or anger try to settle back in, I pull Drake aside and kiss him. It is my reminder that, no matter what, the grass is always greener. If I wouldn't have gone through my banishment, I would have never ended up in Sulfur Heights. I would have never reconnected with my aunt and I would have never found my future. I would have never found Drake, Mia or the rest of the Evans family.

Today is going to be one of those challenging days, but not for me, for Drake. He told me last night after he woke from a dream he is ready to see Presley. I know this is going to be huge. He is ready to confront the loss head on and find acceptance with her death. I know I have to be strong for him today.

Shortly after we reestablished our relationship, Drake admitted to me that he hasn't ever been to her grave. Then, when he told me he wanted me to go with him, I replied that I wouldn't be anywhere else.

The spring air feels good as the wind blows through the window, but the chill brushes across my skin, peaking as Drake pulls the Chevelle into the cemetery and drives up a winding road until we arrive at her grave. I look to the left of Presley's plot and see the grass has grown over my aunt's grave. I'm momentarily reminded of the last time I was here. I miss her everyday and I only hope I am living life like she wanted me to. I hope she's proud of me.

Drake

The past couple of months have been the happiest I can ever remember. I feel guilty saying this, but I'm even happier than when I was with Presley. Although I loved her unconditionally, she was so sad all the time. Back then, I chose not to see it, but after Zoe made me face the pain of losing her, I've done a lot of reflecting on Presley and our relationship. God knows I loved her, I would have died for her, yet when I really think about our relationship, I see that it was one struggle after another.

Maybe if that night never happened and she and I were together now, we'd be just as happy as I am currently, but then again, maybe we wouldn't. She was lost inside herself most of the time and it took her almost dying of a heroin overdose to realize how she needed to climb back out. There was always that chance she would fall back in, though. Most of her life she struggled to keep herself out of the dark and it hurts knowing there was nothing I, or anyone else, could have done to help her.

Knowing Zoe's track record for moving around, I'm a little nervous she'll up and leave. She is definitely a free spirit and has no problem living life on her own, but when I asked her to stay, she simply said okay and went about her business. It was the oddest yet best moment I've had in ages, and I'm so glad she decided to remain in Sulfur Heights.

She told me later on the night I kissed her that she had made up her mind and knew she would never leave. She was just waiting for me to ask. Then she told me if she ever left again, I was in the passenger seat beside her and Mia in the back. This made me happier than I ever expected. Knowing she was going to be here for me and my daughter had my already tender emotions growing more.

Last week, we found Zoe a small two bedroom apartment in a better neighborhood. We spent the next day shopping for furniture and everything else that makes a house a home. She was ecstatic. Jake, Reggie and I just hung back as Darcie, Delilah and Zoe fluttered from aisle to aisle, finding the items to add to her apartment. Even my little Mia was drunk with the happiness of shopping. She walked hand in hand with Zoe, picking out new furnishings and little odds and ends she thought Zoe needed in her new place. It was precious to watch. By the end of the day, Zoe came away with actual things to sit on and every purple decoration known to man. Mia loves purple and assumed Zoe loved it as well.

I couldn't have found a better woman to be around my daughter than Zoe. Mia immediately fell in love with her and always wants to spend time with Zoe. They go on little shopping excursions and together we go to the movies or out to dinner. It feels like we are a family, the three of us. It's the family I desperately tried to have with Presley, and toward the end, I got a taste of.

Zoe and I have agreed to take things slow. Although time has been my enemy, I don't want us to rush each other simply because we might run out of time. I want our feelings toward one another to develop and blossom over time. I want to slow down and take the time to experience every feeling possible with Zoe. I don't want to rush into anything. I just want the more to last. I want us to last.

It is a long week and we were both exhausted from moving her into a bigger apartment, unpacking and assembling furniture. We've spent a good part of the day putting together Mia's room. Considering Mia and I have sleepovers here every weekend, Zoe has decided she'll have a room dedicated only to Mia. She felt pretty special she has two rooms again. Since her Nanny died, Mia has been missing having multiple places to stay over.

Even if I tried, I couldn't keep Mia away from Zoe's apartment. She's a spoiled princess in that respect, but I knew she would be the moment she was born. All of us caved for her honey-brown eyes and precious smile. I've learned to not fall victim to her pleading in such a sweet Mia only way, but my brothers, on the other hand... Yeah, well, they are suckers. Mia only has to bat her eye lashes and she's surrounded by candy and toys or whatever she wants. Jake especially; he's such a pushover for anything Mia, and she knows if she really wants something, Uncle Jake will be the one to give it to her.

Last night, I was physically exhausted from the three hour sex-fest Zoe and I had. We were taking advantage of Mia having a sleepover with her Aunt Delilah and Uncle Jake. We started out in the kitchen, and moment by moment, we made our way down the hallway, into the shower before we eventually ended up on the bed. Three hours spent inside Zoe and I was ready to sleep with her in my arms. And for a couple of hours, that's what I did.

I woke up suddenly when I dreamt of Presley for the first time in months. It wasn't the usual tormenting nightmares of blood and death; it was a remembrance of an actual conversation we had. Shortly after Presley came back from rehab, we would spend the nights awake, talking and reconnecting with one another again.

One night, she had been lying in my arms, snuggled next to my body, when she said, "You know, all I want is for you to be happy, right?" I nodded then I remember being confused, knowing in that moment I couldn't get any happier. She was alive and well, by my side. I was on cloud fucking nine. "I don't want you to be alone, Drake."

I had rolled to my side so I could look into her eyes. My stomach fell to my feet and my heart began to hammer wildly in my chest. I was worried she was starting to slip back into the darkness again. I knew it would always be her war, a constant battle she was forced to face every single day, and I was consistently worried I'd lose her for good. "Why are you talking like this?"

"Because…it's inevitable. I won't be around as long as you. I can feel this evilness always following me, and sooner or later, it will catch up with me." Her voice was hushed and she sounded meek. "I will always love you and I know you'll always love me, but that doesn't mean I want you to spend your nights alone. I want you to be happy." Presley's eyes released a tear as she wore her face of despair.

"Stop…stop talking about this. Nothing is going to happen, okay? And if it does…we will get through it together. I won't lose you." With that, I pulled her into my arms and we got lost in each other.

As I climbed out of Zoe's bed, I slipped on my boxers. I remember feeling overwhelmed with the emotion from that dream—well, not really a dream, but a memory. Presley knew it then that something horrible was going to happen to her; she could sense it and I didn't even see it. I chose to ignore all of the warning signs and saw only what I wanted to see. Could I have stopped it? Could I have prevented the whole fucking night?

I paced Zoe's apartment and found myself standing out on the small balcony off her living room. The spring air was crisp against my skin, but I welcomed the cold. I was starting to feel the pain all over again. Then, it's like she heard me call to her; Zoe was there. She was behind me, wrapped in a blanket. She leaned into my back and laid her head down between my shoulder blades.

"Are you okay?" she whispered to my back.

I stood frozen for a moment, wanting to bottle up the painful feelings stirred up by my dream, however I needed to tell her. I can't heal and move forward unless I talk. So I did.

"I had a dream…or remembered a conversation we had shortly before she died." Zoe unwrapped the blanket from her body and brought her arms around my waist. I could feel her naked breasts against the skin of my back. "She knew something was going to happen to her. She was talking about how she knew she wasn't going to live long. And I ignored it. I chose to ignore it. Could I have stopped all of it?" The guilt was building, followed by the fear and anger.

"No, Drake, there was no way you could have known."

"But, I could've—"

"No, there wasn't. No one could have predicted it, any of it. Life has a way of making us question every situation we face. And with the big ones, we're always wondering what we could have done differently. And truthfully, the answer is nothing. Events like that have a purpose, and there is nothing anyone can do to stop them. The only control we have over stuff like that is how we choose to handle it."

I turned around and wrapped Zoe in my arms. She is special to me and through our pain we've become kindred spirits. I'm not sure where I'd be if I chose to stay away from her, if I chose a different path. And its then that I realized how right she was. I couldn't have stopped Carter from killing Presley; there was no way I would have known his true intentions. He was there to take me out, and in a way, he did.

He killed the part of me. And until Zoe, I thought I could never have it back again. I remember holding Zoe tightly in my arms, and thinking I'm ready. I need to make my peace with that night.

Almost two years later, I'm ready to face her again.

"Will you come with me tomorrow?"

"Sure. Where are we going?" she answered before even knowing where I wanted to take her.

I pulled her back and looked into her eyes. They were warm and welcoming and I fell in. "I'm ready to...to see her. Will you go with me?"

She didn't hesitate with her words a single second, "Yes."

We spent the remaining hours of the night tangled with each other. I remember how powerful it felt to finally admit I was ready to move on.

I'm pleased Zoe recognized how influential the moment is going to be for our future.

As I pull into the cemetery, I drive the Chevelle along the curved roads until I spot the plot where Presley is now resting. The intensity of the moment makes my heart slam into my ribs, constricting my ability to breathe normally. I'm sitting frozen in my seat, scared to get out and face the terrifying conversation.

Zoe's hand comes to my arm and reminds me of why I'm here. Without this, I can't move forward with this woman, and every fiber of my being knows how much I want Zoe to be in my life. I have to do this.

She pulls the flowers from the back seat and encourages me with her eyes. She's telling me it's okay and she will be here for me when I'm done. The thought is reassuring, encouraging me to face my future.

I squeeze her hand and slowly exit the car. The air is unseasonably warm for early March, but the moment my feet connect with the grass, the clouds cover the sun, taking all the warmth away.

Since this is the first time I've been here, I take a moment to look at my surroundings. The cemetery is small. However, the lawn is well manicured, headstones of all shapes and sizes cover the detailed lawn, and resting under a large tree is Presley's plot.

I start to walk toward her. My feet are as heavy as concrete blocks, but I keep putting one boot in front of the other. Before I face this, I notice that Mrs. Fields's grave is next to Presley's. The thought makes me happy knowing that, even in death, Mrs. Fields is looking after her. I pull a white lily from my bouquet and lay it on top of her headstone. I nod my head to her, knowing she's not only looking after Presley, but all of us. I can feel her presence around me. It's comforting.

When I turn to the left, Presley's headstone comes into view. The black granite is rounded on the edges and mounted on a small matching platform. I lay the bundle of colorful lilies on the top of the granite and study every feature it possesses. The headstone itself is not fancy. It's very plain with flowers etched in the upper left corner and the name QUINN across the middle. Just below her name a quote is scrolled into the stone. It reads, "*In life, I survived.*

In death, I am free."

The inscription sends me to my knees as all the looming sadness comes crashing into my heart. I can feel the hurt suffocating me, ripping me practically in half. No other phrase could have explained Presley better. Her life was nothing but survival. She was trying to survive the past one day at a time. As for me, I've been trying to survive my love for her from the moment we met.

The tears well up and release from my eyes as they travel down my cheeks and onto the wet grass. I miss her so much. Every day without her has been hard, an impossible battle I've had to face when I wake up in the morning. I miss her small smile. The way she'd giggle when I gently ran my fingers down her sides. The way her lips always tasted like cherry Chapstick and the way she would always be fastened by my side, looking to me to blanket her fears and give her protection from the impending thoughts.

I can feel myself fall apart a little more as I mourn for the woman I love and the mother of my child. I take a few moments to collect myself. I'm here to finally set my agony free and move forward with the rest of my life. This is what she wanted, this is what she was telling me last night when I dreamt the memory my psyche chose to temporarily forget. I'm ready to be free. I want to move forward and not be stuck in the past, wallowing in pain.

I debated on writing her a letter again so I could organize my thoughts, but I've decided whatever I need to say would be from my heart and she'd appreciate that. And so I begin, "Presley, I miss you." As the tears free fall from my eyes again, I don't wipe them away. I let their moisture remind me of why I'm here—to let go of the pain. "I'm sorry I haven't come to see you, baby, but it's been hard. Every day since you died has been so hard to function, hell, even to breathe because I've been doing it alone. I never thought I would come here. I never thought I could summon the nerve to face you again, but I can't keep living my life in this cloak of sadness." I run my hand down the cool granite, similar to how I had run it over her arms when she needed the comfort.

"I love you so much that my heart breaks whenever I think about you, but I don't want it to break anymore. I'm tired of thinking about that night. I'm tired of seeing your beautiful face covered in blood. I'm ready to remember you from before that night. The girl I fell in love with and the woman I created a child with. I want to remember your smile and the way you'd look at me with the most incredible eyes I'd ever seen. I don't want to remember your pain. I want to remember your happiness, baby." I take a deep breath in and out. My chest hurts and my gut aches, but I need to do this. I need to be free.

"Remember the letter I wrote you? How I was begging you to choose life, well…I guess that's what I'm doing now. I'm choosing to live. I haven't been living since you died, Presley. I've been walking in a constant loop, never going anywhere, only going through the motions of living. So…I'm here to gain your blessing, although I'm not sure how you'll give that to me."

Just as the words pass my lips, the sun peeks out from behind the clouds and lights up her headstone. The chill in my skin instantly warms and I can feel her there. I close my eyes and picture her beautiful face. It's like she's telling me it's okay and that she will always be around. Through the warmth of the sun, Presley is giving me her blessing and the weight of her death finally releases from my body. All that remains is the happiness we shared. The solemn feeling of her depression, her heroin overdose and her death leaves my body as the sun heats up my soul. The good is all that is left.

I stand to my feet and brush the dirt from my jeans. I bend forward and place a kiss to the top of her stone then rest my forehead against the granite. "You will always be with me, baby. I love you. And I promise…to never forget. I will never forget. I love you."

Chapter 24
Zoe

"Happy birthday to you. Happy birthday, dear Mia. Happy birthday to you!" we all sing in unison as Mia stares happily at the three candles on her butterfly cake.

"Make a wish, princess," Drake coos as he strokes the back of her head before placing a kiss to the side of her face.

Mia sucks in a big gasp of air and releases it, blowing out the fire. We all clap and cheer as we celebrate another year of Mia's life.

I pull the candles out and begin cutting the butterfly shaped cake into small servable pieces.

"I want that one, Zoe." She points to the tip of the wing with a small zigzag design on it. I swiftly cut the piece and serve it to the birthday girl. Then Delilah and I serve the rest of the cake to the guests.

It's a small party, consisting only of family, but Mia is lavished upon like she is the queen of England. Jake and Delilah have decided Mia needed a trampoline to add to her collection of outdoor toys, and of course, Jake is the first one to test it out.

"Come on, Axl! Come jump with Uncle." Mia abandons her cake and runs to the backyard of the Evans's family home. The spring air is warm and only a long sleeved shirt is needed to keep the chill away. Jake lifts Mia onto the trampoline and they begin to jump. Mia is giggling with delight as Jake and she hold hands bopping up and down.

Drake was a little uneasy about the trampoline, knowing how easy it would be for her to get hurt, but as he watches her, his smile couldn't possibly get any bigger. He is a good dad and would give Mia his beating heart if she needed it. Drake is the epitome of a great parent. I only wish more kids had parents as loving as Drake is with Mia.

We all stand around and watch the train wreck unfold as Jake starts to show off his non-existent jumping talent. Mia has abandoned him minutes ago to swing on her play set and she's laughing loudly at her uncle showing off.

"You're gonna break your neck, Jake!" Delilah shouts as she tries to coax him off the enclosed death trap. "Get down now!"

"Come on, D! You know how talented I am!" Jake shouts back as he jumps high into the air. He lands and he doesn't get back up. "OW! Mother fucker, son of a bitch, goddamn it, that fucking hurt!"

"Uncie Jake, four dollars for my piggy bank!" Mia shouts from the swing. She's able to hold up her hand, showing Jake the amount of four dollars and has no remorse for Jake's now swelling ankle.

Drake had to invoke a new rule a few days ago when he got a phone call from daycare stating Mia called a boy in her class a fucking d-bag when he stole her chicken nugget at lunch. Drake held a family meeting and said we all needed to watch our mouths around her or else we'd have to pay. Between Jake, Darcie, and sometimes Reggie, Mia has collected about fifty bucks, and if it keeps up at this rate, she will be able to pay for Harvard by the time she graduates high school.

"You stupid fuck! Why do you do dumb shit like that?" Reggie shouts to Jake as Delilah helps him climb down from the trampoline then slaps his hand over his mouth, knowing he's just cursed.

"Three dollars, Uncie Reggie!" Mia reminds him as she holds up three fingers.

"Three? I only said two curse words."

"Stupid is a mean word and my teacher said mean words are like curse words. Three dollars, Uncie!"

Reggie opens his mouth to argue, but Darcie just shakes her head, knowing it's a battle he will never win. Drake just laughs at his brothers' antics as we all sit around the picnic table, laughing and enjoying each other's company.

It's been two weeks since Drake's visit to the cemetery and there's been a recognizable change to his demeanor. It's like a huge weight is gone and he's finally living life again.

He never told me what he said to Presley, and to be honest, I don't want to know. That was a private conversation between the two of them and I don't need to be in the middle of his feelings for her. I know he deeply cares for me and God knows I love him. He will come around eventually. We've got time.

I look over to Drake and fall victim as he flashes me his sparkling brown eyes. When we met, his eyes were always black as coal, absorbed in sadness and pain. Since the cemetery, Drake's eyes have lightened to a devastatingly rich chocolate-brown. Very, very sexy.

"Hey," Drake whispers, getting my attention. "Come inside with me real quick."

Drake

Zoe nods and I start to gather dishes in my hands. I instruct Darcie to keep an eye on Mia while Zoe and I go inside to clean up. I follow her up the back steps and we toss the paper plates in the trash then she starts rinsing off the dishes.

I take a minute to watch her as she works on cleaning up. Moments ago, I've finally come to realize we were meant to find one another. Through our pain, Zoe and I experienced tragedy and loss, and we did it so we could be led to each other. I understand it now. And with Zoe by my side, I've started to slowly heal and accept my life for what it is. She has helped me with that and I want her to know. In this very moment, I want Zoe to know just how precious she is to me.

I wrap my arms around her waist as she finishes rinsing the cake off the silverware. I brush my lips to the back of her neck and feel her slowly melt into me. With my lips, I slowly trail light pecks across the base of her neck until I land on the other side. She spins around and I connect my eyes to hers. They are a faint, light blue that sparkle whenever she looks at me.

I hold her cheeks in my hand and stop thinking, beginning to only feel. "Thank you, Zoe." She looks at me confused so I elaborate. "Thank you for being in my life. I know it hasn't been easy, so thank you for never giving up on me."

"I would never," she whispers back then places her lips

to mine. For a moment, we get lost in each other's touch. It's something we always do; we simply get lost.

"When you came into my life, I felt like I was dying inside. If it wasn't from the pain of losing Presley, it was from the anger toward my brother." Speaking about Jeremy is still very hard for me. I'm not sure when those feelings will ever dissolve, but I can at least function when I push it down and ignore it like he never existed. "But from the moment I met you, it's been getting easier, little by little, day by day." I'm fumbling with my words. I know what I want to say; it's just trying to find the words to say it is difficult. "I guess what I'm trying to say is…I… love you."

Zoe's eyes fill with tears as she smiles her big, radiant smile. I continue to hold her face as the tears fall from her eyes and dampen my hands. "I love you," she whispers.

I can't stand it anymore. I crash my lips into hers. I kiss her like I've never kissed anyone before. I pour every ounce of feeling into that kiss and she does the same. We get lost in the love we've developed for each other. And for the first time, I actually feel like life is going to work out. I feel that, with her by my side, we can overcome and conquer the hate, betrayal and pain that comes from living.

***

Mia is quietly tucked in bed and all the party goers are either alone in their rooms or home for the night. I've kissed Zoe goodbye minutes ago and walked back to my room. This day has been a good one. I finally feel the possibilities my future holds, and my daughter and Zoe will be there with me every step of the way.

I walk deeper into my room and start removing my clothes. I toss the dirty ones in my laundry basket, however when I turn to my dresser to get a clean pair of basketball shorts out, I notice a letter sitting on top. Strange, I don't remember this coming in the mail today.

Then I look at the postmark date and its dated one year after Presley's death. The floor falls out from underneath me. I grasp onto the dresser to keep from falling. I notice the sender, and all my good feelings vanish as the anger sets in.

Jeremy Evans #815.2245
Ionia Correctional Facility
1576 W. Bluewater Highway
Ionia, MI 48846

The letter from my brother is addressed to Mia and me. I pick it up in my hands and it feels like it weighs a hundred pounds. The letter is dingy and worn on the sides, like it's been quietly tucked away for the last couple of years. I can only guess who's had the letter since it arrived. Reggie may think I'm ready to open it, but I'm not so sure.

I walk back to my bed and hold the one piece of my past I don't ever want to forgive or forget. I've dealt with the pain of losing Presley and the guilt of the events that surrounded that night, but I don't—in fact, *won't*—deal with the anger I feel toward my brother. Presley is gone and there is nothing I can do about that, but Jeremy is not. He is living and breathing while Presley is gone.

I start to tremble from the onslaught of ferocity. The paper envelope is shaking in my hand. I have to start expelling deep breaths to calm myself down. Inside is the letter which imprisons his possible apology or explanation for that night. Inside this letter will mostly say how sorry he is or how bad he feels for his involvement with Presley's death. It may even mention he's found Jesus and is now asking for my forgiveness.

It's all there again. In full force—the fury I've kept tightly capped inside of myself is now boiling to a raging ocean that soon will explode.

I squeeze the letter, crushing it in my hand. I close my eyes and attempt to find a sentiment of peace. I search the depths of my brain to find something to bring me out of this raging inferno of hatred. I close them tighter and think of Mia, my precious daughter. The expressions on Mia's face when she opened her gifts today and the gleeful reactions she gives me whenever I come home from work. I think about how she looks to no other to keep her safe, sing her to sleep and brush away her tears. I see my daughter's honey-brown eyes, bouncy brown curls veiling her face and her radiant smile. She is my solace now, her and Zoe, and if I open this letter, I will have nothing but anger and hate.

My nerves are too raw. The conversation I've had with Presley a couple of weeks ago was enough to last me a lifetime of emotional breakdowns. I've only accepted the peace and I can't read this letter and let it disturb what it has taken me two years to find.

I lay the envelope over my knee and smooth out the crinkles. Staring at the black ink for an eternity, I finally stand and tuck the letter into my dresser. I realize that someday I will need to face the anger I have toward my brother. Maybe when he gets out the day of confrontation will come, but until then, I will keep the pains of his betrayal locked away and this letter of his forgiveness trapped in my dresser. I'm not ready to forgive. Not him. Not now. Possibly, not ever. Only time will tell if I have enough of my heart left to accept his betrayal and love my brother once again.

~*The End*~

Surviving Love Playlist

1. "Black Gives Way to Blue" by Alice in Chains
2. "Lovesong" by Adele
3. "Alibi" by Thirty Seconds to Mars
4. "Lullaby" by Billy Joel
5. "Angel" by Jimi Hendrix
6. "Bleeding Me" by Metallica
7. "Bones" by Young Guns
8. "Send me an Angel" by Alicia Keys
9. "Breaking Inside" by Shinedown
10. "Dead & Bloated" by Stone Temple Pilots
11. "For You" by Staind
12. "Happy" by Leona Lewis
13. "I Just Want to Make Love to You" by Etta James
14. "These Arms" by Otis Redding
15. "Gloomy Sunday" by Billie Holiday
16. "Stupid Girl" by Garbage
17. "You" by The Pretty Reckless
18. "ZzyZx Rd." by Stone Sour
19. "Wait" by Seven Mary Three
20. "Love, Reign O'er Me" by Pearl Jam
21. "Black" by Pearl Jam
22. "Let It Be Me" by Ray LaMontagne
23. "Love the Way You Lie" by Skylar Grey
24. "Master of Puppets" Metallica
25. "Waste My Hate" Metallica
26. "I Found You" by Alabama Shakes
27. "Call Me" by Shinedown
28. "Cumbersome" by Seven Mary Three

29. "Drive" by Ziggy Marley

30. "Hats Off to the Bull" Chevelle

31. "Left for Dead" by Citizen Cope

32. "Son's Gonna Rise" by Citizen Cope

33. "Not Meant to Be" by Theory of a Deadman

Acknowledgements

This book would not have existed if it wasn't for my fans that begged and pleaded to give Drake his happily ever after. I would have done it eventually, but not in this format. So I want to tell you *thank you* for making Surviving Love happen. I was hesitant on writing this book knowing I would have to tap into the agony I left behind in Tragic Love. I knew I would have to feel the gut wrenching pain Drake experienced then all the other emotions that accompany the grieving process. It wasn't easy, but like Drake, I started to feel solace in the characters, and by the time I was half way through, fell head over heels in love. I only hope you did the same.

I want to express a big thank you to my personal assistant, Michele, my proofreader, Georgette, street team members, beta readers and editors. You've all worked so hard to promote Surviving Love and I'm eternally grateful. I'm surrounded by the most amazing individuals and I could've asked for a greater collection of people.

Thank you to my family and friends, as well as, all those who give me the encouragement to keep writing. I love you all!

Other Books by M.S. Brannon

Sulfur Heights Series

Scarred Love, available for purchase on Amazon, Barnes
and Noble and KOBO

Tragic Love, available for purchase on Amazon, Barnes
and Noble and KOBO

Blind Love, available for purchase on Amazon, Barnes and
Noble and KOBO

Surviving Love, available for purchase on Amazon, Barnes
and Noble and KOBO

Redeemed Love, coming in June 2014

Stand Alones

Forbidden from You, Forbidden for me, coming in 2014

10375241R00152

Made in the USA
San Bernardino, CA
12 April 2014